This Side Of Forever

Robert Segotta

authorHOUSE®

AuthorHouse™
1663 Liberty Drive
Bloomington, IN 47403
www.authorhouse.com
Phone: 1-800-839-8640

Published by AuthorHouse   11/28/12

ISBN: 978-1-4772-9287-7 (sc)
ISBN: 978-1-4772-9288-4 (e)

Acknowledgements

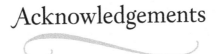

Special thanks to:

Eli Hamlin who inspired me to continue writing and added a youthful perspective to the story as well.

Jeff McConnell who is always a phone call away for technical advice and support.

To **Bob Schmid** who helped in the editing process and gave me daily support.

Cover Art by **Bob Schmid**

Digital imaging of Cover Art by **Esther Eckelman**

Editing by **Robert Segotta**

To Christine and Kyle

And to my entire church family at

Calvary Chapel Salem

This Side Of Forever

Joel 2:28

And it shall come to pass afterward,
that I will pour out my spirit on all flesh;
your sons and your daughters shall prophesy,
your old men shall dream dreams,
and your young men shall see visions.

Prologue

America's past had once shined ever so bright, but her proud label as a beacon for hope had grown dim in the darkest of days. Between her shores turmoil ruled the streets as her tenants scrambled and fought for her remaining glitter and gold. A playground for the fortunate had become a place of unreasonable fear and when that fear turned to violence, the truth of her frailty was revealed. Recovery was the final option to be played in a now darkened cathedral with only, but a few candles remaining in hand.

The collapse had come from nowhere but within. A few wise men had seen the eminent danger, like a storm gathering over a naked plain, but far too many had ignored her warnings. They, like the people before them, in every state and on every corner of this once great land had grown complacent in their ways, and the means in which those ways were sustained. Over a two year period the sheer luxuries of this once fruitful bounty had been left to only a few, while others fought and scurried the plundered plains for the crumbs of the remaining grain.

America's cities had become a depot for the downtrodden of which the numbers were uncountable. Gunfights and prostitution flourished in a way that hadn't been seen since the days of the wild west, and decadence and debauchery became a new normal in the seemingly shattered morality. The labor force had been moved from a service standard to a complex union designed for survival. Beyond the basic necessities, only military, medical and communication personnel were selected at the highest levels to perform the suddenly cherished tasks.

The majority of the Nation's three hundred million strong were left to fend for themselves and their families, while the power of the State rose to unheralded levels.

The world as a whole was faring no better and in many ways much, much worse. Tensions had finally boiled over between Iran and Israel and the first nuclear bomb in sixty five years had fallen over a populated Iranian city and was quickly followed by another. Almost instantaneously Europe was engulfed in a holy war raged by once unchecked and unnoticed Muslims who had been creeping into her belly for centuries. The Europeans had long since lost their will to fight back and in what was to become known as the six month war, nearly fourteen million Europeans had lost their lives. With Iran and Afghanistan obliterated and Iraq in the fallout zone, the stationed US military had retreated into Israel to protect her and themselves from the eminent retaliation.

The third jihad was in full force and this time the European invasion had been successful. Millions of radical Muslims had been joined by converted moderates and were crossing thousands of miles of barren sand to join in the victory dance at virtually every European metropolis. In America, the fight was at first squelched by military forces backed by proud, gun wielding patriots, that seemed to have been waiting their entire life for the battle. During the six month period in which Europe was lost, America had lost nearly forty thousand people, but eventually they slowed the rise of jihad for a period and were hoping to somehow pick up the pieces.

This is a story of a few who lived through these tumultuous times and were brought into a calling that would change their lives forever.

Chapter One

"Flipping through a mental rolodex filled with disappointments is no way to spend your day," John thought to himself as he sat alone at his cluttered kitchen table. It's funny how a man will continue a dialog with himself in complete solitude with voices from the past adding a thought or two along the way. "I know, I know," he would answer his wife's prompting before his despair sent him back into a state of perpetual denial where he was still king and his minutes self absorbed. Day after day he moved about his home, talking to anyone and everyone who would listen except, that is, the only one present who might actually care. John never saw him there, sitting quietly in the darkness; waiting for a sheepish hello, an invitation to an adventure, or a warm cup of coffee and heart filled conversation. But there he was, as loyal as a one minded dog and with a timeless patience reaching to eternity. He would never leave John because He loved John, and in the predetermined time He had set aside for John he would use John, and that time was soon to come.

Colonel John Jerome Robbs was a respected and proud military man to be sure, but he never felt completely comfortable with the formal structure that was a necessary by product. He had fought with conviction in the first Gulf War and was delighted when he was named a special adviser to secretary of defense in 'Operation Iraqi Freedom." John would have died with his boots on living the only life he had ever known, but he was forced into an early retirement when his wife of thirty years was diagnosed with stage four colon cancer. John spent two years watching his wife slowly deteriorate and eventually die from the disease and he hadn't yet recovered when all hell broke out in the world. John found some solace in the fact that his wife was not alive to see the country that they both loved so dearly at its lowest point in history. John, being a staunch conservative, was not your typical African American man. He loved everything about his country, was a registered Republican and was never afraid to admit it. This caused a young Officer in training a lot of undue stress during the early seventies when close friends and relatives dubbed him as an "Uncle Tom" for his political views and patriotic tendencies. John had missed being deployed to Vietnam by a matter of weeks when the war came to an abrupt end, and this led to a change in his nickname to "Chicken Tom" though only muttered by a close few, and always in a playful manner.

When civil unrest became overbearing for military personnel and troops were allocated to domestic duties, John was temporarily removed from retirement along with any other able bodied ex-military personal and was assigned to defend the California coast at Alcatraz. Though it was merely a month long assignment designated to oversee the internal structure of the soon to be base, it ended much too soon for John who would have loved to have stayed on the rock for his remaining days. His time was well spent and being busy for the first time in years allowed him a brief moment to escape the grief that had become his daily deluge of thoughts. The economic collapse nearly one year prior and the loss of his wife six months before that, had left John with no money, no purpose and a renewed desire to simply matter in a world full of chaos.

John and his wife Janice had one son during their years of marriage who hadn't been born until 1996 when John was 43 years old. When John insisted on naming his son Ronald after the former president, it only added to his solidified identity and his close friends had found new ammunition for their ribbing. When John settled in to his new post at Alcatraz Island and warmed his hands around his stainless steel coffee mug. He peered out towards the mouth of the foggy bay while his mind wandered down the coast to the Lompoc Penitentiary where his only Son lay resting on a three by six foot cot.

Ronald Jerome Robbs had been in trouble since his early teens. His trouble began when his father's younger brother had moved from South Carolina to Oakland, California in the spring of 2004. John's Brother Jesse was a military drop-out and had been working in the laborers union when he decided to move his family West to be closer to his older brother and to hopefully gain a grip on his drinking problem. Jesse and his wife Clarice had twin boys who were six months older then Ronald and the three boys became the best of friends overnight. Then, as fate would have it, Uncle Jesse decided to rent a house directly across the street from John and the real trouble soon began. While Ronald feared his father who did his best to keep him in line during the short periods of time that he was home the lure of the laid back environment that his cousins, Johnny and Darrell, enjoyed eventually led him astray. It wasn't long before Ronald found himself doing time in juvenile hall and by the year 2012 he had two priors for drug possession and one for a concealed firearm.

"When you decide to blow off your parole officer it's always best to lay low," RJ, as he had long since been labeled was thinking to himself on the day he was doing just that. Time after time he had gotten away with it. He would use his charisma while pleading his case and then make just enough meetings in a row to again skate on his obligation. But on this day, forever known in his deepest pain as, the day, RJ's luck had run dry. Still deeply on parole for his previous convictions RJ was involved in an altercation at a downtown skate park where a fourteen year old girl had lost her life. A fight had broken out between a couple of Asian kids and a couple of locals that RJ considered friends, although he would be hard pressed to place a name to either one. As his pure bad luck would have it, RJ, who quickly forgot his prior pledge that he had made earlier to himself to lay low, intervened by shoving one of the Asian kids who inadvertently slammed into the poor, unsuspecting girl who then instantly tumbled headfirst into one of the concrete skating bowls. The entire crowd heard as her neck snapped violently as she flopped lifeless to the bottom of the curve. It was an accident to be sure, but Ronald's six foot two, 250 pound frame made it appear as if he were a man amongst boys, a man on parole no less. After the cell phone footage was played before a less than sympathetic jury, Ronald found himself doing eight years for second degree manslaughter and miles away from anyone who might care.

Chapter Two

"Setting up the shooting range was the hardest part," Sadahara mumbled to himself as he raised his daisy BB gun at a shelf in the back of the hallway closet and took aim at another decoratively shaped glass award. *"Another one bites the dust, and another ones down and another ones down, another one bites...."* he would madly sing as he watched his useless life's achievements crash to the floor. Item after item, award after award made their way to closet of doom for their fate filled end. "Eventually," he answered himself as he thought to place the trashcan under the shelf, but for now he was enjoying the crashing sound that symbolized his life and the downward spiral that had brought him here. Playing with BB guns was not the only part of Sadahara's daily routine. He also made paper airplanes with derogatory messages on the wings and sent them flying out the window and on to the street below. He would sometimes super glue household items down to aggravate his wife when she would return home from a hard day of work. Some days he would just spend sleeping, waking just long enough to get the bare minimum of work completed to allow him a roof over his head.

"Why not be everything I failed to be before," he thought as he lined up another glass victim. "Why not be childish, moronic, and lazy," he mumbled as another item exploded and fell to the floor. "I have been persistent, consistent, and diligent my entire life and look where it got me." Sadahara's mind began to drift as he looked around the dilapidated apartment and he soon began to reassess his dire situation and the events that led him here. Sadly, the days fun had ended. He yawned hard, dropped the gun to the floor and stretched out on the couch in disgust and quickly dozed off as his mind went into retreat from his dreaded existence.

During the six month war the use of cellular phones had plummeted. The communication industry in the Western World was quickly taken over by the government of each remaining sovereign country and America was no different. Cell phones that were once in the hands of virtually everyone over the age of sixteen were now used primarily by military personal and a handful of government employees. Sadahara Taganawa was one of the few but was angered by the local radius of its range. Sadahara had been raised in Southern Oregon and had spent many a rainy night staring at his computer screen trying to figure out the inner workings and intricacies of the circuits. After being the valedictorian at his local high school he ventured to Cal Poly and was quickly noticed for his keen intellect in computer design and networking. Sadahara worked hard and by his 30th birthday in 2012 he found himself married to his college sweetheart Akiko and living in a plush six thousand square foot home in the Napa Valley.

Sadahara was drawn to Akiko at first glance. She was a foreign exchange student from Japan and this seemed to fuel Sadahara's desire to know more about his country of origin. Sadahara had been an avid reader of history and the two would engage for hours about his perceived ideas of Japanese life and Akiko's firsthand knowledge. Sadahara was a skinny man with plush black hair, though tightly groomed, and a large pleasing smile. He wore thin glasses with gold frames that he constantly pushed upwards on the bridge of his nose that could never seem to hold the weight of his less than stylish eyewear. Akiko was the ideal and matching counterpart to Sadahara, only with longer hair and minus the glasses. Together they were barely 11 feet tall and just a tad over 230 pounds and they had apparently reached their totals because they both ate like bears. Akiko life had been marred at a very young age and her new found relationship with Sadadhara gave her a sense of stability she desperately needed and had long desired. Akiko became an orphan at the age of six when her parents, while driving their tiny compact Honda on a rainy night had been side swiped by a bus on a busy street in downtown Nagasaki. Two weeks following the fatal crash, a young and confused Akiko was brought to the doorsteps of a loving and caring Aunt Liah who did her best to bring happiness back to her eyes. During her childhood, Akiko did find some happiness in her studies, in her music, and in her many friendships, but she always felt a hidden sorrow for the lost family she never really knew.

Akiko was smitten with Sadahara at first glance and when she ventured to Southern Oregon to meet Sadahara's parents she fell in love with the man, his family and her soon to be country as well. The two dated for two years before they decided to marry after the graduation they would share in the spring of 2007. The early years of marriage were nothing short of blissful for the two young professional. Akiko had earned a nursing degree and put it to use working in Santa Rosa at a homeless shelter. Her pay was minimal and her hours were long, but she had learned at an early age how important it was to help others who were less fortunate. Sadahara, on the other hand, was as ambitious as they come. He worked day and night until he reached the pinnacle of his profession in the communications tech industry, while taking no prisoners along the way. Sadahara had been heavily recruited out of college by Virtual Net, the world's leading corporation in the field of communication, specializing in cellular technology and computer software. By Sadahara's 28th birthday he was named vice president of operations and after his annual bonus was making a seven figure salary along with many fringe benefits. Sadie, as his young bride liked to call him and Akiko had what appeared to be the perfect life and while the sorrow that had plagued Akiko's young life had gone into remission, her deepest troubles in life were yet to be realized.

Chapter Three

"Thirty-five hundred square feet smaller than my last house, but at least this one has a basement," Craig said to himself as he watched the sun come up through the tiny window that perched a mere inch or two above the lawn on the east side of the house. The brick walls of the basement showed the ghostly reminders of taken down items that had rested in place for decades. Craig rubbed his hand over the outline from where a large marlin had once greeted and surely startled the unsuspecting friends that he would lure down the steps as a young boy. The bright blue, oversized fish had been donated to the Salvation Army along with several other cheesy items that Craig suddenly wished to see again. "You can never go home again," he thought as he made his way up the stairs to greet another day. "At least not to the way things used to be."

Craig smiled as he heard his two boys arguing over the bathroom as they did when they were young. As the conversation dwindled and the shower suddenly came on, Craig filled the coffee filter, poured the water, flipped the switch to "on" and then pulled in a deep yawn in an attempt ward off the morning fogginess. "What are we going to do today?" he thought to himself as made his way down the tiny hall to a bedroom where his wife lay sleeping. Again he smiled, as he watched the side of her still and stoic face and wondered what she might yet be dreaming of.

Craig Mitchell was a brilliant home builder. He had learned the craft from his father while cleaning jobsites in his early teens for the family business. In his early twenties his father left his reputation and his company to his only child and Craig took it to a new level. His father had been drawn to building average size homes for the common man, but Craig was more ambitious and he quickly realized that venturing up the coast from their family home in the San Fernando Valley to Santa Barbara would lead to bigger homes with bigger price tags. During the nineties Craig earned a reputation as a quality home builder for the rich and famous who found Santa Barbara to be a refuge from the busy streets of LA in which they made their living.

Craig had been married since he was a very young twenty-one years old. Being a brawny construction worker, with a dark, curly full head of hair and a six foot 220 pound frame, made him appealing to Katie who, after a Friday night at Dodger Stadium found herself pregnant and yet still, entirely Catholic. Katie was a mere nineteen years old, though many more years confident, when she finally caught Craig's attention. They had attended Granada Hills' high school together and although she was considered pretty by most, with a thin athletic build and flowing sandy blonde hair, Craig was oblivious to her attendance at the very school he seemed to rule. Craig spent those years not noticing many things, mostly because he was set apart in popularity by his athletic ability on the football field and, because his never ending charm placed him into a higher echelon of peers. During four full years of high school Craig never once gave Katie a second glance, though she had a watchful eye on him from afar. The circumstances changed when Craig's high school girlfriend left for college and the two arrived simultaneously at a post high school party for those who remained in town the second fall following their graduation. It wasn't long before they were dating and Katie couldn't remind him enough about how he had dismissed her during their school days and Craig would always act confused and playfully say "Are you sure we went to high school together?"

Craig and Katie graduated in 1988 and were married in the fall of 1990. They had an impromptu wedding and moved into the basement of

Craig's childhood home that his father had built shortly after the Cuban missile crisis. By 1994 Craig, through hard work and determination had taken over his father's business and had moved his wife and two boys ninety miles up the coast to Santa Barbara.

Chapter Four

In the early morning of August 4th 2017 the world was engulfed in the worst global economic crisis in history. Businesses were primarily extinct, and in the streets, Americans fought tooth and nail for every scrap of food, work, or hope that they could find. The government had declared Marshall Law months before and those who were not employed by the State were considered enemies if caught conducting commerce in the private sector or black markets. Cable television and home phone service became a right to anybody who lived in a home or an apartment, but the channel surfing had dwindled to two choices; the State news channel that was used primarily for State propaganda and a variety entertainment channel that showed sitcom reruns by day and State sponsored sporting events at night. Telephone service was limited to 30 minutes a day, a ten mile radius and the calls were under constant monitoring. Every other aspect of daily life was ruled by the heavy hand of the Government. Food lines, blanket handouts and water rationing was now a reoccurring daily event with violence awaiting all participants as quickly as the military personnel, would vacated the premises.

John had just awoken from a long nap and flicked on his television. For the last several months John had found it hard to sleep at night in his small single story home on the west side of Oakland. It was mostly out of fear of intruders that he couldn't sleep but also because of the ruckus that the unaccountable National Guard would make during their drunken sweeps of the streets seeking out the curfew breakers. John watched from the kitchen as a State news reporter anxiously reported from the shores of the Red Sea but his sixty six year old ears couldn't make sense of his rambling so he ignored it and went looking for something to eat. John fumbled through his ex-military food ration and let out a sigh when he realized that he would need to make another treacherous trip downtown soon to restock. He sighed and thought about his uselessness that once again engulfed him. He was replaced at Alcatraz two weeks early and he knew deep down that his working days were probably over. John flopped a couple of thin slices of salami on a single slice of wheat bread, rolled it in half to make a bite sized sandwich and grabbed one of last remaining beers from his Costco days, then solemnly headed back to his easy chair.

By now the reporter was worked into frenzy. He was hyperventilating to a point of passing out and pointing out at the bay and when he finally caught his breath he said, "It just exploded in a huge fireball Jim, and nobody here seems to know why or how".. John watched intently and under his breath he muttered, "What now?" Explosions were an everyday event in the rapidly decaying world as something or somebody was always exploding in protests around the globe. The reporter continued, "Once again, what was supposed to be a day of christening celebration for the Israelis in the acquiring of a decommissioned Arleigh Burke Destroyer from the US Navy has gone terribly bad. The vessel which was labeled just last week as the pride of our fleet by the Israeli Prime Minister exploded right here before my eyes." John raised his eyebrows and instantly became focused. He knew that it was just a matter of time before the Middle East went up in flames and this might very well be the spark that ignites it. He had seen the zealotry of the Muslim extremists first hand, and he knew about the hatred they had for the Jewish Nation. John silently watched the footage of the smoldering wreckage for hours and listened to several reports and commentaries until his phone rang and broke him out of his trance.

"Hello," John said in a steady tone and waited for a response, "Who is this," he continued a little louder

"Lieutenant Colonel Carl Ragland, can you hear me sir?"

"Where are you Carl? What's going on over there?"

"I'm at the Pentagon Sir and I've only got a minute for an old buddy, but I thought you should know…"

"Know what Carl?" John replied in a concerned interruption.

"That Destroyer in the Red Sea….It was torpedoed by the Iranians," The Colonel replied. "We don't know how they pulled it off, but we have a good idea why."

"Why's that?" John said as he sat up straighter in his chair and placed his warm beer on his end table.

"Well, it's simple arithmetic Sir. With the West unable to purchase oil these greedy bastards feel it's as good a time as ever to start their next jihad. Basically,

They are calling the Israelis to the mat and it looks like we can't stop them from engaging this time around."

"And what does that mean?"

"Look Sir," the Colonel said with urgency, "We are on the verge of a nuclear war in the Middle East and I just wanted you to know so you could take some necessary precautions. It's gonna get ugly and there's going to be a lot of people panicking. Our troops are scrambling to find any way out of the Israel as we speak. The problem we're having is that we just can't move that many people overnight."

"How do you know it was the Iranians?" John said as he imagined modern soldiers becoming casualties to a conflict that had began over 1400 years before.

"They already took the credit Sir, but that is between you and me and I have to play this recorded conversation to the General before I leave the building. They informed us that we could call certain friends and family and you were cleared on my list."

"Is the pentagon planning on sitting this one out?" John said, prying for last minute information.

"Can't say for sure" the Colonel replied, "But you know as well as anyone that we have moved towards a pacifist stance with this new administration..... Oh, and by the way, before I forget, and I know this is really late in coming, but I was really sorry to hear about Janice, she was always nothing but nice to me Sir, and certainly your better half."

"You got that right, Carl"

How you holding up old buddy?" The Colonel said with genuine concern.

"I'm bored to tears, but I have good neighbors and we try to keep things safe around here. The State takes most of my monthly pension to pay for my utilities and food and they may as well take it all, nothing to buy around here anyway. That is unless you want to pay super inflated State prices or risk buying electronics out of a van at two in the morning."

"Hang in there Sir, and please, if you would, keep a lid on what I told you."

"Thanks Carl, will do and try to call again."

John watched the television day and night for the next several days when suddenly the unthinkable happened.

Chapter Five

Over the last nine months Sadahara had seen his life unravel. Virtual Net had filed bankruptcy and was eventually taken over by the federal government. Though he was deemed a necessity, his pay had been reduced to a little over eighty thousand dollars a year and his home was lost to a loophole in eminent domain. Sadahara wasn't alone when it came to the massive financial and power grab. The State had confiscated the most desirable homes for the higher ups in the new regime and had moved the previous owners far enough away to make their trek home an insurmountable task. Sadahara and Akiko, like most other federal employees were relocated to multi-unit housing projects where Sadahara worked primarily from his one bedroom apartment and Akiko was allotted minimum pay to make neighborhood rounds tending to the elderly. With the government in complete control over commerce their pay was mostly used for basic utilities and their lives and relationship were under tremendous stress.

Sadahara's father was a huge baseball fan and had named him after Sadahara Oh, Japans homerun king. When Ichiro Suzuki had taken American baseball by a storm a decade or so before, Sadahara and his father became instant Mariner fans and would talk almost daily about the season and the play of Ichiro himself. As Sadahara looked up at his Mariner team photo in a stainless steel frame tears welled up in his eyes. "The days of professional athletics has come and gone," Sadahara mumbled to himself in disgust. There were a chosen few who still played the game, but like all other major sports they did so for room and board and actually lived in makeshift dorms in the stadiums in which they performed. Major sporting events took place entirely at the Nation's Capitol and the seats were filled primarilly with drunken government officials and their children. These events were broadcasted throughout the country on a nightly basis and it didn't take long for the public to realize that there were only a few teams for each major sport, and the athletes were second rate.

Late in the afternoon on August 7ᵗʰ 2017 Sadahara and Akiko had just finished another tumultuous screaming match that led to the same results. Sadahara retreated to his computer and Akiko curled up on the couch and silently wept. When Akiko had gained her composer she flipped on the television to the State news and watched as a few commentators spoke of an imminent war breaking out in the Middle East. It had been three days since the Iranians had been so brazen as to take responsibility for killing over six hundred Israelis on board the Destroyer and the U N along with the United States were scrambling to find a way to keep Israel at bay. Akiko had heard of the horror of nuclear war during her childhood from people who had somehow survived the bombing of her home town and she cringed when she thought about the prospects of it happening again. As the talking heads were making their points they were suddenly interrupted by a breaking story:

"This is Brent Rollins with a startling revelation here in Jerusalem. The Israeli Prime Minister has just finished his one sentence news conference and he spoke these words loud and clear and simply walked away from the podium refusing questions. Let's listen to his words."

"The time for talk is over."

"I'm not completely sure what that means, but it doesn't sound good," the reporter said as he was joined by several others who would continue throughout the night analyzing the simple statement as if they were going to find some hidden meaning.

Akiko didn't need to watch the blathering reporters, but she was terribly frightened by the report and she called to Sadahara to come and listen to the news for himself.

"Sadie, come quick," she yelled in her broken English. "Something is going to happen soon."

"What is it Akiko? What is so important?" he said as he slowly entered the room.

"The Israeli Prime Minister said that time for talk is over."

"Good!.. maybe they'll nuke those Morons…… and while they're at it maybe they can bomb this building and end our meager existence."

"Sadie you don't mean that and besides I'm really scared. Doesn't that mean anything to you?"

Sadahara looked at her and felt a moment of compassion that quickly fleeted from his thought process as he stoically turned from her while shaking his head once more in disgust. As Sadahara left the room and went back to his computer screen, Akiko wept again and quietly prayed.

Chapter Six

Craig Mitchell had been out of work for over a year and was living with his wife and two grown boys at his childhood home in Granada Hills. Jason 26, and his little brother James 24, had been living the high life working for their dad when the collapse began. Both had lost their rented homes in Santa Barbara to eminent domain and when their dad lost his luxury self built estate they were all forced into Craig's inherited childhood home. Jason and James were truly a combination of their parents. Both were well built boys, towering over six feet tall and weighing a trim two hundred pounds plus. The boys had sandy blonde hair like their Mom and had her sparkling green eyes as well. Like their Father, they were well tanned by Southern California sun, though more protected by their mothers insistence of sun screen from an early age.

When Craig's Mother had passed away a short eight months after the death of his father a couple of years before, Craig had rented his childhood property to a young Hispanic couple who immediately journeyed back to Mexico at the beginning of the collapse. The home was small and the space was limited, but the family was a tight knit group and they were holding on as best they could.

On the morning of August 9th 2017 Craig and his two boys were dismantling an old shed and planned on using the wood to build a patio cover to help shield the back portion of the house from the blazing sun and the Southern California heat. The new energy Czar had strict limitations on usage and the four Mitchells spent most every summer night sweating in bed while applying and reapplying damp towels over their torsos for relief. At about 9:00 am pacific standard time, just as Katie had finished rinsing of the dishes from a morning feast of cereal and dehydrated milk, the tiny old battery operated Zenith radio in the backyard began bellowing that annoying emergency alert sound.....

"This is Taylor Barnes with a dreaded, but highly expected report. Nuclear war has broken out in the Middle East. Reports indicate that two separate nuclear missiles have exploded over Iranian territory. It is unclear as to the exact location of these separate bombings but it appears as if Tehran has been obliterated as well as a South East portion of the country. The origin of the missiles is not a mystery as the Prime minister of Israel has taken complete credit for the assault and he did so within minutes of the second explosion.

The four Mitchells stood speechless as they heard sirens adding partners in the background and they could hear the sound of neighbors making their way into the tiny cul-de-sac where they called home.

"What does this mean for us Craig?" Katie said as her voice trembled with fear.

"I don't know.........I guess it means that we had better use this wood to board up the house and we need to get as much food and water in there as possible....We need to fill the bath tub and sink with water...... before it becomes impossible."

Craig was doing his best to remain calm and his young boys were following suit, but the realization that the world had taken a drastic turn for the worst showed on each of their faces. Each family member stood there silent for several minutes, each taking periodical glances at each other but unable to find any resolute words for the situation. Then, for no other reason than to break the maddening silence Jason said,

"We better get after it then," and James quickly nodded in agreement.

Chapter Seven

Six months had passed since the Middle Eastern desert had been blanketed with nuclear fallout. Europe was still smoldering from the countless bombings and her dead were being buried in mass unmarked graves. The European Union had been trampled by radical jihadists who eventually took power from South of Spain to the icy border between Finland and Russia. The American troops that were unable to escape the territory prior to the deluge, were hunkered down in Israel listening to daily threats from all surrounding Muslim Nations as well as Russia, China and the newly formed European Islamic Union. Political fallout was encroaching on the United States President for being complacent in protecting Europe but in actuality that battle was won before it started. In America, the previous six months were marked with never before seen riots and upheaval. The murder rates in the States rose to levels that could have never been imagined as Jihadists tried to gain a foothold with the sword while proud Americans fought back with their home supplied arsenals and unfortunately, at times, fired shots at innocent individuals they merely deemed as suspicious. This six month period in American history became known as the "Not in my Backyard" revolution as people raged a bloody war against religious zealots and the new power grabbing government that had shackled them.

Eventually the State won this battle and a sense of normalcy regained a standard. People were placed on even stricter rations and work was performed as a need in the State arose. People with little skill became the laborers and were often sent to untold places and some never returned. Skilled workers who had a particular contact or two were able to keep their families together but were required to be at the ready to relocate at a moment's notice. The equation was simple: the State would keep you fed and dry, provide basic home services, and in return, citizens would become their personal property. Health care was reduced to an allocation of the young as older citizens who could not provide a return of the States investment were left to fend off whatever ailed them. This led to a new drug trafficking problem that quickly became a bloodbath as diabetics and heart patients along with countless others would invest all of their remaining resources to simply stay alive or to provide medicine to a loved one. The State came down hard on these peddlers and their customers, and while a few such private entrepreneurs fought each other for the remaining business, the powers in Washington showed zero compassion and they instituted provision on top of more provisions that made all medical transactions illegal. The private sector of American culture fought these provisions with every fiber of their existence, but eventually they were forced underground and were sought day and night by a power that had no intention of offering them a day in court. Countless were imprisoned and never returned while others were simply gunned down in the dead of night and their bodies burned in incinerators.

John wasted little time after the Iranian bombardment began. That very day he had joined the looters on the streets of Western Oakland and used his six foot four frame to muscle his way into a nearby government owned grocery store and filled two back packs with whatever can goods, vitamins and batteries he could find. When he arrived back home he filled every container he had with water from his hose and boarded up his windows with the two by six planks from his deck. Sweat poured from his body as he hammered the planks securely into place and he realized how poor his condition had became. John was always a big guy, but retirement and the tending to his wife in recent years had left him heavier than ever before and he actually felt a little faint as he pounded the last nail into place. John wiped away his sweat with a work rag and went inside. He would need to use screws to re-secure the planks from the other side, but he would need to wait until the power came back on to charge his power screw driver. John sat back in his suddenly darkened living room and loaded his Ruger .357 magnum and waited for the first intruder to make an attempt at breaking his domestic perimeter. John had figured that he had enough food and water to last him a couple of months, and if he needed to stay put and wait, he would do just that. During the next couple of weeks he lost power several times a day, but amazingly the water and phone service remained working as if nothing had happened. Both network channels were now informative service broadcasts offering strict instructions to the public and an occasional update on U S and world affairs. The civil unrest that blanketed the economic collapse had increased ten-fold and the sound of military personnel making their rounds with pepper spray and bullhorns was now a constant annoyance.

John was sleeping a shallow two hours a day, partly out of fear, but mostly due to unspent energy. He had a few possible intruders try to make their way into his haven but the sound of his .357 firing into the ceiling had held them at bay so far. About a month into Johns darkened stay he had several occasions in which he felt that he was losing his mind. He was in communication with a few neighbors over the phone but any long distant calls were not connected, and his solitude combined with the lack of sunlight was starting to play games with his stability. He had no idea how his brother and other family members were getting along and this "Not knowing" was hard for him to swallow. John also felt a lot of sorrow about his personal disconnect with his brother. He had blamed his son's wrong turn on Jesse and his boys and when the collapse began, Jesse had returned to South Carolina and John never took the time to reconcile or to even say goodbye. Tears filled his eyes when he thought about his wife and how much she loved her son. Her son who was now incarcerated and whom he might never see again.

John had been raised a Baptist, though he had long since stopped practicing, and although he had forgotten God altogether in his twenties, he remembered him again when his wife died, but only to place the blame of her death squarely on his shoulders. John sat there motionless while his mind reeled with thoughts on God. He could surely blame his Son's wrong turn on him too and why not the way the world had become. After all, John thought, "He is supposedly in charge of this mess." Unfortunately for John he knew that he was lying to himself, he knew better, he had always known better.

As John felt the cold emotions of being alone he drifted back to his childhood, to a particular day when his Uncle Amos had been chosen to give a sermon at the family church when the Pastor had fallen ill. Uncle Amos was a devout Christian and read his Bible on a daily basis, but he wasn't the greatest of orators. After a few fumbling and frustrated minutes trying to convey his prepared message Amos, a hunched over, gray haired, retired coal miner, simply closed his notebook and stared intently at the congregation and began to speak straight from his heart.

"Folks, I've been alive for seventy eight years and I've seen many disturbing things. I've seen men beaten down for the color of their skin, I've seen brother rise up against brother and man against wife. I've seen little children die in the arms of their mothers while doctors and on lookers scratched their heads and wondered why. Yes, I've seen many things in my life, some beautiful, some...not so much, but this black book and the power of prayer is what kept me going through it all. Don't let the dust overcome these pages people, open it, read it, and keep it close to your heart."

Suddenly, John felt a nudging and unexplainable desire to revisit those pages and before long he was fumbling through some old boxes in the garage until he eventually found his old Bible that he received upon his confirmation into the faith. Before he opened the book John fell to his knees and for the first time in years he prayed...

"God, it's me John Robbs. I'm so alone and so frightened. I want to believe that you are there and that you have a purpose for me, but I don't know what to do. I can't take this solitude much longer. Please God, if you are there help me, please help me!"

John had finished his prayer and sat back in his easy chair expecting nothing in the way of a response when his phone suddenly rang. John jumped like a startled cat, but just as quickly took a deep sigh when caller ID revealed that it was his next door neighbor Sherlynn who was always watching the street though a makeshift peephole that she had made and was always ready to divulge useless information to John's not so receptive ears.

"What's up Sherlynn?" John said in a disappointed tone.

"There's a kid sitting on your back porch John, and I'm not sure......... but I think it might be RJ" She excitedly replied.

"Nobody is going to see RJ for about six and a half years Sherlynn... What is this kid doing?"

"Well…. he gets up every now and again and appears to be about to knock and then sits back down, he's been out there for a while, at first glance I thought it was you. He's a bigger guy an....."

"Hang on," John said to stop her rambling, "I'll take a look"

John had a small hole carved out of his bathroom window and a tiny Dentist mirror he used to look both ways. As he stuck his mirror out the golf ball sized hole, twisted it to the right angle that would give him the needed view, he suddenly gasped in shock, jumped backwards and almost lost his balance as he dropped the phone to the floor.

"My God that is RJ," He said in a moment of complete shock.

John picked up the phone and told Sherlynn he would call her back as he practically floated around the few obstacles to make his way to the boarded sliding glass doors.

"RJ is that you?" John shouted in an overly excited tone.

"It's me Dad, can I come in?"

"Ya, just hang on and don't go anywhere."

"I don't have anywhere to go Dad," RJ replied as he rolled his shoulders upward and his eyes followed suit.

John used his cordless screwdriver to remove the two inch wood screws holding up the first few planks and opened the door. The two men starred at each other for a moment and then embraced in a long overdue hug.

"What are?…How did you?…How did you get?…….You're not a fugitive are you?

"No Dad," RJ said as he began to play the disappointing Son role once more. They let me out two months ago, said they had bigger fish to fry and needed the room. They reviewed my case and said I could go."

"Well… where have you been? How come you didn't call?"

"It's a long story Pops, but if you got something cold to drink I'll tell you all about it."

RJ explained that the penitentiary was getting inundated with young Muslim extremists and that for every 10 new arrivals there were at least two radical Muslim clerics at the ready to expand their numbers. The war inside the prison walls grew out of control and eventually they separated the Muslims from all other inmates. RJ went on to explain that it took him three days of constant interrogation to prove that he was not a Muslim and that he had in fact recently became a Christian.

"You became a Christian RJ, how did that happen?"

"By God's grace Pops, but if you want to hear the longer version I guess we have time."

"Absolutely I want to hear it. I've been alone in here for weeks now, I'll listen to anything as long as a real live person is telling me the story."

The two men sat back in the darken living room and with sweat glazing on their foreheads from the stuffy and elevated room temperature, RJ methodically told his story.

"About six months ago I was lying on my cot when a new depression hit me. I had been depressed before, you know, when I heard about mom and all, but never like this...I mean this was different Ya know, deep down kind of stuff.... Anyway....... I felt like offing myself....... 'cause I had done nothing good in my life and had caused you and mom so much pain. Then about an hour later I felt even worse, I had to vomit five times before I could take my next breath... After I finished, I just sat there next to the toilet sweating and I began to cry and that's when it happened....."

"What happened RJ?" John said as he looked on with complete attention.

"Well, I prayed. I prayed to an invisible God that I really didn't believe in, and that He might help me, you know, give me a sign or something..."

"And..."

"Well, a few minutes later my cell door opened and my new cell mate stepped in. He took one look at me sitting there half covered with vomit and crying and said, "We'll have to fix that won't we?"

"Who was he RJ?"

"He was the biggest white guy I'd ever seen. His name was Michael Timms, but everybody just called him "Trouble"..... but it's not what you think Pops, I mean, they called this guy trouble because he was saving souls in there and most of the guys didn't want anything to do with him. So when they would see him strolling down the hall with his Bible in hand they would say", *"Here comes Trouble"*..And that was about all they would say....cause, like I said, this guy was huge."

"And" John said, knowing his talkative son's tendency to take his conversations down bunny holes.

"So" RJ continued sensing his Dad's annoyance, "When the door slammed shut again he sat back on the lower cot and said, 'Let me know when you're finished?' I looked at the bowl and flushed it before I almost vomited again from the visual and told him that I don't have anything else to give. He smirked and said, "Tell me when you're finished talking to God, boy."

"Did he hear you praying?" John said in a leading tone.

"No, that's just it," RJ said as his excitement grew in his voice, "I was praying in silence and there was no way he could see me........ he just knew."

"So then what happened?" John said in a friendly, but once again prompting way.

"Well...to make a long story short. Michael explained to me why I was feeling sick and why the world seemed to be going to hell. He actually took the time to explain the gospels to me Dad. Have you ever read the gospels Pops?"

"In my youth RJ, in my youth."

"The things that Trouble told me made sense to me in a lot of ways, but after a few weeks of reading and praying I felt those same feelings of depression, only this time it was worse. It wasn't long before I was barfing my guts out again while Trouble just sat there smiling. Eventually... he looked down at me and said, "It's about time boy, let me know when you want to really talk with God". After a few more dry heaves I looked at Trouble and said, 'Now would be good.' With that Trouble laid a hand on the back of my head and he began to pray.

John was listening intently to his son tell his story of redemption while he fidgeted back and forth in his seat. Religious talk had always made John feel uncomfortable and he had always preferred to avoid it like the plague or the funeral of distant relative. But in this particular moment, he found himself longing for more, and as RJ's pause extended a little long for John's liking, he sat up straight and pushed him onward.

"Well.....What did he say?"

"He just prayed the sinners' prayer with me and asked me if I believed with all my heart, soul and mind that Jesus is Lord and God, and that he rose from the dead..... unbelievably, I did!"

"A couple weeks later," RJ continued after a long silence, "They let me out and I hitchhiked my way up here to Oakland and I've been working at the church around the corner ever since, you know, helping feed the nomads and all"....RJ lowered his voice and spoke softly when he said...

"I wanted to come home right away, but I wasn't sure you wanted to see me until today."

"Why, whaaat happened today RJ," John said with his curiosity rising.

"I don't know" RJ replied, "I just felt that today you wanted to see me, and here I am."

John sat there speechless as his mind was reeling with emotion. He knew for the first time in his adult life that there was something beyond the physical realm. He knew that the day's events were more than just a coincidence and that his life, however meager it would remain, had changed forever. He had prayed for relief from his solitude and God had answered his prayer and left him with little doubt of His existence. As RJ looked on, John rolled his eyes towards the top of his head and fell to his knees and began to cry. When RJ knelt beside him he looked up at the shadowless ceiling and silently muttered these words, "Thank you God, Thank you God."

During the next few months John and RJ worked at the corner church and eventually became members. John accepted God's grace, like his Son before him, and both men were baptized into the faith. It was risky to venture out into the raging streets of Oakland, but they did so every day and safely returned. They had several run-ins with local trouble makers but after the first month of the "Not in my Backyard" revolution the streets became manageable for two men totaling five hundred plus pounds.

Chapter Eight

Sadahara and Akiko had become strangers living in the same one bedroom apartment. The days were long and the tension between the two had made their stuffy apartment into a prison of sorrow. In time Akiko had adapted to walking on eggshells but she came to cherish her time away from the man she had sworn to love, honor and obey. Their street and apartment complex were under constant surveillance and it was relatively safe to be outside during daylight hours, although there was nothing to see but military personnel and government cargo vans driving at reckless speeds. Their needs were met on a weekly basis as the military would deliver and distribute food to the building's occupants and usually take a well bodied person or two with them for grunt work on a nearby base. Sadahara had been commissioned to work on anti-virus software and was never called to duty elsewhere, but Akiko was taken to the base a few times a week to assist military doctors that would care for the fortunate few who actually received treatment. Knowing that Sadahara was a useful citizen of the State made her returns safe and in a timely manner, though neither seemed to care.

On a particularly foggy East Bay day, while Akiko was out working, Sadahara received a phone call from a State official who didn't bother reciting his name. He informed Sadahara that he and Akiko were to be ready to leave at six am the next morning and that they were not to return. They were to bring only their clothes and whatever belongings they could fit into a couple of suitcases. Sadahara paused in a momentary confusion and asked where they were going and the nameless official replied, "Somewhere in the Sierras, and that's all I know." Sadahara spent about a half minute processing the information when a big smile came over his face.."Anywhere is better than here"

When Akiko arrived home she went straight to the shower and ignored Sadahara's excitement. Sadahara stomped down the tiny hall, flung open the bathroom door with disgust and shouted loud through the running water and heavy steam…

"I thought that you might want to know that we are leaving in the morning and we're not coming back."

Akiko didn't catch all of what he said, but she had heard enough. She heard the word *leaving* and it had gotten her attention. She quickly shut off the water and flung her shampoo engulfed head around the pulled back shower curtain and said..

"What?"

"They're sending us to the Sierras and that's all I know," Sadahara yelled even louder as he made his way back to the living room.

"They can't just send us away like that," Akiko said through the half opened door, still confused.

"We've gone over this a thousand times," Sadahara said as he let out one of his patented, 'You're an idiot' sighs. They can do whatever they want, whenever they want, and thereforrrrre, we need to be ready at six am."

Akiko rinsed the shampoo out of her hair and dried her body in record time. She jumped into a pair of faded, worn out gray sweats, pulled a Cal Poly T shirt over her head and hurried into the living room where Sadahara and his Mariners were annihilating the Angels in a game of EA sports MVP baseball.

"What are we going to do in the Sierras?" She asked, mostly to herself, while looking downward in a thinking pose.

"I already told you that 'I DON'T KNOW' is that good enough English for you."

"Why do you have to be such a jerk, Sadie?"

"Hey" he said in a loud and pointed manner, "I might be a jerk, but I'm getting the hell out of here and that suits me fine."

"Why do they want the both of us?" She said under her breath..

"I TOLD YOU...."

Sadahara stopped talking and simply shook his head in disgust. Akiko's eyes welled up and she went into the bedroom and cried. As she laid there she began to feel an awkward sympathy for Sadahara. He had lost contact with his parents at the start of the revolution and he had no way of knowing of their situation. The State had closed interstate five at Bridge Bay near the Southern portion of Shasta Lake and only previously cleared personnel were allowed over. She had tried to use the phones at the base to call Southern Oregon, but they were coded and she was reprimanded for trying. She knew she had to be strong. They had survived the worst; their house had been confiscated, their careers had been reduced to a service for the State and they had lost contact with friends and family. She wasn't going to give up on Sadahara, they had made it alive through six months of hell and she still loved him. She rose from the bed, wiped away her tears and began to quietly pack her belongings.

The next morning the two awoke at 5:00am and barely spoke a word to one another as they made their final rounds through the apartment stuffing whatever they could into bulging suitcases. At 6:00am the military cargo van was screeching its horn in the street and they hurried to climb aboard. Akiko immediately realized that it was the same van and the same driver that had been picking her up almost every other day for the past few months, but for Sadahara it was a new experience. Once they were seated Sadahara asked...

"Any chance we can make a phone call when we get where we're going?"

The driver looked back over his shoulder, grinned and shouted...

"The way I hear it, everybody heading to the mountains is getting a new clearance ID and, with it, you can call anywhere in the country."

Sadahara's mood changed from excitement to a boyish anticipation, but just as quickly he hid his happiness when Akiko rubbed his arm to show support.

It didn't take long for Akiko to notice they were headed for the base. She was a little perplexed to watch the driver head directly to the tarmac instead of stopping at the main headquarters. The driver pulled up to a helicopter with its blades spinning and simply said with a smile...

"Have a nice flight."

Sadahara had been on corporate helicopters before and was giddish when he hopped on board. Akiko, on the other hand, was a little apprehensive when boarding and her fear was apparent to the other three passengers already strapped in. There were two doctors that she had seen at the base, but had never worked with and a Hispanic lady in her mid-forties that she was not familiar with at all. When the lady saw that Akiko was a little intimidated by the flight she quickly changed her seat and sat next to frightened girl and grabbed her hand...

"You're going to be fine Sweetie. First time on a helicopter?"

"Yeah," Akiko said in a barely audible tone, while scoping the interior of the bird.

"Well, my name is Maria and I made my first two flights yesterday. It won't be long until you get used to it and after a while, it actually becomes quite invigorating."

"Do you know where we're going?" Akiko asked, hoping for answers.

"Actually I do," Maria said with a hopeful smile, "We are on our way to the SETI facility just outside of Hat Creek California."

""SETI," Akiko proclaimed, "The extra-terrestrial place?"

"Oh you've heard of it," Maria said in amazement, "Well, you're one step ahead of where I was a couple of days ago."

"I've seen it on the History Channel," Akiko replied, "But why are we going there?"

"Well, from what I hear the reasons are twofold. First we are going to convert those satellite dishes into some sort of missile surveillance technology and secondly we are going to start work on "Project Americana.""

"Project Americana, What in the world is that?"

"You'll see dear, you'll see," Maria said as the chopper lifted slowly to a high point, dropped its nose and then swept down low to propel it forward. Akiko closed her eyes and felt a lightness fill her head as she held on tight to her new friends hand.

Chapter Nine

In Southern California the "Not in my Backyard" revolution took a tremendous toll. The large population of Hispanic Catholics proved to be a great Ally to the State at the beginning of the jihadist uprising. When that threat came and for the most part went, a new struggle for power ensued on virtually every LA Street. Supply lines were cut from Santa Barbara in the North to Oceanside to the South as virtually all commerce was controlled by Mexican drug cartels that had inhabited the streets prior to the initial collapse. The strong military force in the San Diego area had secured the lower part of the state but LA seemed to be a lost cause as it had become a crime riddled region too dangerous to secure. Whatever good people that remained alive were doing so on pure luck, the bartering system and whatever skill they could find useful. The US Government along with the puppet State of California had proposed shutting down power to the entire area but had not yet reached that critical point. The idea was passed on time and again mostly out of fear of what might pour into the surrounding towns that were finally regaining some sense of order. Many arguments had led to no set conclusions as to the "LA" problem, but it was certainly moving towards a battleground, and the good citizens and the murderous street thugs could both sense it coming.

Craig Mitchell was a shadow of the man he was just two years before. His life had been reduced an unenviable task of protecting his family and that meant remaining, for the better part of every day, dormant. Craig felt the slightest bit fortunate that he was home, in his childhood neighborhood, when things became their bleakest. He knew most of the people in his cul-de-sac and they worked together to fend off the cartels the best they could with bartering and for the most part remaining neutral. Unfortunately, like most people living in the LA, everyone he knew had incurred casualties, and in time he would have his own.

Craig, his two boys, and about twelve other men made daily trips into local fields to gather whatever produce remained and then crept into downtown Granada Hills to trade their daily findings with local thugs who had stock piled canned goods and other supplies. The Mitchells and their cul-de-sac clan had been fortunate that the Walkers, an elderly couple who owned Walker Family Pharmacy lived at the top of the street corner. They had seen the collapse coming and had been stock piling antibiotic's, insulin, and other basic medical supplies for over two years. Their pharmacy had long since been looted but their personal supply gave the Mitchells and their closest neighbors bartering chips in exchange for protecting the aging entrepreneurs.

On one particular afternoon while Jason and James were filling their backpacks with walnuts on a nearby farm, a lone heavy set Hispanic man walked up to them and lit a cigarette.

"Is there a reason you guys are stealing my walnuts?" the man said in a menacing tone.

"I knew the man who owned these trees and he was 80 years old and Irish," Jason said while staring directly into the outnumbered man's eyes. "Besides that, you look like you've been eating pretty well with your belly hanging out like that."

The other men quickly surrounded the stranger and asked him to move on. Craig was immediately disturbed that the man was wearing an overcoat in the midday sun and he quickly realized that the odds of their newly found stranger not to be carrying a gun was low. The men knew that bringing a gun along with them on their journeys had some benefits but the loss of the home defense armory would be great. They only had a few firearms and a couple of boxes of ammo left and their supply was dwindling nightly with much needed warning shots. The man looked at his situation and realized he was largely outnumbered and so he flicked his cigarette at the feet of Jason, spit heavily on the ground and began to walk away. James, being the fiery one of the two boys, muttered something under his breath which gave the stranger a renewed bravery and he spun like a top and fired two shots, point blank, into youngest Mitchell's chest, the second one ripping through his heart as the breath was sucked from his lungs. James died in his father's arms in an instant as Jason and the others beat the man half to death with baseball bats and golf clubs.

As the men looted the half dead body of his fire arm and ammo they knew that there was little time to mourn. The gunshots would bring others to the area and they needed to move. With blood soaked arms they carried James body back to their make shift camp at the cul-de-sac where Katie simply collapsed upon their arrival. The next day the men buried James in a field where they had buried fourteen others during the past six months. They made a cross out of used two by fours and wept for another that had fallen.

Time simply stopped for the Mitchells during the next few weeks while heavy tensions grew between Jason and his father. They felt tremendous guilt that the youngest of their family had died and yet they remained alive. James was a fully grown man and yet to Craig and Jason he would always be a kid; a kid they failed to protect. Katie started her grieving the moment she saw her blood soaked Son and it got worse every day as she would simply lie on her side and weep until exhaustion gave her relief as she would fall into short periods of sleep. She would talk about suicide almost daily and it got to the point that Craig was afraid to leave her side. Craig would pace back and forth in the basement, occasionally exchanging glaring glances at Jason who spent the better part of his days tinkering with old electronically vintage devices he had found in dusty boxes. Craig was filled with hatred that he didn't know was possible for a man to feel. At times he wanted to run into the streets with guns blazing and take as many scumbags out with him as possible, but in the end he realized that he needed to protect his remaining family. The three Mitchells ate their rations and drank their water but barely spoke a word to one another as their grief had paralyzed their emotions and hardened their hearts.

Jason had been feeling stir crazy much before his Brother's death, but now it was becoming hard to breathe. The frequent trips to town had halted and we're reduced to 3:00 am deals with other neighborhoods whose men who had not become targets. Jason spent his days listening to State reports on his radio and doing whatever helped his Mom cope with her grief. At night he would lie awake and think about Jennifer, his Brother's girlfriend who had left Santa Barbara in the winter of 2014 for an internship at New York Providence Medical Center and was unreachable after the long distance phones went dead. Jason didn't share in his Brother's optimisms'. He fancied himself a realist, and he really, really believed that things were not going to get better any time soon. James always said that once they found a new footing on this torrid wreckage, once known as America, that he and Jennifer would be reunited, married and would start a family of their own. Knowing that his little Brother's hope had been in vain only added to his despair. Jason wanted to tell Jennifer about how courageous James had been during the collapse and ensuing chaos. He wanted to let her know how much he had loved her and how he always kept his head held high in a hope of them being side by side once again. Frustration set in again as his eyes began to well; He thought about his ex wife and how she might be faring in the State of Washington, he thought about what kind of future might lie ahead, but mostly he thought of his Brother and felt sorrow followed by shame and followed again by rage.

Craig busied himself with remedial tasks that he performed over and over again in what could only be explained in the manner of an obsessive. He would clean an area of the house and before anyone had made a finger print he was cleaning it again. It had been two weeks since he saw the precious life leave his son's breath and he wasn't sure if he himself, had taken one since. The neighbors would stop by every now and again to bring supplies and offer words of hope but it seemed to make little if any impact on Craig. He needed something to do and if he didn't find something soon he was going to make true on his impulses of going out "guns a blazing'"

On a particularly warm afternoon in March Craig was putting his ninth coat of poly urethane on his wooden kayak in the garage when the phone rang. The Mitchells never hurried to the phone because they had learned long ago that the only calls that they received were from neighbors who never seemed to have anything prudent to say. So when Katie answered with a low toned "hello" she was shocked to hear who was on the other end of the line....

"That you Katie?"

"Ricky?" Oh my god, Ricky where are you?"

Ricky was Craig's childhood friend who had joined the Marines a few months before she and Craig had gotten together and decided to make the military a career. Ricky popped in from time to time and was actually the boys Godfather; a tradition that Katie's parents had insisted upon and one that Craig didn't understand nor hardly cared about. Nobody had heard from Ricky since the bombs had fallen in Iran and it was assumed that he was in Israel.

"I'm in Omaha Baby Doll," Ricky replied, "How are you guys holding up? I hear it's a mess out there"

Katie had not yet shared the information of James death with anyone that didn't see it first hand, and before she could even begin she burst into tears..

"Katie?"......Ricky said in a suddenly alarmed tone, "Settle down...... and tell me what's going on. Are you guys okay?"

After a few silent moments and several sniffles and low sobs, Katie regained her composer and began to speak...

"James was killed Rick, he was shot down by one of those Cartel idiots down by the old Milner's walnut farm"

Ricky didn't know how to respond to that so he sat there silent for solid minute before he quietly said...

"Katie I am so sorry...... I am so sorry that I wasn't there for you guys."

"I know, I know, we've all been wondering about you," she said before clearing her sinuses with a soft blow.

Ricky took several deep breaths and thought about how much pain his friends were in and how he wasn't there to help. His mind started rolling through scenarios that would allow him to do something now, although a little late...

"Are you still there Rick?" Katie said to break the silence of his deep thoughts

"Sorry," he said softly while regaining his memory of where he had left off, "I just got back from Jordan two days ago and I couldn't call you until now. I tried your cell phones over the past few months but like most people I know, they were no longer in service. I don't know, I should have sent somebody in there for you guys, My God, I'm so sorry."

"How did you know where we were, Rick?"

"I scoped the old neighborhood with a government map and counted down the houses in the cul-de-sac and called the existing number.... Katie, is Craig there with you now?"

"Hang on Rick."

Katie opened the door to the garage and found Craig lying on his back putting even strokes of varnish on the underside of his boat. He didn't even take the time look up to see who had joined him, but when Katie said, "Ricky is on the phone" he inadvertently slammed his head into the glistening varnish on the side of his project and spilled the last few ounces of varnish out of his two gallon bucket. Craig popped up quickly, and in great excitement replied, "Ricky Smalls?" Katie just nodded her yes and set the cordless phone down on the workbench and went back to her room.

"Ricky, where the hell are you man?" Craig blurted out the exact second he retrieved the phone.

"I'm in Omaha Craig, but I'm going to be landing in the old neighborhood cul-de-sac tomorrow morning...... Katie told me about James, and I feel like I'm going to vomit."

"I tried that... It didn't help.... Did you say that you're coming here, Ricky?"

"Yeah, tomorrow morning. Is Jason there with you guys?"

"He's here somewhere and he's really pissed off.....Wait, wait, wait... Tomorrow..when?"

"Tomorrow morning at 4:00am and I'm getting you guys out of there. I just wish it were a couple of weeks earlier..... I'm so sorry Craig."

"Wait.... I don't understand, where are we going?"

"We're heading to the Sierras buddy, we've got work to do and listen, does your Dads old basement have any room left in it?"

"It's sqeaky clean actually, my Mom cleaned all the old fishing gear out of there when Dad died and turned it into a guest room."

"Good. I can't go into too much detail over the phone, but the cartels that have been holding you guys and the better part of SO Cal ransom, only have a couple of weeks to live. On Cinco de Mayo were taking back the city."

"On Cinco de Mayo?"

"Yeah... I guess the President has retained a sense of humor. 4:00 am Craig and don't tell any of the neighbors. I'll give them instructions when I land, and Craig, be ready to go I plan on being on the ground less than a minute. Just be wearing clothes and that's all you'll need."

"Okay Rick.......uh.......I guess I'll see you then."

Craig pressed the end button and went looking for Katie. He couldn't help but to feel a little excited and for the first time since James had died he felt a sense of relief. He found Katie where she had been since the burial; lying on her side looking at family pictures that hung on the wall in their bedroom.

"Katie," Craig called as he crept down the hall.

"Ricky is coming here in the morning to get us out of here."

"What?" Katie said as she rolled onto her back and looked up at her husband.

"He's going to land here in the cul-de-sac at 4:00am and we're getting the hell out of here."

After a long pause Katie quietly replied through tear filled eyes....

"You guys can take me where ever you want, but I'm never going to really leave here. My life ended here and this is where I'll always be."

"Katie" Craig said with a suddenly fleeting amount of sympathy, "I know you're hurting, Jason and I are hurting too, but now is not the time to be melodramatic."

It was as if Katie had been waiting for this opportunity to erupt. She had been mourning her son's death in a darkened room and her mind had been filling with rage. She flung her legs over the edge of the bed and used them as a counterweight to propel her body upright to her feet and within inches of her husband's face and she shouted in the deepest of tones she could muster...

"Melodramatic!! Are you serious? Our son had two baseball size holes blown through him and you're going to tell me not to be melodramatic. I don't even know who you are anymore Craig, but if you want take me on some new adventure with you, please excuse me for not showing my share of enthusiasm."

Craig realized that he had that coming. The Mitchells had lived the good life before the collapse and they never paid much attention to anything beyond that. Craig knew in the back of his mind that if tragedy ever struck his family they would have zero idea of how to deal with it. While Katie had been alone in the bedroom praying to a God she had long since abandoned, Craig was cursing him under his breath. Now, when he needed someone to lean on he turned inward because he felt that if there was a God he certainly wasn't doing him any favors. With Katie safely back in her position on the bed, Craig walked to door and said, "I'm sorry Honey, we're leaving at 4:00 am."

Chapter Ten

ohn and RJ had finished loading donated bags of canned goods and batteries onto the large church pantry shelves and were talking with Pastor Albert in his office. "It's simply incredible the amazing grace that God fearing people show in making contributions in a world where supplies were so limited." John said as they continued to talk and give God praise. The men were in deep prayer when they heard a military truck pull up in front of the church and abruptly stop with screeching tires. This was an odd occurance because they usually made their rounds in the neighborhood without stopping unless they needed to harass somebody or arrest them without cause. The church was a clearly peaceful place in the devastated community and it was mostly left alone except for the occasional thievery that the church dealt with by their own means with their many volunteers. The three men walked to the window and looked down at the parking lot two stories below and saw four men with assault rifles headed up the entry stairs towards the door. Upon hearing the loud rapping on the double hand crafted mahogany doors, Lefty, an elderly African American man who had been cleaning the sanctuary for over twenty years opened the doors and was greeted with four assault rifle barrels pointing directly at his head. Pastor Albert hurried down the stairs from his office with John and RJ in hot pursuit. Albert an elderly man himself, mustered up as much bass as he could summon and shouted…

"What's the problem here?"

The four men quickly lowered their rifles and solemnly lowered their heads in a momentary shame. The youngest of the men reached into his pocket and retrieved a notepad. He looked at his notes and then directly at John and said…

"Are you Colonel Robbs sir?"

"I'm Colonel Robbs, what is this all about?" John said while eyeing the young soldier up and down.

"I'm Captain Robert Dylan with the US army and we have orders to take you with us sir."

"Take me where?..... Wait a minute, did you say Robert Dylan?"

"That's the rumor and the ridicule Sir. I try to use Robert whenever possible."

"So it's Bob then?" John said with a devilish grin.

"For the most part that is true Sir. Will you come with us or do we need to detain you?"

"Detain me," John said as he stepped closer and puffed his chest outward, "Good luck with that, young man."

"Sir, we are only doing our job and we have strict orders. Will you come with us?"

"I don't know Bobby, maybe the answer is blowing in the wind," was John's sarcastic reply.

Pastor Albert broke into a slight laughter while RJ stood there confused, staring at his dad as if the old man had finally lost his marbles. After an awkward silence RJ said…

"You guys are freaking me out, what's the big deal about this guy's name?"

With that proclamation everybody started laughing and John looked at his son in amazement and said…

"You've never heard of Bob Dylan?"

"Not until he walked in the room, Pops."

The men laughed more and RJ simply rolled his eyes and sat down in the closet pew and figured that he would sit this one out. John turned his attention back to the matter at hand and stepped in close to the young Captain and said…

"Listen Captain, I'm retired and I have work to do here. A few weeks ago I would have jumped at the chance to get out of here, but I have a newfound purpose and that purpose is here."

As the uniformed men conversed on their dilemma, Pastor Albert quietly walked to the cross that hung behind the pulpit and knelt. John turned and watched as his new Pastor whispered his prayer and was agitated in not being able to hear over the voices of the soldiers and their chatter. John, clearly agitated, broke in….

"What's the deal with you guys coming in here pointing guns at people? This is a church, not a meth lab!"

"Sir" the young Captain said, "With all due respect, there are no safe places anymore, and we've lost many good men in churches just like this. We are ordered to be prepared for the worst at every turn. I would hope that you, of all people, could understand that…. Sir!"

John looked down at the polished hardwood floor, acknowledging the truth in Dylan's statement. He looked up and nodded his agreement and said...

"I guess your right son, but I sure hope that someday soon we can move past this insanity."

"Amen to that Sir."

John looked back over his shoulder and saw that Pastor Albert had left the sanctuary and apparently RJ had gone with him because John was left alone with the soldiers...

"It's good to know I have full support in here," John then raised his voice to a new decibel and repeated... "I said, It's good to know that I have full support in here!"

"We're coming, we're coming, the elderly pastor yelled as he and RJ made their way down the steps from the office.

"What are you guys doing up there?" John said in a curious voice.

"I wanted to give your son something before he left here and it looked as if I was running out of time," the Good pastor said through heavy panting..

"First off Pastor," John said, "They only want me to go with them, and secondly, I don't plan on going anywhere."

Pastor Albert solemnly walked up to John and placed his hand gently on the big man's broad shoulder, and then looked directly into his eyes, and said....

"When RJ first came into this sanctuary he was a broken young man. He had accepted God's forgiveness but he felt that he didn't deserve yours. I prayed with him that day and every other day that he came to see me.

Finally one day he said that he knew it was time to reunite with you, and so he did. Then he started bringing you with him and I've seen a change in you since you've been here....Anyway, I'm an old man and I don't want to belabor my point but the thing is....I've known for many days that you would be leaving and that RJ would remain at your side."

"You've known? What do you mean you've known?" John took a quick glance at the soldiers and swung his head back to the Pastor. "You've been in contact with these guys Pastor?"

"No, no... nothing like that John, but I've had dreams lately that appear to be more like visions."

"And you've seen RJ and me leaving with these guys to God only knows where?" John said in a disbelieving tone.

"I haven't seen you leave John, but I've seen where you are going. I prayed many hours about this and my answer is always the same."

"What answer is that Pastor? That I need to go with these guys?" John said as he was allowing his temper to slightly rise while his voice followed suit.

"Just that my vision is correct, and from God," the Pastor said with resolution.

John was wondering if the old timer had finally lost it when more questions arose in his mind...

"Okay mister wizard, then where exactly is it that we are going?"

"Hat Creek," came an instant reply from the Pastor.

When the soldiers, conferring near the front door to the sanctuary, heard the mention of the very town where they had orders to transport the Colonel, they walked to a darkened corner of the church and formed a tight huddle. John watched intently as Captain Dylan broke from the huddle and used his radio in a quiet voice as to not be heard by the others. After a few moments and several nods from the young man he walked back to the front of the church and said…

"If your son can swing a hammer he is welcome to come with us Sir."

"And where exactly would we be going young man?"

Captain Dylan glared at the old man of God with a mixture of wonder and suspicion and said…

"Hat Creek Sir."

"Come back in an hour young man," John said without offering any form of a commitment and then he turned his attention to his Pastor. He placed his hand on his shoulder and steered him away from the others while whispering in his ear, "Tell me about this dream."

Chapter Eleven

Akiko's first helicopter ride was a turbulent one. The winds blew at thirty knots and the bird fluttered up and down like a roller coaster. Maria held her hand the entire time and could feel the young woman's pulse race through her ever tightening and somewhat sweaty grip. Sadahara was oblivious to Akiko's anxiety as he peered through the tiny window with excitement of his new journey and a chance to reconnect with his family. When the flight had ended a military jeep was waiting for the passengers and the two young privates quickly loaded the back with the suitcases and backpacks. Just as the passengers began to wonder how they were all going to fit into the small vehicle a van pulled up behind them and the driver yelled through the open window..."Are you guys coming or what?"

The van followed close behind the jeep up one hill and down another until it reached a well fenced and well fortified gated check point. The driver of the jeep simply waved as he passed through and the van along with its occupants pulled to side of the station and waited.

"Why did we stop?" one of the doctors asked.

"Gotta check you guys in," the driver replied as he leaped from his seat and made his way to the station attendants window. A few minutes later he walked back to the sliding door of the van and opened it….

"Doctor James Narwald?"

"That's me," came a reply from the back seat.

"Could you step outside with me sir, I just have a few questions."

One by one the passengers were taken out of the van and interrogated about their true identity, their religious background and any possible affiliations. The questions ranged from early childhood acquaintances to their preferred coffee. It became apparent to the group that these guys knew much more about the new arrivals then anyone of them had ever dreamed possible. As more and more returned to the van the chatter began to rise. Everyone on board felt as if they were being verbally intruded and somehow violated. They wondered what kind of living arrangements they were in store for and what kind of people would be running the compound that was just inside the heavily guarded gate. After about an hour of annoying questions and tiresome waiting the driver hopped back into the van and said...

"Sorry about that folks. Just need to make sure we have the right people."

The van made its way through several winding dirt roads and finally up a large incline that brought into view a valley with giant satellite dishes sprawling for what seemed like miles. A collective "whoa" was sounded by the passengers as they brushed under the first of many on their way to the main building. Upon exiting, the three doctors were hurried off in one direction, while Maria, Akiko and Sadahara were promptly greeted by an elderly Hispanic military man and led into a warm conference room with a wooden open beamed ceiling. The room appeared to be more of a lodge than anything else. It had a fireplace occupying a roaring fire, a large bookcase, sofas, and a stainless steel espresso machine complete with glass tubs containing a variety of fragrant beans. In the middle of the room there was a long table with about sixteen cushion swivel chairs and a whiteboard for detailing ideas. The three new arrivals were pleasantly asked to sit and the orientation began in a classic monotone military voice.

"I am Lieutenant Colonel Ramos and I'm here to explain why you're here, what you will be doing, and most importantly what you won't be doing. Your personal belongings are being transported to your new homes as we speak and there will be further instructions and orders awaiting you there" This base is designed to serve two purposes; first we are going to convert these enormous satellites dishes into missile defensive grid systems allowing us to pinpoint trajectories from missiles barely aloft, the search for ET has been put on hold indefinitely. Secondly, we are going to build a new city in the town of Hat Creek which you flew over upon your arrival. The reason for building this city is simple, we plan on turning back the pages of this once great country in an effort titled "Project Americana" The US military in a joint effort with the Traditional foundation has deemed it necessary to rebuild from within and there are currently seventy five new cities being built or about to be built. We are bringing in contractors from every field of expertise, nurses, doctors, technicians, firemen, you name it. Hell, we even have early entrepreneurs like the Joker who had this crazy coffee machine flown in. Along with the wonders of this valley there are some guidelines that you would do yourself well to remember. First and foremost is this, it is a privilege to be here and the US military, who is the law inside these gates, will have zero reservations about throwing your butts out of here.

Luitenant Colonel Ramos paused to look at his notes, took a deep breath, let out a sigh and said….

"I could go through all this nonsense for you but you three look like you know how to read. Just go through this stuff tonight and let me know if you have any questions."

"I have a question Sir," Sadahara said while raising hand like a school child.

"What's that son?"

"I heard that we can make a phone call."

"Tomorrow you will have working phones in your quarters, and yes, they'll ring anywhere in the lower forty eight," The Lieutenant Colonel replied as he flipped his binder under his arm and left the room.

Moments later Sadahara and Akiko were back in the van circling around the back of the base to several rows of temporary housing units. The structures were long single story boxes about two hundred feet long and sixty feet wide each, and there appeared to be about a dozen of them. When they walked up to the front of building "C" a young private no older then nineteen years old, touting a huge welcoming smile, greeted them with a handshake and asked them to follow him down the long hallway in the center of the building...

"Where Ya from?" asked the young soldier.

"Napa Valley," Sadahara mutely replied as he looked around at the walls and ceilings of the most boring building that he had ever seen.

Noticing the saddened look on Sadaharas face the young private showed a smirk that cleverly hid what he knew would come as a huge surprise to the two new recruits. When they reached the door marked C-09 he paused before opening it and said...

"What they failed to provide in exterior beauty is heavily compensated for in interior design."

When the door was fully opened Sadahara and Akiko gasped at the site of their new home. The first glance showed a beautiful ten foot open beam ceiling, hardwood floors in the main room and lightly textured walls decorated with colorful art. There was a large California king-sized bed in the bedroom with deep red bedding and a neatly placed plethora of fluffy pillows. The room was complete with two well lit walk-in closets on the opposite end of the room and a sitting ottoman in each. The office was large with several bookshelves and a solid maple desk shadowing two plush chairs in either corner. The desk top was complete with a computer and an extra laptop already on and humming quietly alongside every other office supply imaginable. On the reverse side of the living quarters there was a state of the art kitchen with polished stainless steel appliances, a living room with a forty-two inch flat screen TV and a plush leather couch with a matching love seat. In the corner stood a black wood burning stove near a sliding glass door that led to a private concrete porch. Down the hall there were side by side bathrooms painted in distinct his and hers colors with decor to match..

"Wow," Akiko said in a shocked tone and Sadahara added, "Who knew?" as they made round after round exploring their new dwelling.

"If you're wondering why this unit seems to be a bit more luxurious then you expected I can explain. General Thompson who runs this project wants to keep morale high and he knows that many of the people coming here will have lost everything and in some unfortunate cases............. Everyone. He knows that this project is going to take more than a few years to complete and he is doing everything in his power to make the long stay here enjoyable. We have a rec hall, a movie theater, three different restaurants, and even a gymnasium.....You name it.."

"What about a phone?" Sadahara piped in.

"Tomorrow morning Sir. Unless you want to be bothered with them setting it up now."

"Bothered? By all means bother us," Sadahara excitedly replied.

"Okay, I'll send somebody down within the hour and please make sure to read the all the paperwork. You'll find that all the rules and regulations are there along with maps of both the base and the proposed town."

As Sadahara fumbled through the initial setting requirements of the high definition television, Akiko buried herself into the half inch thick stack of paperwork lying on the dining room table. Beyond the basic rules of conduct it clearly explained the point system that they were to adhere to. Akiko and Sadahara were to each receive a card, linked to one another, that allotted them a determined amount of points monthly and that those points were to be deducted for groceries, entertainment, and dining out. Alcoholic beverages were only allowed at the restaurants and there was a limit of two drinks nightly per person and they were costly in points. Workers were expected to work six days a week with an extra day off every other week. Basically, the rules stated that at full capacity there would be over a thousand workers present to work the defense system and to build a new town and that it would take complete cooperation from everyone at the base to make it work. On the final page it had worker ID numbers and instructions of where and when to receive their cards and orders which happened to be at six am the next day at the main building.

"These people don't mess around," Akiko mumbled to herself as she came to the realization that her new job would begin in less than twelve hours....

Sadahara had already flipped on the television to a State run propaganda documentary about religious tolerance towards Muslims and was literally pacing back and forth waiting for the phone guy when Akiko asked if he had any interest in knowing what the papers said…

"I'll read them myself Akiko, you probably mixed up the words anyway."

"I don't know exactly why you are so full of anger for me Sadie," Akiko said as she slammed the papers down in a heap on the freshly polished table. "But I think they look at us as a pair and I don't think that we have much choice in the matter."

Sadahara gave her a disgusted look and kept right on pacing until the silence was lifted with an abrupt knock at the door...

"Just a second," Sadahara said as he hurried to open the door.

"Need a phone?"

"A phone would be great. Any chance you could link me online with somebody other than the government?"

"The internet doesn't really exist anymore Sir. Nobody can afford to maintain a site and there is nobody that can afford to visit it if there was one. Plus, for security reasons obviously."

"I'll settle for the phone."

"Just take a few minutes."

Sadahara had been waiting months for this moment. He hadn't spoken with his family in Southern Oregon in nearly a year and as the technician was completing his work Sadahara felt the anxiety of actually making the call home. Were his parents even alive? What about his younger brother who worked as a commodities broker and lived on the other side of town. Was he, and his wife, and little girl okay? Sadahara had several family members living in the greater Rogue Valley of Southern Oregon. They had migrated there at the end of World War Two and endured vast racism from every corner of the American culture. Sadahara's grandfather spoke about the early fifties and how he was arrested almost monthly for bogus charges and how he was treated behind closed doors. Amazingly his grandfather understood the racism and was always quick to proclaim that his hardship was for his family, and that his new country would be a place for great prosperity for his children. Sadahara's parents made the best of their lot in life and were able to purchase a home in White City when Sadahara was two years old and they had lived there ever since.

When the phone had came alive with a dial tone the technician under handed the cordless receiver to Sadahara and said....

"There Ya go, let me know if there are any problems," and he promptly left the room.

Sadahara held the phone in his hand and looked over at Akiko who was just as curious and concerned as he was.....

"Call Sadie."

"I will.........just give me a second."

Chapter Twelve

At exactly 4:00am the tiny San Fernando Valley cul-de-sac was illuminated with a bright light and the sound of chopper blades that surely woke several adjoining neighborhoods. The three Mitchells, as instructed hurried to the craft and after a swift embrace from Ricky boarded without incident. Craig looked out the window as he buckled himself in and saw his neighbors, dazed and confused in their front yards and staring directly at him. He felt shame and disloyalty but he needed to take his one opportunity. Katie sat sandwiched between Craig and Jason and was quietly weeping with her head between her legs. Ricky ran to over to Bill Richards a particular neighbor that he remembered from his childhood and handed him a box, said a few words and sprinted back to the co-pilot seat and gave the universal take-off sign of the twirling fingers and away they went.

The bird flew through the valley, followed Interstate 5 for about two hours and then darted northeast into the mountains. From there they floated through large puffy clouds as the sun began to rise and the outline of the enormous Sierras came into view. Craig had tried to communicate with Ricky at the start of the flight but the combination of Ricky's headset and Craig's lack thereof made it virtually impossible, so he relaxed and settled himself into a sightseer and let his mind drift. Craig had no idea what lay in store, but he trusted his old friend and knew that better days were certainly ahead. An hour later as Craig stepped out into the fresh mountain air, stretched his cramped legs and yawned deep to shake his early morning awakening from his brain. He couldn't help but feel his first tinge of excitement in over two years, though he knew better than to let his wife see that excitement on his face...

"Listen guys. I know it was hard leaving your neighbors, but they're going to get help soon. That box I gave to old man Richards has instructions of what they need to do to prepare for the 5th and it also has a secured cell phone that they can use to keep in communication with the military. It also has instructions to start a chain reaction of the alert to other neighborhoods and we can only hope that it stays secure.... They're going to be okay."

"Why us Rick?" Katie said with a look of contempt.

"See that little town at the bottom of the hill. You guys are going to help build a city down there."

"But why us Rick?" Katie asked for a second time with an extra emphasis on the word "us."

"Because I love you guys," Ricky replied as he walked to the back of the bird to retrieve the cargo.

Katie followed him and kept inquiring.....

"Was there some kind of lottery Rick? Were we chosen because of our good looks? Or are you just feeling sor..."

"Katie stop!! I could and I did, end of story."

Craig walked between the two and Katie wandered a few feet away and performed a slow 180 to take in the breathtaking view that she was in no mood to enjoy. Jason joined her and began to rub her shoulders and she released some of her tension while leaning back into her son. Katie watched the early morning wildlife begin to wake and move about as she contemplated the very meaning to it all. Craig helped Ricky unload the bags and whispered that she just need some more time and that eventually she would come around…

"Everybody here has a lot of work to do Craigo. I think that this is exactly what you guys need."

"Tell me about this city. What's the deal?"

"I'll come by tonight and fill you guys in with all the details but for now we need to get you settled in."

After the interrogation proceedings the Mitchells were taken to their new home that was similar in every way to the Taganawa's with the exception of an extra bedroom. Katie had been informed that the following day she could call her parents and Sister Jamie who had left Southern California years before to open a restaurant in Miami. Katie's Sister had studied culinary abroad and when her parents decided to retire in Florida they invested a large portion of their retirement fund to open a sidewalk café on the seaside boardwalk. Jamie had always had an entrepreneurial type of heart and with hard work she made the business flourish, but the last time the two sisters had spoken the restaurant was close to failure and Mom and Dad were close to broke.

Fifteen minutes after they were left alone in their new abode a knock sounded lightly on the door and when Ricky appeared at the other side, Craig said…

"That was quick. I thought you said tonight?"

"I did my man, but I'm here for Katie. Whadda Ya say Katie, want to take a ride?"

"Where?" Katie replied with her voice now only half full of anger.

"You'll see. Come on, the fresh air isn't gonna get any warmer."

Katie dropped the clothes that she was unpacking back into her suitcase and followed Ricky out the door. They hopped into a two seat jeep convertible and sped around the row of housing units and up a steep incline and down another. After only a couple of minutes of winding their way through heavy woods they came upon a giant A framed building with a sprawling exterior that sprawled several hundred feet in each direction from the A. Ricky pulled up to the front of the building and said.....

"Quiet here isn't it?" as he looked at his watch.

"I guess so...what is this place?" Katie said in no mood for riddles.

Again Ricky looked at his watch and said...

"In about forty seconds you'll find out."

Forty seconds later a loud bell rang out that echoed through the nearby canyons and a couple hundred kids came running out the side doors of the exterior and into the plentiful yards that were filled with massive trees and playgrounds...

"Some of these kids belong to people stationed here Kate, but the truth is, most of them are orphans."

"Orphans?"

"Yep" The guys from the Traditional foundation have been rounding them up for months and bringing them to facilities like this all over the country. This is just the beginning too. We're gonna need to build a second building like this one pretty soon because by the time we're done with this town we might have five times as many kids. Anyway, I just thought that you might want to see where you'll be working."

"Me?"

Robert Segotta

"Everyday Katie. These kids need role models and teachers, and you can be both."

"I'm not sure that I'm ready for this kind of responsibility Rick."

"Nobody is ready for anything anymore, Baby doll…..We just do what we can."

Katie watched the children at play. Their eyes were filled with wonder as they climbed trees and kicked soccer balls on the lightly snow covered ground. Her mind danced between her own childhood and that of her two boys and she began to feel the sorrow that had only temporarily left her when her eyes began to well once again. Ricky, feeling awkward, asked her if she wanted to see inside…

"Another time Rick, I'm sorry I'm just not ready for any potential joy."

Later that night as the Mitchells made dinner from the food that was provided in their refrigerator and pantry upon their arrival, Rick came calling again as promised. They gathered in the living room and Rick spent the next hour explaining "Project Americana" and the soon to be recapturing of the greater Los Angeles basin. Rick told the Mitchells that there has been a struggle between the progressives and traditionalists in DC since the collapse began and the divide grew much deeper after the war and ensuing uprising that came as an obvious result. The progressives have a set agenda of rebuilding America in a completely secular way because they blame everything that has happened in the past couple of years on the world's religions. Ricky explained that the primary problem that the progressives are having in achieving their goal is that much of the energy resources, primarily oil, is locked into the hands of traditional Billionaires who are being protected by a band of ex-military personnel with an arsenal that they had been stockpiling for decades. The progressives need energy, so they needed to make some concessions. "Project Americana" is one of those concessions. He went on to explain that the real world shakers are entrenched in a battle of ideologies. On one side we have the secular progressives that are trying to take full advantage of the situation and turn our sovereignty over to a global commission. On the other side of the coin we have traditionalists who feel that the only problem we have as a Nation is the progressive movement in the first place. Obviously we have a progressive President in a rapidly becoming progressive world, but in the meantime he won't get too far in Air Force One if the pipelines shut down."

Craig seemed a bit confused and asked…

"So the president of the United States wants a one world government?"

"Maybe, but for now he'll settle for a global commission that will supersede our constitution and bill of rights. Basically we will be answering to French diplomats when we misbehave."

"That's the end of the world stuff that James used to talk about," Jason said as he went back for a second helping of spaghetti.

Craig watched Jason doing the spoon and fork twist and as his mind did a temporary drift, he thought about the times that James would ramble on about what he had learned at church. James attended regularly with Jennifer and even joined a home group Bible study that met twice a week. Craig and Jason were annoyed at best when James would start talking about his faith and their lack thereof. After several attempts and with little success, he eventually stopped bugging them. His mother on the other hand enjoyed the discussion, but she too turned away from the boy and his insight when he revealed his questioning of her Catholic upbringing. When the brief flashback session ended Craig sighed, brought his attention back to Ricky and asked….

"So what exactly is "Project Americana?"

"Well," Ricky continued "The idea was first introduced to what remained of congress about four months ago by a couple of big time players that are never named. The plan is to rebuild America one town at a time in remote locations where the sustainability of each town is self contained. The idea was to prove that Americans, if left alone, will flourish and prosper. Obviously this will take an effort from the US military to secure the area, which is why this former SETI base is a perfect location. The military secures the boundaries, reworks the satellite dishes into a high tech missile defense grid; basically giving them something to do, and a town gets built in the process. We have fifty of these projects under way and several more planned. They are entirely funded by sources unknown and the funds seem unlimited."

"So this is a safe location?" Katie asked.

"It can't get any safer Katie," Ricky said as he looked at her still mournful eyes, "There is only one road in here and that is highway 89 which winds its way towards the top of Lassen Peak to the south and moves north to Mount Shasta. The Military has secured both locations and have actually destroyed a major portion of highway 44 that heads east from here towards Susanville. Put it this way, if you make it to this base the military knows about it."

"How did we end up here? And furthermore how did you end up here Ricky?" Craig asked.

"I had been following the developments on my secured military laptop and when they announced the go ahead for the projects, I did a lot of begging, and as far as you guys...........I actually had no clearance to bring you here when I told you that I'd be picking you up this morning. In fact I didn't have permission to fly into the LA area at all, but after I hung up the phone with you last night I devised a plan to present to Colonel Fields, my commanding officer. In that briefing I described what an amazing asset you would be in the construction and what benefits that could come from giving the good people of LA a "heads up" It took about three hours but eventually he agreed, and just in time too, because we barely made it there in time."

"So you're here to stay for awhile?"

"As long as they let me Craigo."

Chapter Thirteen

On May 3rd 2017 Colonel Robbs and his son arrived at the base outside of Hat Creek. John was introduced to Brigadier General Gerald Thompson, a man John had always heard about but never met. John had heard stories about the Generals legendary temper and his sometimes unbridled anger, but he also knew about his amazing bravery and valor. The General informed John that he would be second in command of the entire operation while RJ was to report to the architecture office for further instructions. As John and RJ were settling into their new apartment John was still trying to make sense of the discussion he had only hours before with Pastor Albert. The Pastor, an elderly African American man who appeared to be on his way out of this life had, in no uncertain terms, explained his prophetic dream to John and his son and it had jostled John's mind and left it reeling. John's uneasiness came first in the form of religious jargon that he didn't understand but mostly because of the supernatural ability the man seemed to have in forecasting the future. John had always mocked the idea of psychics and their so-called predictions and always looked forward to their failed forecasts. In all his years he had never thought of the vast prophesies that were foretold in the Bible and the reliability of each and every one. To John, the Bible had been a book of morals at best and all the rest was for the experts to discuss and argue about. Now he believed and had built a relationship with the author, and as time wore on, he knew that all things were possible.

Back in Albert's office the Pastor had read from Joel 2:28-32 and told

John that he believed that for the first time in his life he was experiencing an old man's dream as prophesized in Joel.

"You see John," the Pastor explained, "It says here that after the day of Pentecost that 'your old men will dream dreams' and I have no doubt that I have dreamt a dream that came from the Lord."

"What exactly did you dream Pastor?" John remembered asking...

"My dream is always the same. I see you and RJ laughing and having a good time in a large courtyard in the middle of a beautiful town. I look over and I see a tall clock tower and underneath it is a plaque that reads *Hat Creek, reestablished 2018.* Then I feel a sense of trouble and I see you two in a small church with worry showing on your faces. There is a young Asian women lying on her back screaming while others are attending to her. Then I feel a rumble and a shaking and a sense that something horrible is about to happen........."

"Then what?" John had asked.

"Just as I feel this awful fright there is a great light that wakes me every time. But the strange part is that I am always fearful up until that point, but when I wake I am always as calm as I can be, completely relaxed and at peace."

John hated the ending of Albert's dream. He wanted answers that his Pastor simply didn't have. It left him fidgety the first time he heard it and his anxiety only grew from there. Now that he was sitting in a new apartment on a hill, overlooking the ghost town of Hat Creek, he knew his God had plans specifically for him. He would do his best to be a simple servant, but his past failings and insecurities were making it hard for him to function in what was a surreal and unpredictable environment.

John finished unpacking and settled into his new living room waiting for RJ to finish his shower so he could talk more about the dream. John knew that his son was not an expert on the Bible, but he knew more than he did. When RJ finished his shower he emerged wearing his oversized gray sweat suit and his Oakland A's hat that had been part of his everyday apparel for as long as John could remember...

"What do you make of that dream RJ?" John said, never allowing it to wander far from his thoughts.

"It's spooky... why, what do you make of it?"

"I think that it's spooky too. How did he know that we would end up here in Hat Creek?"

"I don't think that he knew Pops. I think God knew and he used Pastor Albert to direct us here."

"But what about the shaking and rumbling? What about the Asian girl and the light? John said, hoping for a new answer.

"Who do I look like to you, Billy Graham?" RJ said as he started clipping his nails with a brand new nail clipper he had found in the bathroom drawer.

"I can't believe that you know who Billy Graham is," John said sarcastically.

"I didn't until a month ago when I started reading one of his books during my breaks at the church."

"And?" John said in his now, customary leading way.

"Nothing really. It just helped me understand some things, you know, he put some troubling ideas into basic language that even a drop out like me could understand."

"Do you still have this book?" John asked in a more sincere tone.

"Nope. It was a signed edition for Pastor Albert, but I do have a few Ravi Zacharias tapes and a couple of CS Lewis books. Plus I have this.."

RJ reached into his bag and pulled out a brand new Bible with his name embossed at the bottom and handed it to John.

"Pastor Albert knew that I wouldn't be around much longer and he wanted me to have this for my journey."

"That's a good looking Bible son," John said as he held it in his hand.

"It has a brother too," RJ said as he pulled a second Bible from his bag and handed it to his father.

John took the second Bible from his son's hand and noticed immediately that his name appeared at the bottom. He held it there for a moment pondering how his faith had grown in such a short period of time and how much shame he felt for ever doubting God in the first place and the shame he felt for still doubting today.

"I think he wrote something inside Pops."

John opened the book and in the extra space of the first page was written, *"Always keep this close to your heart"* the exact words that his uncle Amos had used so many years before. John sat there with tears welling up in his eyes and he bowed his head and began to pray…How his God could communicate directly to his heart, in the very moment he needed answers, was beyond his comprehension. John continued to pray with RJ at his side and a new peace overcame them both and they settled back, ready to embrace whatever lay in store.

The next morning John reported to General Thompson's office for his first official briefing. General Thompson had a long and distinguished military career and was an angry and ornery old man a little overdue for retirement. The General was a big man with short gray hair, though it appeared as if he had never lost a single one. He stood about six foot three and weighed well over 240 pounds and used his size to add to his already position driven intimidation. He had little patience for the upheaval that was commonplace on the streets of America today and he was a staunch opponent of "Project Americana." The General was a traditionalist in many ways but he couldn't find the reasoning to build new cities when there were perfectly good ones that were there for the taking. The General was also a committed atheist who had hidden his belief system from the military for years. Whenever the topic arose General Thompson made a quick response that he was raised Catholic and then abruptly changed the subject. As the General sipped from his stainless steel USS Arizona memorial coffee mug his intercom began to chirp at exactly 6 hundred hours…

"Colonel Robbs and Lieutenant Colonel Smalls are here to see you Sir."

"Send 'em in Christine."

The General's office was large with giant windows that opened to a view of the enormous satellite dishes below. The room reeked of cigars and the cloud of the mornings first had not yet dissipated. After the official military greeting the two men were instructed to sit across from the General's desk as he wasted no time in starting his rant…

"I wish I could tell you two what exactly it is we are doing here but I can't. Reworking those satellite dishes is a purposeful idea and we have all the tech geeks in the world to do it and plenty of personnel to protect them while it gets done. I could see why we need somebody in charge of this project but it hardly requires a General. I fought in Viet Nam for crying out loud and now they have me up here camping in the woods. Anyway, as for this ridiculous "Project Americana," I need you guys to handle all that construction garbage because the thought of it makes me sick. Smalls, I want you to deal with those damn kids. Figure out what they need, keep 'em quiet, and keep 'em away from here. Colonel Robbs I need you to keep the peace at that waste of time building site down there. Talk with the architects and builders and make whatever orders for supplies that are needed. There shouldn't be too much because apparently we already have almost double the materials we need due to lack of planning and misguided ordering. Whatever is left over can be used in or around the school or here at the base and I'll leave all of that to your discretion Robbs, as long as I don't have to hear about it. First and foremost, we need to figure out who is going to be in charge down there, 'cause I'm sick of all the bickering that keeps coming from those undisciplined civilians. We have already decided the head architect and we've had ground crews forming slabs to their specs for a couple of months since the bulk of the snow was cleared, but we need to find somebody to be the project manager"

The General leaned in close to make his next point...

"Listen Robbs, we have over a thousand workers either here or on their way here and this town needs to be built in a year. Now it starts to snow in late October so the framing and the roofing needs to be done. You can spend the winter working the interiors and then next spring you can start building homes, starting with mine!!"

"General Thompson, if I may sir," Ricky said in his most straight forward voice.

"What is it Smalls?"

"As you might already know Sir I brought a personal friend here who is the best damn builder you'll ever meet and since it won't be a conflict of interest with me up at the school I would like to endorse him to be the head builder. I'd stake my reputation on him Sir."

General Thompson opened a notebook and said...

71

"What's his name Smalls?"

"Craig Mitchell Sir. And his son Jason works alongside him and is a great builder in his own right."

General Thompson opened his file cabinet that contained pretty much the life story of everybody present at the base and grabbed the Mitchell's file. He looked it over and saw the added notes that Ricky had made at the end. Everybody's file was incomplete because the whereabouts and happenings of the last 18 months were unobtainable by military personnel.

"It says here that he recently lost a son to those scoundrels in the LA basin."

"Yes Sir, my Godson," Ricky said as he looked down in a sorrow filled reminder.

"Well the bastards responsible probably won't be breathing by this time tomorrow," the General replied with delight glowing in his well aged eyes.

"Excuse me Sir?" John interjected into the conversation.

"Is there something that I'm missing?

"You haven't heard Colonel. We're taking back LA at three am tomorrow. We have strategic strikes planned and an army of thousands surrounding the city ready to conquer and destroy any morons that get in there way."

"What about the not so moronic Sir?" John said in a low tone.

"We've done our best to inform them Colonel but I'm not going to lie to you. There will be many causalities. Too bad we don't apply these tactics in every city and turn the page once and for all on this debauchery. Anyway, we can all watch that on the news tomorrow morning..... so what do you think Robbs, is Mitchell your guy?"

"Sounds good enough to give him a try Sir," John said while still trying to ingest the earlier information.

"Give him a try for a week Robbs and if you replace him with somebody else you better be sure. I don't want anarchy down there. There are two jeeps outside, keys are in 'em, take your pick. Here's your orders and here's a cell phone for each of you, you'll find a directory in your papers there so call whoever you need to contact and get the ball rolling. Meet me here each morning at 6 hundred hours. That'll be all."

When John and Ricky made their way outside to where the jeeps were parked they felt the awkwardness of being in such close proximity only moments before and not really having a second or two to become acquainted....

"Sir, you're going to like Craig Mitchell and his Son, they're good men."

"What's your first name son?" John replied.

"Rick Sir, but people call me Ricky."

"Tell me about the other son Ricky, what happened to him?"

"I never got too many details Sir. Too early to pry. I know he was gunned down in broad daylight by a cartel member...and that's about all I know."

"Did you say that you were his Godfather?"

"That is correct Sir. Craig and I were childhood friends."

"Are you a religious man Smalls?"

"I guess so Sir. I believe there is some sort of God."

"Maybe now would be a good time to identify him Son.... By the way Ricky when we're not in the presence of Mister stuffy in there, it's John. I'm too old to care and I'm still pretending to be retired, I don't need to have my ego inflated when I'm in the process of learning humility."

Ricky reached out his hand and gave the big man a firm handshake and said..

"Sounds good to me John."

Chapter Fourteen

It had been two weeks since Sadahara had made that fateful phone call; The call that would push him even farther away from where his heart needed to be and to a place where retrieval would become the test of a lifetime. Sadahara had found his parents number disconnected so he called his Aunt Ginny who lived in Grants Pass, Oregon about thirty miles away from his childhood home when he heard the horrific news. His Father had died almost a year before when he suffered a heart attack during an altercation at a food bank in downtown Medford. Apparently a couple of local thugs were attempting to steal jewelry from people in line and Sadahara's father had intervened and a scuffle ensued. A moment later he was lying on his back with several good souls trying to revive him, but he never regained conscientious. Sadahara's Mother had moved in with his Aunt and her two teenage sons while his Brother and his family had moved North to look for work and no one knew their whereabouts. When Sadahara spoke with his Mother she was not recognizable to him. She spoke quietly and repeated herself over and over again. She would whisper that she loved her son so much and then ask why he wasn't here. After she rambled on for a few more minutes Aunt Ginny took the phone from her and said….

"Your Mom is a little confused Sweetie."

Sadahara was again replaying the fateful call in his mind as he finished his coffee and walked out into the beautiful mountain air. The late Spring world was coming to life right before his eyes. Birds were soaring and diving, streams could be heard in the distance, as the light breeze was rustling through the mighty pines and yet to Sadahara it meant nothing. He simply walked down the hill towards the main building as he had done every day for the last two weeks. Once inside he would bury himself in the electronic world where no one could touch him. Sadahara was using his talents to transfer the use of the enormous satellite dishes from their intended use to a more practical one and while the work was intriguing, forming a crisscross grid of relaying satellite zones to narrowly pin point incoming missiles, Sadahara had lost his ability to care. He had been there for only two weeks and he had already gained a reputation as a sour puss, and was quickly becoming the office pariah. There were many military technicians at the base as well as many talented civilians but to Sadahara they were all idiots and he had zero problem expressing his views, and belittling every person who did not have the authority to send him packing.

Sadahara spent his hours alone. He ate his lunch alone, he ate his dinner alone and slept on the couch each night watching television until he finally dozed off. He spoke few words to his wife who had became a stranger living in the next room. Every evening and every morning she would try to talk with him but he merely grunted a response and would ignore her to the best of his abilities. He knew deep inside that she was hurting too but he wasn't ready to share his grief with her, nor anyone else for that matter. Sadahara had seen his world turn upside down in a matter of months and his once prestigious existence had been reduced to a fading shadow of its prior self. He looked at others at the base with contempt. They surely didn't work as hard as he did, they didn't sacrifice the time that he once did and they didn't deserve the life he once knew and sorely missed. Sadahara began to see others as mere obstacles to overcome. If he were to find any happiness in this world he would need to rise to the top of this newly forming town and conquer it.

Ricky drove his jeep towards the temporary housing units and saw Jason outside the building running laps around its perimeter…Jason had always been an athlete and his slender yet muscular six foot frame showed years of training.

"What's going on Jay Dog? Where's Mom and Dad?"

"Inside," Jason replied while holding his hands to his knees trying to catch his breath.

"Well, I need to talk with them. Are you almost done?"

"A couple more times around, I'll see you inside," Jason said as he regained his stride.

Ricky lightly rapped on the Mitchell's door and Katie opened it a second later as if she were waiting for a reason…

"That was quick," Ricky said as he made his way inside.

"She gets sick with worry when ever anybody leaves her sight Rick," Craig said from the kitchen table as he finished gobbling down his apple.

"Well, I can understand that," Ricky said with compassion, "But there is little reason to worry about trouble here. This place is secure. Anyway, I've got some news for you guys. It just so happens that the big man in charge of this base hasn't decided who will be the project manager is going to be and he doesn't want anything to do with the decision either. So I had a meeting with the guy who will be making the decisions and I suggested you…"

"And?" Craig said with a perking interest.

"Well, his name is Colonel John Robbs, a big black guy and he doesn't know the first thing about constructing anything little yet a town so he's going to give you the first crack at it. I figure you can fool him for awhile anyway, whaddya think?"

"Well, obviously I think that it's great. I'd rather be making decisions then carrying out ridiculous ones. Unfortunately Jason and I are not allowed to be happy about anything quite yet."

"Stop it right now Craig," Katie said as she poured herself a second cup of coffee. "Forgive me for feeling a little awkward about all our good fortune when we left loving neighbors to fend for themselves."

"Oh, that reminds me," Ricky chirped in. "Tomorrow morning our boys are going to take back the city. As long as your neighbors do what we instructed them to do they should be fine."

"And what exactly did you instruct them to do Ricky?" Jason said as he walked into the kitchen wiping the sweat from his face with a towel.

"Simple really. Get down in your Grandfathers' old basement and stay there until the seventh. After that, the military will pick them up and take them somewhere safe."

"What does safe mean Rick?" Katie said with a look of suspicion in her eyes. "A camp?"

"Look Katie, we'll start with getting them somewhere safe and we'll take it from there. Has anyone tried to call old man Richards?"

"They just hooked up the phone this morning and I've been talking with my parents and my Sister. Haven't had time to call LA yet," Katie responded.

"How are they doing Katie?" Ricky asked.

"Thankfully, they're all fine. One of my Sisters best customers was also one of her wine suppliers who has a vineyard and a large house attached to it in Virginia. When things got really ugly he invited the three of them to move into the guest house. I guess he has his own helicopter because he personally flew them from his vacation home in Florida to his vineyard which is pretty well fortified from what I understand."

"How did you know how to find them?" Ricky curiously asked.

"That's the amazing part Rick. When I called the house a Hispanic man answered who couldn't speak a word of English. I asked him if he knew the people who lived there before but he couldn't understand me. I was about to hang up the phone when he said my name in severely broken English. I said yes, yes this is Katie do you know where my family is? And he mumbled the number to me, thankfully I remember the first ten numbers in Spanish and he had it right too, because I found them. My sister said that when they left the house they knew that somebody would eventually move in so she wrote several notes around the house and on the walls…"

> *We are leaving now, please enjoy the house as it was once filled with laughter and joy. We are missing persons dear to us, Katie and her family. Please, please if she calls this number give her this new number………..*

"Couldn't they have left you a message on the answering machine Mom?" Jason said with a twinge of sarcasm.

"They did that too Jason, they're not idiots, but it doesn't take a PHD in logic to realize that phone messages can be deleted."

"Listen Guys," Ricky said. "We've got work to do. Katie and I need to get you up to the school to meet with a Maria Gonzales. She's in charge of the school administrations and I'm in charge of keeping the kids in line up there, and you two need to get a vehicle at the main building and head down to the site to meet with Colonel Robbs."

"Wait a minute," Jason said. "My Mom is going to be working for a Mexican?"

"Not all Mexicans are bad people Jay. From what I understand she is an extraordinarily nice lady and well qualified too."

"Excuse me and my racist tendencies, but I just watched a dirty Mexican shoot my brother to death and I'm not quite ready to forget that... as of yet."

"Jason," Ricky replied through a deep sigh. "I spent several years on foreign soil and I've seen things that would make just about anybody sick to their stomach, but if I learned one thing in all those years it is this; there are good people and bad people of every color and creed. Learn to love the person for who they are individually, otherwise you'll be choking in anger for the rest of your days."

Jason gave a semi polite nod and headed off to the shower while Katie hung her head showing the pain she felt in being reminded of her loss. Ricky felt the awkwardness and broke the silence with a proclamation…

"Katie I'll pick you up in an hour or so and Craig you guys need to get down to that site."

Chapter Fifteen

ohn picked up RJ and drove his jeep to the site where he saw what appeared to be miles of foundations ready for framing. He saw hundreds of workers working the grounds running pipes for sewage while electricians brought power to each slab from temporary power poles. At the end of the first row of slabs he saw several trailers with men wearing red shirts bustling around pointing and chatting with one another. John had no idea what or where he was supposed to go so he simply pulled right in front of the set of trailers and he and RJ hopped out of the jeep and made their way to the first and largest one. John didn't notice that the door had his name on it but RJ was quick to point out the revelation.

"Looks like they knew you were coming Pops," RJ said as he pointed to the door.

"Imagine that" John said as he opened the door to find several more red shirts working behind drafting desks. John had not yet donned his uniform because it was being resized to fit his larger self and the architects who were busy at work showed little respect or patience for the abrupt intrusion.

"Ever heard of knocking?" came a response from the back of the room where it appeared the guy in charge was seated based on the size of his desk and demeanor in his voice.

"Didn't know I needed to knock on a door with my name on it son."

Ryan Teagarden a master architect in his mid forties, half bald and wearing thick geek squad glasses sprung his tiny frame from his seat in the back of the room and quickly offered an apology and a handshake.

"I'm sorry Sir. You must be Colonel Robbs."

"I am, but this is hardly a military operation son, so unless the General or another suit is present, you can call me John and this is my son RJ."

"Good to meet both of you," Ryan said with a sheepish grin still hiding his embarrassment from showing disrespect. "We sure are glad to have you here Sir."

"And why is that son? I don't know the first thing about building a dog house. What is my purpose here? Why does it seem so important to have a formerly retired Colonel babysitting a jobsite?"

"Because it's anarchy out there Sir. We have so many workers from different locations that all think they know what's best. We told the General that we needed more intervention to keep order down here if we expect to make our deadlines but he never seemed to care. Apparently that all changed when he was informed that the funding would slow if he couldn't keep the scheduled pace so he went looking for a second in command, and I guess he found him. They just put that name plate on the door this morning and I never guessed that you would be here so soon. Once again I want to offer my apologies."

John looked out the small window at the workers bustling about and asked...

"Who's in charge of operations right now?"

"That's just it Sir...I mean John, we are! and architects and construction workers don't always see eye to eye. We just draw it and they build it, but to be honest we don't always know how they build it."

"What does that mean?" John asked as he spun around and looked at Ryan with inquisitive eyes.

"These guys are some of the best ground crews that I've ever seen, but they do things in unconventional ways, at least some of them do. Anyway, if we try to redirect them in any way they just laugh at us and tell us to take our bowling shirts to the lanes where they belong. That of course is a minor problem compared to the arguing amongst the crews themselves. We've had too many fights to count out there and now that we're ready to start framing, we've got over a hundred builders that think they have the best plan...Its gonna get ugly unless we get some kind of order."

"I already have a project manager in line to take over immediately," John said with authority.

"Great, and who is that John?"

"I believe that would be me," Craig said as he walked into the room with Jason following close behind. "You must be Colonel Robbs."

"I am," John said as he accepted Craig's hearty handshake.

"I am Craig Mitchell and this is my son Jason. Who's drawing this project?"

"I'm the head architect," Ryan said as he reached out his hand to shake Craig's.

"Do you have a general drawing of the project I can look at?"

"It's right over here on the wall. Let's take a look."

The men moved over towards the back of the wall and looked at several drawings that showed an entire town from different angles. The town had everything: Shops, a grocery store, a theater, a large courtyard, a town hall, restaurants, a sports park, and more. Ryan went on to explain that they had already expanded the highway to four lanes and that the center of town would have a roundabout that would circle the enormous courtyard in the middle…

"Where's the clock tower going to be?" RJ chimed in.

"The clock tower is going to sit….wait a minute," Ryan said after a brief pause. "How did you know about the clock tower?" Did the General tell you guys about that?"

"Nah, I never even met the General, I'm not too good with authority figures and from what my Pops tells me he's kinda scary."

"So how did you know then?"

"Let's just say an old friend told me. A very wise old friend."

Once again John had that convicting feeling of belief stir inside him and before he knew it the obvious question came from his mouth.

"Are we building a church?"

"Ahhh no," Ryan said while still trying to come to grips with the clock tower revelation.. We had planned on building one but it was a concession for the progressives in Washington that we don't."

"So what about all the people who are going to live here? What if they decide they want to worship?" John asked.

"I really don't know. I guess they need to do it in private."

"I'm not a religious man but I can't imagine a town without a church," Craig said as he looked over the drawings.

"Does it look buildable Mr. Mitchell?" Ryan asked, trying to change the subject.

"It's Craig, and I can build anything you can draw as long as it's possible and if it's not I'll let you know."

"I like your confidence Craig," Ryan said.

"Oh he's got an abundance of that," Jason said with a smirk as his Dad gave him an evil eye.

"Well, we need to get these guys together and let them know who's in charge," John said. He then looked to Ryan and said "Why don't you call for a mandatory meeting tomorrow around 10:00am and I'll introduce myself and Mitchell here."

"It's done John, we'll see you in the morning and I'll have my things moved out of your desk."

As the two Robbs and the two Mitchells left the trailer to a bright sun with large puffy white clouds John took Craig aside with a light pull of the arm and asked him if RJ could be of any assistance to either himself or his son. He informed him that RJ had no experience in construction but that he was sure that he would do his best. John simply didn't want RJ to end up impaled on chunk of metal or falling off a roof. Craig assured him that he would keep an eye on him and keep him close at hand. Then a few minutes after that conversation Craig performed his first act of delegation when he informed Jason that RJ was his responsibility.

Chapter Sixteen

Ricky picked Katie up a few minutes before Craig and Jason had returned and drove her to the school to meet Maria Gonzales. Maria, a heavy set Hispanic woman with caring eyes and a welcoming smile instantly took Katie by the hand and began to walk her around and introduce her to the teachers and staff members. Ricky found his office to be just where Maria had directed him and he started going through his duties that were laid out in his stack of paperwork that he had received earlier. Maria was about as kind as a person could be and she showed that kindness with every word she spoke...

"We've got an amazing opportunity here Dear. These kids are going to have their first chance at a normal life and it is up to us to give them that chance. This building used to be a Christian camp years ago but it turned into a lodge for the SETI personal when somebody decided that it was more important to look for ET then to look for God. Are you a believer Dear?"

"I was raised Catholic, I guess I believe some of it," Katie replied.

"You see Dear we have something in common already. I was raised Catholic too, but shushhh..Don't tell anybody.......I left the church and became a Christian."

"What's the difference?"

"Well, it was explained to me this way. If you and I are each holding a good egg but one of us is holding it incorrectly it doesn't necessarily make the egg bad. However, holding it correctly is always a good idea."

"Okay, maybe we can expand on that over lunch sometime soon" Katie said with a confused look.

"Here we are Dear. This is where you'll be working." Maria opened the doors to a small medical station with a waiting room and a glass partition that separated the room. Behind the glass stood an Asian girl taking the temperature of a small boy with bleach blonde hair…

"Akiko, this is Katie. Katie this is Akiko. Akiko and I actually flew in here together a couple of weeks ago and she is already my dear friend. I just know you two are going to hit it off. Akiko needs somebody to take care of the station when she is down at the makeshift hospital at the base and to help her with some basic tasks."

"But I don't have any medical training," Katie said.

Akiko looked deeply into the green eyes of the rapidly aging woman. She could tell that she had, at onetime been a beauty queen with a petite yet full figure. She quickly studied the lines of sadness on her California perma-tanned face and knew that she would need to show her the line of kindness that Maria had undoubtedly begun.

"That's okay," Akiko said after a brief yet telling silence, "I'll teach you the basics; CPR, temperature taking, how we wipe noses" Akiko let out a slight laugh and said, "We just take care of the kids like Timothy here, right Timothy?"

Timothy hopped down from cot and said….

"Where's my sucker Mrs. Taganawa?" Akiko held out a bowl with many colorful suckers and Timothy grabbed one and quickly ran out of the room.

"Doesn't appear to be anything wrong with that one," Maria said.

"Just a little cold," Akiko said with a smile.

"Good. I'm going to leave you young gals to get acquainted and I'll stop by and see you during my rounds."

Katie stood there silent like a schoolgirl in detention not knowing what to do. She felt out of place and as nervous as could be. Akiko quickly sensed her nervousness and broke the silence with an offer to walk around and meet some of the kids. Katie smiled and nodded in agreement but as they were heading towards the door it flew open and Mrs. Peterson, one of the original teachers, hurried in carrying a small six year old girl who had blood gushing from her head. Katie froze in horrified shock as Akiko sprung into action…

"Call the doctor Mrs. Peterson," she said as she grabbed the sobbing child from her arms and quickly carried her to a stainless steel table in the back.

Katie watched in horror as Akiko applied pressure with a cloth and with her free hand grabbed a bottle hydrogen peroxide…

"Open this for me will you Katie."

Katie grabbed the bottle, opened it with shaking hands and handed it back to Akiko who then asked her to keep a pressure hold on the blood soaked cloth. Katie thought that she was going to lose it between the sobs and the blood but she pressed down on the wound anyway…

"Okay," Akiko said, "When I say so, lift the cloth so I can disinfect the wound and then apply the pressure again with this clean cloth."

Akiko poured a liberal amount of the solution onto a clean sponge and motioned to Katie to remove the cloth. It was then that Katie had her first glimpse of a four inch gash behind the girls ear that ran up to the top of her forehead. There was a momentary pause in the gushing blood when she pulled the cloth away but when Akiko squeezed the sponge over the wound it unleashed an avalanche of diluted blood and Katie nearly fainted....

"Put pressure again," Akiko said, and Katie quickly reapplied the pressure while holding back convulsions to vomit.

Akiko grabbed a clean cloth from a drawer and told Katie that she had it from here. The two changed places and Akiko was now applying the pressure...

"What happened to her Mrs. Peterson?" Akiko asked.

"I don't know exactly, but I guess one of the boys threw a rock at her."

"It must have been a big rock," Akiko said as she comforted the young girl with some quiet humming and gentle rocking.

A moment later a young Doctor came in and took one look at the wound and decided that it was best that he attend to her at the base's make shift hospital. Akiko went to the maintenance closet and brought out a gurney and unfolded it. She and the doctor lifted the young girl off the table and onto the bed with wheels and whisked her down the hall. Akiko looked back over her shoulder and said to Katie...

"I should be back soon. Push nine on the phone and it'll ring down at the hospital."

Katie looked at Mrs. Peterson and said in a frightened voice...

"Ahhh I'm going to freak out if that happens again and I'm alone in here."

Chapter Seventeen

Craig was fumbling through a set of blueprints that he had gotten from Ryan while Jason was watching the National news channel wondering why there was not a single mention of the LA situation when it occurred to him how obvious the answer was. The thugs in LA have televisions too. Jason flipped off the set and made his way into the kitchen to make a sandwich when there was a knock at the door. Jason opened the door and was surprised to see RJ standing at the threshold…

"Hey man," RJ said, "Wanna go check out the scenes?"

"Whadda Ya mean check out the scenes?"

"I don't know. I just know that we are the only people here who have this day off and my Pops gave me the keys to his jeep. I looked you up and here I am. It wasn't a long walk cause we live right down the hall but I went out of my way just the same."

"I'm not so sure that I want to go anywhere right now," Jason said as he slowly started to close the door and waited for the polite "Okay" response.

"Come on man, they got a river up by that school and plenty of poles. What else are you going to do?"

Jason took a deep breath and realized that he really didn't know what he was going to do with the rest of his day but he hadn't planned on making a new friend with a black kid several years his junior...

"Look man," RJ said with his million dollar smile, "If we get really bored we can roll the jeep off a cliff and I'll tell my Dad that it was my idea. He's used to me screwing up...Come on let's get out of here."

Jason sighed and after another long pause he said "Alright, but if I really get bored will you fly off the cliff with the jeep?"

Jason let out a grin and RJ showed off his smile once more and said...

"It's a deal man..... You will be there at the bottom to put me back together, right?"

RJ and Jason began to laugh and made their way down the hall to the gravel parking lot.

Craig couldn't believe the intricacy of the drawings that lay before him. Every building was to be unique and stand apart from the next. The angles were amazing as were the drawings themselves. He actually had to lift his head a couple of times and mutter "Wow" when he saw the plans for this new town. It truly would be something to marvel at when it was complete and he was excited to begin while feeling blessed to have the opportunity. At that moment, alone in his new apartment his mind began to wander. He thought about being blessed and then he thought about the actual word "bless." Before long he started thinking about who was blessing him. Craig had always felt that his hard work and skills had brought about all his good fortune. He had heard James say on many occasions that he felt so blessed but Craig never paid much attention to his son and his growing faith. Craig leaned back and remembered a particular occasion when James had a spring of unbelievable bad luck. In a short span of three days James had his truck stolen, he had stepped on a nail and his foot got infected and grew to the size of a cantaloupe and the next day his girlfriend's Sister had been killed in a car crash.

James was down, but he and Jenny, through their grief, still proclaimed to be sincerely blessed. Craig was deep in thought when his phone rang for the first time. It actually startled him and brought him back from his minds wandering...

"This is Craig Mitchell?"

"Craig, John Robbs here. Listen I want to go over a few things before we have our little meeting tomorrow. I need to check in with the General at 6am can we get together at that café around 7?"

"Which one is that John?" Craig asked.

"The only one that serves breakfast." John said as he looked over the take home menus for each restaurant.

"I'll see you there. Oh, and by the way how many points is it for breakfast?"

"Beats me son," John said with a low chuckle, "I still have a couple of twenties in my wallet."

"Perfect, we can leave them as a memorabilia tip," Craig said while adding a soft chuckle of his own.

"Sounds like a plan, I'll see you at seven."

RJ drove like a wild man until it prompted Jason to ask...

"Do you even have a license?"

"Nope.... Never did either." RJ said with a growing grin.

"Then why are you driving?"

"Cause I need the practice, isn't it obvious?" RJ said while letting out a wild man's laugh.

"Yeah it's obvious alright, but just remember it's supposed to be you at the bottom of that cliff not both of us."

RJ drove the jeep up the steep incline and down the other side towards the school. He only had vague directions and they were forced to back out of a few wayward roads overgrown with brush and fallen branches until they finally saw the school come into view. RJ hopped out and said....

"Let's find those poles and find that river."

"Do you even know how to fish RJ?" Jason asked.

"Nope, but I've seen it on TV. You remember that show with the guy in the orange hat with the letter "T" on it. I've seen that guy pull in all kinds of fish. Besides, I'll bet you know how to fish."

"What makes you say that?" Jason said with a genuine look of curiosity.

"White people are always fishin' or golfin' or doing something outdoors."

Jason couldn't help but smile as they headed towards the doors of the giant A frame. He also couldn't help but like RJ and he knew that he was going to be friends with him and it was probably best to just let it happen. At the main entrance they ran into Ricky who was asking the personnel about the incident that occurred earlier with the young girl...

"Hey Rick," Jason said as he walked up behind him and touched him on his shoulder.

"J Dog, what are you doing up here?"

"This is my new...This is RJ and he said that we can find a river near here and some fishing poles."

Ricky looked at an elderly lady who worked at the front desk with an implied question on his face and she responded that there were some poles and gear down by the river in an old shack but they would need the key. She fumbled through a drawer and finally produced it..

"Here you go. Just make sure to return it."

"Jason, aren't you guys supposed to be working?" Ricky asked.

"Our sentence starts tomorrow," RJ replied. "This is the final day off for sheriff Bart and his trusty side kick the Waco Kid."

"Blazing Saddles...ahhh, I remember that" Ricky said with a grin. "You didn't find that movie offensive?"

"Not at all," RJ replied, "I found it offensive how much they butchered it for cable."

Once again Jason was smiling. It became apparent to him that he hadn't had any fun in months and he couldn't remember being this amused in consecutive moments for over two years. When RJ started whistling the theme to Blazing Saddles as the two made their way towards the river he had Jason in stitches and it prompted Jason to say in as high a voice as he could muster...

"Listen Bart," and the two were rolling with laughter...

Jason showed RJ how to tie a lure and how to cast and reel without landing a hook in his head and they settled into a day of fishing in the full river nestled against a backdrop of fifty foot pines. They didn't have much luck catching fish but they kept themselves amused with stories of the prior world they both had experienced...After a pause in the conversation RJ pulled a 180 and said...

"What's the deal with those guys making a town without a church? That's like a village without a village idiot. And I should know because I was the village idiot of West Oakland. After I went into the slammer the place was never quite the same."

"You were in Jail RJ?" Jason said quietly with surprise.

"Prison to be truthful. I went to jail a bunch of times, but that was only for a few days or so but prison, that was a whole new cat to tackle."

"Okay, I want to know all about prison but first you need to explain that phrase...A cat to tackle?"

"Ever thought about tackling a cat. The things just gonna roll over on its back and claw the tar nation out of Ya. Tackling a cat is a hard thing to do and so was prison."

Jason paused long enough to imagine his childhood cat Cyrus shredding his belly through his T-shirt when he re-focused.

"So how did you end up there, in prison I mean?"

"Well," RJ continued, "Because I used to be a degenerate and I didn't do what I was supposed to do......ever. Then one day I was supposed to be meeting with my parole officer Larry, when at the last minute I decided to skip it to hang with my two loser cousins at the mall, and when they bailed out on me I went to the skate park where a fight broke out....RJ let his sadness show for only a fleeting moment.....And to make a long story short... I pushed a guy who slammed into a young girl who fell into one of those skate bowls and she broke her neck and died."

"Oh my God RJ, that's horrible," Jason said while quickly darting his eyes back to the river and his line to hide his awkwardness.

"I know, I vomited out half my insides thinking about it for months. I've found peace with it now. Pastor Albert says that God had a plan for that girl and he has a plan for me too. He told me that God has forgiven me and that walking around in sorrow isn't going to help anybody's cause and it sure won't shed a good light on the Kingdom that I am now a part of..... And you know what else?" RJ said as his million dollar smile returned, "That little girl, Shayla.....that was her name, she is rooting for me right now in heaven. This might sound crazy, but I can't wait to meet her."

"I didn't know that you were a religious guy RJ," Jason said with rolled up eye brows.

"I wasn't until a few months ago."

RJ went on to explain about his conversion and his father's new found faith and it left Jason feeling awkward and ready to leave…

"You don't like talking about God do you Jason?"

"Nahhh, it's just that my kid brother always talked about God and look what that got him. Two rounds to the chest and an early grave."

"My pop's told me about that," RJ said softly and then paused for a moment and then gently added....Ever wonder why it wasn't you?"

"Whadda you mean?" Jason said with a narrowed eye look at his new friend.

"Well, maybe your brother was ready to go home and maybe you're not," RJ said with rolled shoulders.

"Look RJ, you're a funny guy and I like you, but I'm not ready to be lectured on the whole God topic from a kid who just got out of prison… No offense, it clearly sounded like an accident."

"None taken, but you need to revisit Blazing Saddles…. The Kid was the white guy."

Jason found himself laughing again and as the sun grew lower the two figured that if there were any fish in the river they must have been sleeping and they decided to call it a day. As Jason walked back into his apartment he found his Dad on the phone with old man Richards. Craig was trying to explain the circumstances that had separated he and his family from the rest of the group but he could tell that his father was having trouble relaying the message. When he finally hung up the phone Jason asked…

"Everything okay down there dad?"

"Yeah they're fine. They're in our basement waiting for the war to begin and they're all really ticked off at us."

"Where's Mom?" Jason said in a low voice, knowing that news would upset her.

"She's taking a shower and she's got a story to tell you when she gets out."

Chapter Eighteen

In the wee hours of the morning on May 5th the military forces that had surrounded the city of LA were awaiting the call to action. The aerial assault got the party started with strategic bombings of lush hotels in the downtown area where the cartels had made their makeshift kingdom. Almost instantaneously over a hundred other strikes lit up the dawns early sky that were targeted as strongholds that had been pointed out by the best surveillance intelligence available. The strikes were widespread from Agoura Hills to the north all the way down to Angels Stadium to the South. After the rocking of the civilian shock and awe the ground troops simply went to work and by the following afternoon the military had recaptured the city. The news cast showed a lighter side of the engagement where they claimed only a small percentage of casualties, but to anybody on the ground, or anybody who knew the region, the place was surely a mess and it would be that way for a while.

Craig wanted to call his old house but the entire area was going to be blacked out of power and communication during the raid and for several days later so he would need to wait. He watched the news until about 6:45am and headed out the door to meet Colonel Robbs for breakfast. As he was leaving he told Jason to call RJ and be ready to go when he got back. As Jason fumbled through the directory he heard an old familiar sound resonating from his parents' bedroom. It was his Mom and she was whistling as she used to do when he was young. He placed down the directory and crept up to the door and peered in to the room between the door that was slightly ajar and the jamb. He watched as his

Mom brushed her hair and put on some modest makeup…Jason did the make believe clearing the throat thing and she responded without even turning her head…

"Need something Jason?"

"You seem to be in a good mood today Mom." Jason replied softly.

"I feel better. I'm not quite sure why but I do feel better."

"Maybe it's because you have something to do," he replied.

"Could be, but I think it's more about the people that I'll be working with. I really like those women and I think they have some kind of blind faith in me."

"What does blind faith mean Mom?"

"I don't know," she continued, It's just that they seem to trust me and I haven't given them any reason to do so…..Maybe Rick inflated my resume a bit before I got there…I don't know."

"Well I'm glad you're feeling better Mom." Jason said as he turned to walk away.

"Jason," Katie said as she walked to open the door completely. "I just wanted you to know that I haven't forgotten you or your Dad."

"I know Mom."

"Jason listen to me please. Come in and sit down," Jason walked in slowly and sat on the edge of the bed and his Mom sat next to him with tears welling up in her eyes….

"Yesterday I saw that little girl with a giant gash in her head. She was frightened, in pain, and crying uncontrollably and after she left to the hospital I realized that she didn't have a mother or a father to care for her......She looked so alone and so scared and then it hit me.....I'm scared too. I'm scared of being alone in a world without my family. I've been so frightened that I used my sorrow to deny my love for you and your father and I just wanted you to know this...and I already told your Father." Katie paused and stared directly into her son's eyes and said, "I will never again neglect you like I have in recent days.....I love you so much Jason."

By now Jason's eyes were filled with tears too because although he would never admit it, he was scared too. He was scared that his Mom would never snap out of her sorrow and would never again be a portion of the rock that made up his world. The two embraced and for the first time since James had died Jason began to feel whole again.

Craig walked by the Italian restaurant and the Mexican one too until he reached the door of the "Café of the Woods." All three restaurants were makeshift at best but the breakfast that Craig and John enjoyed was anything but. They used their points to eat and were pleasantly surprised that there was no limit to what they could enjoy. They had buttermilk pancakes, eggs Benedict, and the best biscuits and gravy that either of them had ever had. When they had finished John told Craig that he would need to be as authoritative as possible when dealing with the other builders. It would be a power struggle for a while and he would need to gain their trust through a test of his will. John knew about these types of struggles first hand as the Army was the ultimate test with the chain of command always at the forefront. John went on to explain that he would need to delegate authority to best fit the talent of each builder and that it was his job to figure that out. Then John leaned back and nestled his coffee cup against his stomach and said...

"To be honest with you Craig I have another reason why I wanted to meet with you today."

"Which is?" Craig said.

"Well, this is going to sound strange....well.... really strange I suppose, but yesterday when we left the meeting at the Generals office I went home to go over my briefings and I started to fight the sandman. I haven't slept too well in months and I finally felt a sense of calm and safety and before I knew it I was sound asleep in the middle of the afternoon on that comfy new sofa. You got one of those pillow top sofas in your place Craig?"

"It's unbelievable, yes."

"Anyway," John continued, "I'm sleeping like a baby and I have this strange dream."

"Yeah...... let's hear it."

"Okay, but like I said before its gonna sound weird" John took a deep breath and contemplated keeping his dream to himself but he knew he had already gone too far for that..

"I dreamt that I was in some really deep woods, I mean really deep. The kind of woods where you can barely tell whether it is day or night.... Anyway, all of a sudden I see James Earl Jones and he walks up to me an...."

"The actor James Earl Jones?" Craig said with a growing grin.

"Yeah.... James Earl Jones, Field of Dreams, Darth Vader....... James Earl Jones..."

"Ya know John you kind of look like James Earl Jones," Craig said with a smirk on his face.

"I know I get that a lot....Do you want to hear about my dream or not?"

"I absolutely want to hear about you and James Earl Jones alone together in the woods," Craig said with a now hard to hide, widening smile.

"Ha ha ha....Anyway, I'm in the woods and Jones comes up to me and says, 'Do you know where you are John?' I said no, so he walks me to a clearing and I can see the school at the bottom of one hill and the jobsite and highway at the bottom of the other and he says 'Can you find your way back here John?' I looked around and realized that I could easily find my way back to this spot. It might have been a over a mile from the base but I'm pretty good with bearings........Then he says to me.....And this is where you'll probably get your best laugh........"

"What did he say John?"

John took a deep breath and was genuinely worried that Craig would think that he had lost his mind but as he had realized before he had passed the point of no return...

"He said if you build it he will come. And then he turned me around and showed me a small church nestled in a small clearing of the thick woods. It was the most beautiful building that I had ever seen. It was all natural wood, lightly stained and had a beautiful round stained glass window decorating the front.......Then I woke up and called you."

"Why did you call me?" Craig said with a curious look.

"Two reasons Son. First I need somebody to help me build this church and secondly I had written your name and number on a piece of paper and left it on the kitchen table...apparently, while I was asleep, a breeze must have blown through my place, because that little piece of paper was resting on my belly when I woke up."

"Whoa John, you're really into this supernatural stuff aren't you?" Craig said as he slightly shifted back in his seat.

"You don't know the half of it Son."

"I'm not so sure I want to hear the other half John. It's kinda creeping me out."

"Do you believe in God Craig?" John said as he leaned in a bit.

"Kinda, I mean I guess I do."

"It's not a guessing game Craig either you believe or you don't. I didn't believe until a couple of months ago but since then some crazy things have been happening to me."

"What kinda stuff is that John?" Craig replied, feeling more and more awkward.

"Well for starters did you ever wonder how my Son knew that this town was going to have a clock tower. Would you be surprised if I told you that I already know what the plaque at the base of that clock will read?"

"Okay John, this is getting a little weird for me."

"I'm just telling you that I know that there will be a plaque at the base of that clock tower and I know what it will read." "Craig" John said as he leaned in even closer, "It's gonna read *Hat Creek reestablished 2018.*"

John knew that he had let the cat out of the bag and he felt that maybe he had picked the wrong man to devise his plan with, so he closed his eyes momentarily and said a quick prayer for a miracle and then he continued…

"Will you help me build a church in those woods Craig?"

"Won't we get thrown out of here if we try to sneak out there and create a new building?" Craig replied looking for a quick excuse.

"I spent all night devising the plan and I think that it's almost foolproof and besides, in a roundabout way I already got the go ahead from the General himself. It's what we will be building that will get us in trouble."

"I gotta hear this," Craig said just as the door opened to the diner and a few Red Shirts made their way in with the cool morning air. The two men simply ignored them until they overheard them talking about a plaque that they had decided to place at the base of the clock tower. John and Craig sat there motionless listening to the conversation that was getting heated by the minute..

"We don't want it to read like a novel Dale," one of the architects said.

"And I guess that we all agree that there are way too many people responsible for this project to name names," another said.

"Look," the large Philippino guy sitting in the middle of his dwarfed coworkers said, "We have plenty of time to decide if we want to replace it down the road, but for now let's just settle with *Hat Creek Reestablished 2018* and let's just hope we get it done by then…

John leaned over towards Craig's shoulder and whispered in his ear.….

"There's more."

Craig sat there silent for a moment and uttered.….

"Dinner at my house tonight?"

"Want me to bring RJ?"

"Absolutely."

Chapter Nineteen

Ricky picked up Katie at 8:00am as he promised to do each morning and they made their way towards the school...

"Did you hear about that little girl Rick? Is she going to be okay?"

"Yeah, she'll be fine. She had a minor concussion and she'll have a bad headache for a while but she'll be fine."

"Did you figure out who threw the rock?" She asked with her mother's inquest.

"No, and that's just it. These kids have been through the ringer so many times that they've learned how to lie like a CIA operative, and if there were any witnesses they must be afraid to come forward."

"Got any suspects officer?" Katie said with a sly yet playful look on her face.

Ricky noticed her smile and felt a sense of relief as the Katie he knew and loved was beginning to reemerge and said...

"Not yet... but I haven't ruled you out Baby doll."

Katie smiled and hopped out of the jeep and said....

"Lunch today Rick?"

"Sounds good to me, should we say about eleven thirty?"

"It's my first full day Rick. How about you come by at eleven thirty and I'll see if I can get away."

"Deal," he said as they parted ways in the lobby of the sprawling wooden lodge.

Katie walked into the little medical station and found Akiko with a solemn look on her face…

"What's wrong Akiko?" Katie asked shyly.

"Oh it's nothing, just an argument that I have every morning with my husband….that is, when he actually decides to talk to me. I usually snap out of it by my second cup of coffee and it's almost ready."

Katie didn't feel that it was right to pry into the life of a person that she had just met the day before but she knew that there was more to the story then a simple argument…

"Well, what do you need me to do?" She asked changing the subject out of respect.

"For starters we need to make that walk that we never got to make yesterday. I need to check on a couple of kids who had minor fevers anyway. Come on it'll be fun, and it will give the coffee a moment to cool."

The two ladies left the room and headed down a long hallway to a large gymnasium that was filled to the hilt with cots..,

"This is where most of these kids sleep. Now that the weather is good they leave these cots here all day but before I got here when the weather was bad they had to push all these cots out of here in the morning to give the kids a place to play, and even then they needed two shifts."

"How long have these kids been here?" Katie asked.

"I guess some of them have been here for six months or more. They started rounding them up after the war began.…They say that there are more than twenty thousand living in Boys Town in Omaha."

"Whoa, I'd hate to see the line for the bathrooms there," Katie said as her first one liner in months.

Akiko let out her childish laughter and motioned Katie to follow her…

"Were going to stop by and see the older kids first."

Akiko opened the door of a large banquet room where there seemed to be several dozen kids sitting at desks facing the four different corners of the room.

"These are our nine and ten year olds. The oldest kids that we currently have here. We have four teachers working with these 60 kids and most of them have never been taught anything beyond the basics of math, reading and so on."

"60! It looked more like two hundred." Katie said while her eyes panned the room.

"It's an optical illusion. It fooled me at first too. I think it had something to do with how they are sitting, facing different directions and all."

"I hope this question doesn't reach beyond my boundaries, but what about the eleven year olds and the twelve year olds? There must be orphaned kids of older ages."

Akiko sighed and after a long pause she said.….

"It's so sad, and it was the first question that I asked too. I guess that it came down to resources and necessity. We didn't have the resources for all the kids and these kids were more in need............I know......I try not to think about it."

"I'm starting to realize that this is a crapshoot being here," Katie said with raised eyebrows.

"It is. I think. Does crapshoot mean lucky?"

"It does Akiko and we are some of the lucky ones."

"Somehow I don't feel too lucky these days," she replied looking towards the ground while slowly closing her eyes during her brief sigh.

"If you ever want to talk about it I guess that I'll be here awhile to listen," Katie said in her best well practiced caring voice.

"Thank You."

The gals made their rounds and met with some of the kids that knew Akiko by her surname. They even stopped to shoot a few baskets with the eight year olds as they were on their recess. On their way back to the station Akiko mustered up the courage and uttered a few words of her discontent and as Katie opened the door to the station, she realized the invitation and said…

"Come on sweetie tell me all about it"

At 10:00am a group of nearly 400 gathered in front of the work trailers and Ryan Teagarden introduced Colonel Robbs to the men. John, after a quick speech, introduced Craig as the project manager and the crowd

became a little restless. It only took a moment for the pride of a few to begin their dissenting tones. Craig had remembered what John had told him and began his introduction with a stern warning...

"How are you guys doing? I'm Craig Mitchell and I'm in charge of the construction here. You guys are obviously talented or you wouldn't be here. I'm open to suggestions but your suggestions will remain suggestions unless I decide to implement them. Every worker here is to answer to me and all decisions are to run through me. Any change orders or architectural requests are to be honored after they are run by me. I will be working side by side with Ryan Teagarden who is our head architect and he and his staff are to be respected as your superiors because they are. Everyone present here today is under the guidance of Colonel John Robbs, and he has the final say in all matters involving the project. I will be delegating authority of the framing to a few builders that I have chosen based on their resume' and their cooperation since they've been here. Apparently some of you guys would rather fight then work...That stops today! Colonel Robbs has informed me that he will have little patience for persons who involve themselves with petty differences and cause problems for others. If we work together and respect our different ways of doing things then we can complete this project on time and possibly learn a thing or two from one another. If you have a problem with that, then we have helicopters ready to fly you out of here. If I call your name, you have a meeting in ten minutes in the main trailer here. The rest of you guys, start evenly distributing the lumber alongside the slabs. We start framing today.

Craig called a few names to the heckling of others and retreated into the trailer with John and Ryan...

"You sure you were never in the military Craig. You were kinda scary out there," John said with an amazed look.

"I guarantee you that it wasn't as scary as that stuff you threw at me earlier this morning," Craig replied still trying to digest the information.

As the men came in one by one Craig gave them specific instructions of the particular buildings that they were to be overseeing. He gave them blueprints and sent them on their way. Craig saved the clock tower and the courthouse building for himself and Jason. It was by far the most intricate of all the drawings and Craig's competitive nature wanted to prove something. He told Jason to handpick a dozen or so guys to work on their crew and he told him to assert himself as foremen. RJ asked if he was supposed to hang with Jason and Craig simply looked at the boy and said…."Just do what he needs you to do and don't get impaled on anything or you'll make me a promise breaker." John grinned and headed to his desk to run through the stack of request orders left there by Ryan. As Jason and RJ were heading towards the door Craig shouted to them…

"Hey!, before I forget, you guys need to go down to the edge of town and find us a truck, I have no idea where, but apparently there is a lot with trucks on it and we need one."

Akiko was a skinny young lady but her eyes were big and bright and she had an extremely warm and caring smile. Unfortunately today her eyes were filled with sorrow and her smile was nowhere to be found. When the ladies were back at the station Katie got right to the point….

"Tell me what's going on?"

"It's just my husband. He's not the same anymore," Akiko said quietly.

"How so?"

"He's just so bitter. He thinks that he's smarter than everyone else and he thinks that he deserves more then he has......Anyway, he hardly even talks to me and sometimes I get so lonely."

"He doesn't hit you or anything does he?" Katie asked with growing concern.

"No, no... Sadie is not violent, just angry."

"Why do you think he's so angry?"

"It's because we used to be very rich.... We had a big house, all the money and all the toys and then we were put into a small apartment where we needed to work just to keep the lights on and have food at the table. It was a hard transition for me too, but I figured that at least we had each other......I don't know, maybe he never really loved me."

"Didn't coming here help lift his mood any?" Katie asked.

"At first it did, but when he found out that his father had died of a heart attack he slipped even further away from me...........It all goes back to that day at the clinic......I saw him drift away from me and he's never come back."

"At the clinic?" Katie asked, not really knowing what to expect, but was betting on it being bad.

"A couple of years ago, just before the collapse, Sadie had decided that it was the right time to have children. He always wanted to wait, wait, wait and when he was finally ready we found out that I was unable........... He has never looked at me the same way since."

Akiko started to cry and Katie quickly put her arms around her and comforted her....

"Every now and then," Akiko continued through tears and snuffles "He wants to have sex with me. He won't talk to me for weeks and then he wants sex. Afterwards he pretends that I don't exist."

"Maybe it's time for you guys to talk to somebody. I saw in the directory that they have a couple of counselors up here," Katie said, trying to hide the fact that she was , only days before looking for one herself.

"You don't know Sadahara, he won't go to a counselor, he is too proud."

"Well I don't know what else to tell you Akiko."

"I'll just continue to love him and Maria and I will continue to pray for him each morning," Akiko said while nodding her head.

"Ahhh." feeling that uncomfortable God thing Katie replied, "You guys get together and pray every morning?"

"We go to Bible study together too, but that is kind of a secret."

"What do you mean it's a secret?" Katie asked curiously.

"One of the doctors here is the son of a pastor and he saw Maria and I praying one morning and he asked us if we wanted to study the word with him and his wife. We've been meeting at his house for the last few Tuesdays and Thursdays at 7:00 pm. I just tell Sadie that I'm going to work and when Maria shows up at the door he never thinks twice about it."

"But you didn't tell me why it is a secret," Katie inquired further.

"Oh sorry, it's just that Jeff thinks that in these days it is best to be discreet....you know with the end of time coming and all."

"The end of time? Akiko do you think that we are in the end times?"

"I don't know enough to really know, but Jeff and Maria are convinced and they seem pretty smart to me…."Hey!" Akiko said as her eyes lit up a bit, "Maybe you can come sometime."

"Maybe…. we'll see" Katie replied as a fear of the unknown swept through her mind. She had heard about end times her whole life but had never really given it much thought. Suddenly she felt as if maybe she should.

Jason and RJ went down to the massive parking lot at the end of town where they were to find a new truck to use. New was not the right word for these trucks, they were donated pieces of junk, but luckily they only needed to move a handful of miles a day. When they found a mechanic lying on his back underneath one of the jeeps cursing and spitting mad, they figured it was best to talk to somebody else. After roaming around the lot for about ten minutes they realized that the mechanic was the only guy there so they needed to annoy him with their request….

"How's it going down there?" Jason directed his voice through the open hood.

Carlos, a skinny Salvadorian with a pencil thin mustache was the only mechanic working what seemed to be an endless amount of projects. He rolled out from underneath the jeep and said…

"What do you guys need?"

"A truck," Jason said abruptly.

"Well take your pick they all have keys in 'em."

"Any truck huh," the boys said as they looked over their shoulders at the many to choose from, and made their way out of the garage and back towards the lot.

The boys started heading towards a fairly new Chevy Crew cab with a ladder rack and utility boxes........

"You're not going to want that one," Carlos said with a sheepish grin.

"Why's that" RJ said.

"Because it don't run. All the rest of the trucks you see on the front lot don't run either."

"So where do we find a truck that does run?" Jason said with sarcasm running high and his patience moving in the opposite direction.

"All the running trucks are in the back and we've only got a few left," Carlos said as he motioned the boys in the other direction with a wave of the arm.

The three began to walk around the back of the old pint sized dealership while Carlos started in on his daily rant.........

"All these trucks were donated and 90% percent of them are trash...This place is more of a tire store than anything else. That is what I'm gonna do with all those trucks, use 'em as spare parts for the running trucks. I don't have the equipment or the resources to bring many of 'em back to life so I guess they'll just sit there...They're supposed to send me another mechanic but I kind of lost hope for that a few months ago.... guess they didn't figure on much need for transportation........I don't know......Anyway,... here they are, take your pick. I'd suggest "Old Blue" there but nobody seems to want her......Anyway take your pick, I need to get back to my jeep."

Jason and RJ looked at the three remaining trucks and realized that they were a little late to the candy store. The first truck that they looked at was a Toyota mini pick-up with a cracked windshield and had metal coils sticking through the seat cushions and they ruled it out immediately. The second truck was an older model full size dodge but it was a single cab with bucket seats and Jason knew that his Dad wouldn't be happy using a truck with only two seats. Plus it had no ladder rack and no utility boxes and "Old Blue" had both. "Old Blue" was a 95 Chevy crew cab that seemed perfect for their needs with one exception…..It was completely blue. The truck was blue, the hubcaps were blue. The ladder rack had been painted blue and the boxes were painted blue. The interior was blue right down to the carpet and the dashboard. The seats had covers on them that were two shades of blue and even the steering wheel was blue.

"This is one ugly truck Jason," RJ said as he slowly assessed the vehicle. "It would be bad enough with all this blue," he continued, "But man!.... This is weirdest, palest, baby blue I've ever seen, you mind if I hide in one of them boxes when we roll in this thing?"

Jason walked around the truck looking at it in complete amazement…

"I didn't even know they made blue steering wheels," he said after shaking his head a few times. "My Dad is gonna freak out when he see's us come back with this thing." Jason sighed and squinted his eyes while shading them with his hand and looked a little deeper at the faded paint……"It's so blue that it almost looks purple…if that's even possible."

"Does that mean were taking it, cause I saw an old abandoned paint store down the street and we could drive this thing through the window and see if we can add a few tones to this rig," RJ said while rolling his eyes upward before continuing, "I knew I should have been a Royals fan, my ball cap is gonna clash against all this blue."

"We should probably drive it through the window of that paint store and leave it," Jason replied through a sly grin.

As the boys hopped into the truck and fired it up Carlos walked up to the window while he was wiping his hands with a solvent drenched rag. He smiled, spit his used up snuff on the ground and said…

"Takin' "Old Blue" eh'……She's the best running truck up here so don't let anybody give you a hard time now"…."Have a good day Blue Bonnet Boys," he yelled as the boys pulled out of the lot listening to the fading laughter.

It was about a mile and a half back to the work trailers and when they pulled around the graded, soon to be round-about the other workers were already pointing and laughing hysterically. Jason just continued to drive past them towards the trailers. RJ pulled his A's cap down over his eyes and said….

"I wasn't kiddin' about that paint store Jay. We can be there in two minutes."

When they pulled up in front of the trailer, Craig was outside with Ryan going over some logistics and they both froze when the blue machine pulled up alongside them. It truly was the ugliest truck that anyone had ever seen…….Jason hopped out of the truck, walked up to his father and said, "Old Blue," this is my Dad, Dad this is "Old Blue," I don't want to hear it, so you might as well save it and he just walked on past while Craig and Ryan hadn't moved from the shock of what lay before them.

Chapter Twenty

Katie was a little surprised when she found out that they were having guests for dinner but she went about making scalloped potatoes and a vegetable dish pleasantly enough. It helped that Craig and Jason had stopped by the store and got a couple of tri-tips and were making good use of the propane BBQ that they hadn't until earlier that morning noticed was in the utility closet outside their small concrete porch. When the Robbs arrived they ate and laughed at RJ's amusing tales and were intrigued by John's stories of the first Gulf war. After dinner they retreated into the living room and watched the live feed from the streets of LA……..

"You guys have friends down there don't you?" John said.

"Yeah… and they're hiding in my basement and we can't get a hold of them," Craig said with a down turned face.

"When was the last time you tried?" John asked quietly.

"On my way to the bathroom about six minutes ago," Craig replied with upturned palms.

"He's been calling every ten minutes since he's been home," Katie said as she brought some slices of store baked apple pie to the coffee table.

"Well sometimes you just have to have faith," RJ chimed in. "Why don't we go down to that rec hall Jay and let these old people digest their food."

"They have a rec hall here?" Jason said with a look of surprise.

"Yeah... let's get out of here you inflatable homebody."

"I'm inflatable, what are you pushing, 250, 260?" Jason ribbed.

"That aint my fault. Look at my Pops, it's clearly a genetic problem."

The two young men went to leave and John gave them a stern look and said...

"Most of those guys down there know who you two are so you better try to stay out of trouble."

"Trouble used to be my middle name Pops, now we just need to work on changing yours to 'Trust."

"He really is a charismatic boy isn't he John," Katie said with a warm smile after the boys closed the door behind them...

"He is now, young lady, but he used to be a handful."

When Craig and Katie were alone with John, Craig got straight to the point. He wanted to know more about the supernatural happenings that John was experiencing. He hadn't had any real time to discuss the matter with Katie so he informed her that John had some things to tell them that were going to seem a little weird at first. John went on to explain RJ's conversion and how he prayed for an end to his solitude and how his prayer was answered in an awesome and convicting manner. He then explained in detail Pastor Albert's dream and how prophetic it was. He told them about his new Bible and the words that were inscribed inside the cover and how it was the exact words that his Uncle Amos had used to address his childhood congregation. Finally, he told them about the plaque and the architects from earlier in the day and the whole story left Katie speechless and Craig wanting more....

"Either you are the biggest liar I've ever met John and you are trying to screw with our minds or something really strange is happening here," Craig said as he leaned back into the sofa and realized that he hadn't been breathing too much in recent minutes.

"Well son, I've never been much of a liar and this stuff is new to me too, but I wouldn't call it strange, I'd call it God and we've all been estranged from him for far too long."

Craig sat back up straight and said…

"So tell me your plan for this church."

"I thought there wasn't going to be a church Hon," Katie asked.

"According to John here we're going to build one off the grid. After we hear his plan of course…. So?"

"Well for starters we need a story if we get caught. If they find us working on that church we tell them that it's a surprise for the General. You know, a hunting slash fishing getaway cabin. It won't be until we decorate the inside and put that stained glass window in that anyone will recognize it as a church. Secondly we are going to need to recruit other believers to help…

"I'm not even sure if I'm a believer John," Craig said.

"You will be Son," John said with conviction.

"Are you sure of that Oracle man?" Craig replied.

"It's one of the few things that I am sure of. You'll both be believers and so will Jason."

"I know of a few Christians up here," Katie said much to the surprise of her husband.

"You do? we've only been here a few days," Craig said.

"I met an Asian girl named Akiko who attends Bible study twice a week with a doctor who's dad is a pastor.........Oh my gosh!! I just realized.... Your Pastors dream...The Asian girl screaming on the floor.......Is that going to be Akiko?"

"I have no idea Katie. It wasn't my dream," John said with the universal frown of not knowing.

Craig leaned back again in the sofa and was trying to make sense of all that he had heard when a little voice inside him said... "Just go with it." It startled Craig because it wasn't the typical voice inside his head, it was a voice that he hadn't heard before. He instantly sat up straight and said......

"I'm feeling a little weird, maybe we should continue this conversation later."

"You okay Son?" John asked.

"Yeah....... just a little overloaded right now."

Just then, as if on cue, Jason and RJ walked back in to the apartment and RJ announced that he was the king of the pool table and if they still used money all of Jason's would be safely in his pocket.......RJ noticed the awkwardness and the silence that his humor had no effect on and he said...

"Freaked 'em out didn't Ya Pops? No worries... it'll get easier to digest with time. Try some pepto, it helped me swallow the enchilada."

As the Robbs said their goodbyes and left the apartment for their own, Jason found himself perplexed at the mood of his parents that he was quick to inherit. Craig and Katie told him about everything they had learned earlier that evening as well as the plan for the church. Jason took a deep breath, leaned back in his seat and said...

"Whoa, maybe I do need some pepto."

Chapter Twenty-One

Ricky Smalls was a busy man. He had always been busy. He had a huge heart for a man with such meager beginnings. His early childhood was wondrous growing up in the cul-de-sac, two doors down from Craig and his family. He and Craig were the best of friends and they did everything together, but when Ricky was twelve his Dad left his Mom and his only son, and never returned. Eventually the bank foreclosed on their home and his Mom moved them to an apartment complex in Van Nuys. Ricky's Mom eventually became an alcoholic and unwittingly seemed to blame Ricky for everything that had happened. Ricky would ride his bike seven miles to be at the Mitchells and it got to the point that he was practically living there. His Mom didn't seem to care and Craig's Dad would often drive him to school in Van Nuys when he would stay over on week nights. Ricky learned to loath his Mother and when she died of liver disease while Ricky was a few years into his military career he didn't even return for the funeral. Ricky had married once when he was in his early thirties but since he had no idea how to be a husband it didn't last long. Ricky was a bit of a player, but a player with an truly caring personality that he had soaked up from the years he had spent with the Mitchells. It was said that he had a different girlfriend on every continent and he never said anything in denial of the rumor. So when he found himself working mostly alone with a bunch of kids he began to grow restless and needed to find some relief.

A mere two weeks into his stay, and not a moment too soon, Ricky would find that old familiar feeling once more. He was making his final rounds at the school while the kids were in line for dinner when he noticed a new face in the crowd. He moved towards and then peered into the faculty lounge to get a closer look. There before him was the tallest, leanest and most beautiful women he had ever seen. Ricky, not one to be intimidated was surprised to find himself nervous as he could be when she walked straight up to him and said....

"Hi!, I can tell by the uniform that you must be Lieutenant Colonel Smalls. I'm Caroline Walker. I'm new here. They needed extra teachers and my Sister sponsored me, and wallah, here I am."

"Nice to meet you Ma'am. Who's your Sister? does she work here?"

"Yeah she's around here somewhere or maybe my Brother in Law Jeff already picked her up."

"Is that Jeff Wrigley, the Doctor?"

"Yeah, do you know him?"

"I met him a couple of times when he's been here to get your Sister...I've met her too.... she's the accountant right?"

"Yep....Hey! Were you looking for someone? I saw you glance in here and then I noticed that you crept in for a closer look."

"No....ahhh....I just....I don't know, I just thought I recognized you that's all."

"Well the next time you see me I hope you do," She said in what he was sure a flirting tone.

Ricky walked out to his jeep on cloud nine. Caroline was beautiful with wavy red hair and sparkling green eyes and seemed to be as sweet as she could be. She seemed to be receptive to him as well. He pondered what she had said as she turned away and he concluded for his hearts sake that it was an invitation.

The very next day Ricky couldn't wait to get to the school. He asked Katie about four times if he looked alright and she finally proclaimed yes with a little extra emphasis on the affirmative. Ricky told Katie about his encounter the previous evening and she just rolled her eyes and said in a playful manner as she hopped out of the jeep....

"Another in the long line of the Richard Eugene Small's conquests.... Remember to practice safe sex little Ricky."

"Okay Ma," he shouted as she made her way into the school.

To be honest Ricky was more than enamored with this woman. He hadn't felt this way in a long time. Once again he was nervous but he would hit his nerves head on and ask her to dinner the moment he saw her. It didn't take long because when he opened the doors to the A-frame there she was at the front desk getting supplies from the behind the counter...She looked up and smiled at him and said...

"See somebody you recognize Mr. Smalls?"

"As a matter of fact I do. I see somebody who might want to have dinner with me tonight."

"I don't think that is a very good idea Mr. Smalls. You see I am a very busy woman."

Ricky stood there in his awkwardness not quite sure how to reply to that when Caroline broke the silence....

"Tonight!"

"Excuse me?" Ricky said with genuine confusion.

"I am busy tonight, how does tomorrow sound?"

"Great! After work then."

"You got a car Sailor? Have me home by ten?" She said with twinkle in her playful eyes.

"Tomorrow then," Ricky said as he felt a few too many eyes watching him from behind the counter and felt it was time to leave…..

Caroline had always been the adventurous type. She had a habit of jumping in with both feet if the time felt right. Up until now it had served her well, and she was ready and excited to roll the dice once more. Caroline Walker had come down from icy town of Nome, Alaska. She had been widowed for almost ten years when her husband had left for a fishing trip and simply vanished like so many before him in the rugged terrain. After about two weeks it was deemed that her husband and his two buddies along with their guide had perished, though they never did find the bodies. Caroline raised her two children alone until they eventually left home and married young. In Alaska, the collapse was felt the same as anywhere else but the people in the frozen northern terrain were used to sharing and caring for one another and therefore the upheaval was limited. Overall, besides the inherited dangers, it was a safe place to be after the war. Caroline had turned forty-five in the winter of 2017 and when her Sister called her in early spring to join them in this new project she was ready for a new adventure. Caroline had worked with disabled children since she had graduated from UC Irvine when she was twenty two and her career had just began when she found herself married, pregnant and moving to Alaska with her geologist husband. Luckily she found her skills in high demand in the little town hidden in the middle of nowhere and she never missed a beat. Caroline was a devout Christian as was her entire family. She knew better then to tend to her own needs when her children were still at home but when she met Ricky she felt that young girl feeling once more and she could barely contain her excitement.

Katie asked Akiko if she could join them for Bible study later that night and Akiko's eyes lit up and she said…

"Of course. I was praying that you would ask."

"Can I bring some friends and family members?" Katie asked.

"How many people are we talking about?"

"Five including me, and we've got a story to tell."

Akiko walked over to the phone and pushed 9 on the receiver and gave Katie the universal "Shush" motion with a finger to the mouth…"Doctor Wrigley please."

"Hi Jeff its Akiko. I have some people who want to join us tonight…. uhuh….yes………….five…...uhuh……….okay…….uhuh……….I'll tell them, thanks Jeff…….He says that it's fine but you all have to promise to keep it a secret."

"After what we tell him he won't have to worry about us keeping a secret," Katie said with a grin.

"What do you need to say?" Akiko whispered quietly.

"Sweetie we wouldn't get anything done today if I started to explain this and I wouldn't even know where to begin."

The day flew by fast and at 7:00 pm sharp the three Mitchells and the two Robbs were knocking on the door of Jeff and Courtney Wrigley's apartment. Jeff and Courtney were in their early fifties, both of typical stature and condition for their age. Jeff was a take charge guy with strong features and full head of graying dark brown hair. Courtney was a beautiful woman like her Sister as they could almost pass as twins, although the 6 year difference showed in the lines on her face. Jeff was a noted neurosurgeon and Courtney was a certified public accountant who worked at the school trying to make sense of what was left behind by the SETI personnel. They had three grown children who were doing okay in different locations around the country and each of them had families of their own. Once inside, the new comers were introduced to Maria Gonzales, Akiko, and Courtney's Sister Caroline…

"Obviously our group has doubled in one night" Jeff said as he moved some furniture around to make some extra room. "Before we begin here tonight I need to ask," Jeff continued. "How many of you are sure that you believe in the resurrected Christ?"

RJ and John raised their hands while the Mitchells froze having not expected to be put on the spot so quickly…..

"That's okay," Jeff said. "You're here and that's a start…. So maybe someone can tell me why you're here?"

John went on to explain his reuniting with RJ, Pastor Albert's dream, the church and the story of the plaque complete with the details of the happening at the café. Craig had heard the story two times in the previous few days but he listened just as intently as the others. When John had finished everyone in the room sat quietly waiting for someone to break the silence….

"That's an amazing story," Caroline said as she placed her hand under her chin.

"It's also a supernatural story," Jeff chimed in. "The only question that remains is if the story is good or bad."

"What does that mean?" John said slightly irritated by the response.

"Well," Jeff said as he leaned forward to punctuate his point. "When we are dealing with something supernatural it is either entirely good or entirely evil. I personally have no doubt that this is coming from God, but I want to make sure that we are all in agreement before moving on."

Everyone was quick to agree except for the three Mitchells who were not yet convinced that a God, who they were not familiar with, was behind all these apparent coincidences. All eyes turned towards the non-believers when Katie ended her silence and abruptly said...

"I believe it. I believe that God is trying to send us a message and I believe that he wants us here right now to hear it."

The room fell silent for a moment as the two sisters and Akiko moved closer to Katie and began to pray around her. Jason found this unbelievably uncomfortable and left the room while Craig sat there motionless...

"What about you Craig?" Jeff asked. "Are you ready to believe in a higher power or are you going to continue denying his purpose for you?"

"I'll start by building him a church Jeff, but I'm not ready for that stuff quite yet," Craig said as he pointed over to the ladies who were now formed into a tight circle praying with his wife who was down on her knees.

Craig rose up from his chair and abruptly left the apartment without looking back. He closed the door behind him and headed towards the gravel parking lot while John followed close behind...

"Craig wait a minute," John shouted as he tried to gain ground on the younger and fitter man.

Craig looked back over his shoulder but kept moving until he reached the parking lot. He walked over to "Old Blue" dropped the tailgate and sat down with a deep sigh and began his long look at the ground between his knees...

"Craig," John said as he joined him at the tail end of the truck. "I know this is hard for you right now but you need to understand what is happening inside with your wife."

"And what's that John? My wife is going into a trance with complete strangers."

"She's accepting God's free gift of grace Craig and that is a beautiful thing Son," John said without a hint of shame.

"What is grace? I hear that word all the time from religious types and I don't even know what it means," Craig asked.

"It means that she is being saved into the kingdom through God's grace even though she doesn't deserve it."

"What do you mean she doesn't deserve it?" Craig said with a renewed fire in his voice. "If anyone deserves to go to heaven it's her."

"That's just how it is....nobody deserves forgiveness Craig, it's just a free gift to those who accept it, and based on my own acceptance, I'm pretty sure that Katie is accepting it right now."

"So that's it then. Wallah! And she's a Christian," Craig said while sarcastically making light of the simplicity of the happenings inside.

"I can't say it's easy Son," John continued, "It took me three quarters of my life to acknowledge God and it took the love and pressures from my Son, his Pastor and several others before I found myself on my knees. I will tell you this though, it was the greatest day of my life and I've never felt as free as I do today."

"What if I never find the faith? How will I know when the time is right?" Craig asked.

"Have you ever felt blessed young man? Have you ever wondered where that blessing came from in the first place?"

Craig almost exploded in a response but quickly decided to hide his emotions. It had only been a couple of days since he sat alone on his couch wondering about being blessed and where it stemmed from. It was almost as if God himself was knocking on the door to his heart and he was doing everything possible to avoid answering....

"I'm feeling a little freaked out right now John. I think I need to take a little walk."

"Mind if I tag along?"

Craig was reeling with emotions. On one hand he felt like being alone but on the other hand he felt a closeness to John that he hadn't felt since the death of his father. He wanted John's company and something inside him told him that he might need it...

"Sure, why not."

The two men began walking up the steep grade that led towards the school. It was a typical late spring night in the Sierras. A cool breeze rustled through the mighty pines and the sound of the crickets could be heard through the blasting sounds of the hammers echoing through the valley from the night shift working down below. A low moon illuminated the road and creeping shadows from the trees spotted each and every step…

"Beautiful night isn't it," John said while trying to keep up with the younger man.

"It is at that John, it is at that."

"Ever wonder about the beauty that exists son?" John said as he gulped in the high altitude air.

"Sometimes, but it always gets interrupted by a death or a bill or a project that is running late," Craig answered.

John felt that it was best to remain quiet and let Craig lead the conversation and when they reached the top of the grade he was pleased to hear Craig say that maybe they could just hang out there for a while and watch the construction lights in the distance. John was completely out of breath and simply plopped down on a nicely rounded rock and said….

"I'm glad that we didn't go down the other side 'cause I'd be sleeping with those kids tonight waiting for a ride home in the morning."

The two men sat there for over an hour talking about their life's stories while avoiding the inevitable until it finally came back to the forefront in the most unexpected way. After a long pause in the conversation Craig said in a monotone voice…

"I felt jealous."

"Excuse me," John said with genuine curiosity.

"Earlier at Jeff's house. I felt jealous of you guys."

"And your wife?" John asked.

"I felt that she abandoned me...... You know John, I guess that I always felt a little jealous of James too. Jason and I used to make fun of him behind his back when he would start in on the whole God thing, but secretly I always wanted that kind of faith. Maybe God won't give me any because of the way I used to ridicule one of his own."

"Craig,..... I'm not an biblical expert, but I know enough to know that God isn't keeping you away.... you are. And trust me, your wife didn't abandon you she is probably praying for you just like me."

"What do you mean you're praying for me?" Craig asked as he looked a little deeper into the dirt scribbling he was making with a stick.

"I've been praying for both of us this whole time Son. For your salvation and for me to be given the right words to help."

"How's that working out for you?" Craig said as he gave John an attentive look.

"You tell me," John said and then paused long enough to look out at the stars that illuminated the passing clouds before continuing.

"Look Craig, do you believe that everything happens for a reason?"

"I don't know, I guess so.....why?"

"Well," John said, "Why do you think that you're sitting up here on this hill with a retired military black man? Why do you think the world is going to hell right before our eyes? Why do you think we are getting a reprieve from the madness?"

133

"I guess we just got lucky," Craig replied.

"Why do you think it was James who was shot and not Jason?" John said before he could bring the words back from their now physical existence.

The question shot through Craig like an arrow and seemed to pierce his very fragile existence. He was literally gasping for air between shallow breaths and before he knew it he was lowering his head between his legs. Quietly, Craig began to mutter to himself..."It should have been me. It should have been me" and then suddenly, without warning, he began to cry a cry that was long overdue. Craig had been holding back his emotions of grief to protect his remaining family and, in that very moment, he realized that he had become vulnerable and he released his pain right before the caring eyes of his new friend. John gently placed a hand on his shoulder and whispered into his ears....

"You will see him again Son. I promise."

When Craig had composed himself as best as could be expected, he looked at John and muttered...

"How can you be so sure that I'll see him again?"

"Because I believe that you believe, that James is alive and well. What I refuse to believe is that if there is a way to be with him that you will ignore it. James was taken because he was ready to go home and his death is paving a way home for you and the rest of your family....."

"Craig," John said after a short pause, "I'm old, fat and tired, but still, I knew that I had to come up here with you tonight. God has changed me into a new person. A person who actually cares about others. If you think all this is crazy, you should have tried to sell me on it a couple of months ago. I would have told you to pound sand and yet here we are....."

You trying to make your last stand against God, a futile one I might add, and me hoping that I'm saying the right words."

Craig listened to every word but waited a while to respond. After a couple of false starts and thought gathering he said in a low voice...

"Every time I feel my lowest I get this undeniable feeling. It felt foreign to me at first, but now it is as true to me as anything I've ever felt, and it brings me comfort."

"What's that Craig?"

"Since the moment James took his last breath I've known that I would see him again. I never knew how or why, but I knew. The problem is, I don't know anything about God. I wasn't raised in a religious home like Katie. I don't even know where to begin"

"You can begin by saying you're sorry for neglecting Him and living a sinful life. You can admit that you believe that He exists, that he died for your sins, rose again and that you're ready to trust Him with everything you have, including your life. After that Son, He'll pretty much take care of the rest."

Craig sat there looking off in the distance in deep thought. He was rewinding his life and not liking much of what he saw. He realized for the first time just how dirty he was, how much he needed to be cleansed. He felt more alone in that moment then he had ever felt in his life, and he found himself to be completely helpless. He reached for John with a trembling hand and said..

"I need God John, I need him now."

Chapter Twenty-Two

Over the course of the next few weeks Jason had committed his life to the Lord, though kicking and screaming while endlessly looking for more evidence, and the small group of believers had grown into more than twenty. Four men from Craig's crew had joined in the study as well as several from the school and hospital. Maria had cleared out an old gymnastics arena and the group now had plenty of room for growth. Tensions between General Thompson and Colonel Robbs had become troublesome due to the General's distain for religion and John's disregard for the secularists daily bulletins. Religion was becoming the primary target for the military and the General was leading the local march. The secularists had gained the majority of control over social matters and they had deemed religion to be the ultimate threat. General Thompson was delighted when he received a memo direct from the oval office that declared a State run religious system that made it illegal to practice any form of religion outside of a newly labeled Universal State Religious System or USRS. In these new places of worship no names or symbols were to be used to identify any particular god and there was to be no mention of holy books or any references to a deity except for that of a universal higher power. John had mocked the memo and the General took notice.

The framing was swinging into high gear and it was beginning to take form. Craig had a few problems with a handful of prima donnas but with John's help they quickly squelched the uprisings. Craig and Jason worked together like never before and they quickly realized that they were indeed building something special. The courthouse was small by courthouse standards but it was to be built in an ancient Greek Doric style on top of a parade of steps with six columns in front and the familiar Greek triangle design at the top of the structure. The Clock Tower was to be built in the same fashion with four longer columns to present a slimmer design and with a lightly illuminated dark blue clock with gold roman numerals in the center of its own triangle. Craig had sought out the best mason on the project to finish the columns with a hybrid of concrete and fiberglass to present a finished product that appeared to be solid stone. The real problem was in making the molds to spray the mixture of concrete and fiberglass into. Craig eventually used 36 inch PVC pipes as forms for the columns and stacked them in eight foot sections one on top of the other. In the center of the hollowed forms he had an "I" beam running the entire length. After the columns were in place they were sanded at the joints and then finished by an elderly Mexican mason, who could only be explained as a true artist, to appear as solid stone. The entire exterior facing of both buildings were to be finished the same way, but for now the crew needed to focus on the remaining framing and securing rooftops on their half built structures.

Craig was amazed at the finished columns sitting atop the steps and was surprised how good they looked without a base. Ryan had explained to Craig that he was modeling the buildings after the Temple of Delians on the Greek Island of Delos. It was a temple built for the God Apollo and it had no base at the bottom or top of the columns. Craig looked at the drawings before he actually began to build the columns and thought they would look ridiculous. Now with the columns in place atop the concrete steps that were poured before his arrival he marveled at their beauty. Craig had Jason and RJ cover the ten columns with ten mil plastic and secure it with duct tape to await the framing that needed to be completed above.

On the first Tuesday in June the group of believers met in their usual setting in a small arena behind the gymnasium at the school. Ricky, who hadn't made the final leap yet was still smitten with Caroline and attended every gathering and was useful in lowering the decibels of the children when the study began. Also in attendance each Tuesday and Thursday were Doctors Frank Daly and Janet Tippins who befriended the Wrigleys at one of the early social luncheons and were both long time Christians. Maria's personal assistant Bridget who had lost her entire family in England during the Six month war while she was studying abroad in San Francisco. And the four Mexican American brothers from Craig's crew who were Catholic but felt as if they needed to find fellowship somewhere on the mountain.

The Brothers' Ortiz were an amazing group with an even more amazing story. They had stumbled upon the jobsite by accident while camping in the woods nearby. Juan, the oldest at 30 had told his younger brothers; Roberto, Alex, and Paulie that they needed to learn to live off the land after the collapse. They had an inspiring landscape business in Susanville, California that crumbled almost instantaneously when the work went dry. Then, just as dominos fall, the home that they were renting was confiscated by the owner who needed a place to call home himself. The Ortiz brothers were first generation Americans who truly loved American life and they never got caught up in the gang riddled street scene. The two older boys had wives and small children who they had found safe homesteads for at a North of Lake Tahoe hotel. The ladies worked the rooms occupied by government personnel on hunting vacations and were compensated with room and board. With their families safe, the boys headed out north to seek out work. Juan had told the group how he didn't believe in remaining idle and that every night while living off the land he prayed for a purpose for his hands and those of his Brothers. Amazingly they found work at a small dairy farm near Lake Britton which provided them shelter for the winter. The boys knew that they would have probably died in the mountains if it hadn't of been for some unbelievable good luck and they all believed that it was more than just luck that they happened upon the project on their way back south in the Spring.

Akiko had told Sadahara that she needed to work late on Tuesdays and Thursdays and Maria reworked her schedule to suit the deception. She felt tremendous guilt in lying to her husband and, he himself was becoming more and more of a worry to the group. Sadahara was delighted to see the news report about the State run religion and had actually formed an alliance with several other military tech geeks who were forming a tight inner circle with the General himself. Sadahara would brag about his personal connection with General Thompson and how he was first in line whenever a problem arose in any area of communication at the base. Sadahara soaked in, and truly believed the message of religion being at the core of the worlds dismay and loathed any zealot who might have been responsible for taking him away from his plush lifestyle. Akiko and the others prayed for Sadahara but felt it best to avoid confronting him at this point.

Maria had informed all school personnel that they were attending a board meeting on the nights they gathered and that they were not to be disturbed. The General knew they were there and so too did most of the base personnel, but none of them knew why. They locked the doors and closed the blinds and focused on the Lord and what lay before them. What lay before them was a church to build with only a few skilled hands, a couple of borrowed construction lights and a single blue truck to deliver supplies in the dead of night. Craig had decided to build the church with a raised foundation and without electricity or running water. They would quickly call it a fishing cabin if anybody stumbled upon before they completed it with the alter or pews. The stained glass window that had been carefully taken from Johns mind to a piece of paper was in God's hands because they knew of only one person on the site who could produce it and she was an avid secularist who had made her way from a military private to an artist in charge of enhancing the newly formed village down below. When the group had finally gathered together Jeff led them in a short prayer and as was the newly found custom they went over the business at hand before opening the Word.

"How are we looking on supplies Craig?" Jeff asked.

"Well, we've got everything we need at the site to build a foundation, but I'm a little concerned about the noise. Also it would be suspicious if we all had the same hours off so I'm gonna need to separate my hours from Jason's to make it work."

"Why don't we test it tonight?" John said. "If we get Jason and RJ up there with some walkie talkies you and I can soar around to different locations and have them pound some hammers into some lumber and we'll see where we can hear 'em and where we can't."

"That would work John," Craig said "Besides we need a little covert operation to make you feel useful."

"I'm useful, I make lumber and nails disappear from invoices like nobody's business and I've been practicing swallowing my pride just to get a closer look into the Generals inner workings."

"The guy is really starting to scare me," Ricky said while returning from peeking a view into the Gymnasium from the blinds in the window that separates the two rooms. "He actually wants to persecute people like us. I think he's looking forward to it."

"I'm not sure which side you've settled on yet Rick," Katie said with a slight smile.

"Me either," Caroline said with raised eyebrows.

"I'm on your side okay," Ricky said with gentle contempt. "Just because I haven't figured this whole thing out yet doesn't mean that I would ever turn against my friends."

Ricky was clearly agitated and thought it was best to leave it alone but Caroline took an unexpected step…

"You know Ricky, you keep saying that you're trying to figure God out, like he's a puzzle or something. Figuring out God won't bring you home safely, but if it will help lead you in the right direction, I have a challenge for you."

"What's that?" Ricky said with a look of sarcastic rejection before even hearing the challenge.

"I have some software that goes into great detail examining the death and resurrection of Jesus. It has commentaries from the world's best known skeptics both living and dead. It has all possible accounts of what happened a couple thousand years ago after Jesus died. It is completely unbiased and it covers every base. I think that you should spend some time studying it and see if you can find a plausible explanation for why we are all sitting in this room that differs from the Biblical account."

"Computer software?" Ricky asked.

"Yep," Caroline said. "And I've even got an old laptop that you can destroy along with the software when you're done. It's probably not a good idea to download it onto your office computer."

"I'll take a look at it," Ricky replied. "And for the record, I'm not a hardened skeptic. I…just like to be sure, that's all."

After the group finished studying prophecies from the Old Testament and aligning them with the New, Jason and RJ took "Old Blue" up to the site where they had cleverly hidden supplies under fallen pine branches and heavy brush. Craig and John decided to stay where they were and see if they could be heard in different areas of the school. About ten minutes after the boys left to the darkened site the walkie talkie chirped in Craig's hand…

"Whadda you want me to do Dad, just pound on a board?"

"Yeah, but elevate it on top of a couple of logs to make an echo. Make it as loud as you can."

It was Almost ten o'clock and the kids were in bed as John and Craig crept into the Gym and they couldn't hear a thing. They made their way around the school signaling the boys to pound away for about ten seconds at a time and they soon realized that they would not be heard at the school. When they walked out to the playground area behind the school their luck was not as good. The sound of the pounding could be heard loud and clear.

"Stop, stop, stop," Craig quietly said through his hand held radio. "That is going to be a problem from here."

"Do you want to try some other areas Dad?"

"No. I just remembered that when you sit on the ridge between here and the base all you can hear is the sound of the construction below. As long as we get our framing done up here, before they quit swinging hammers down there, nobody at the base or at the village will hear us. We just need to worry about the school."

"So what do you want us to do Dad? Jason said abruptly. "It's kind of creepy out here."

"Have em turn on the battery powered lights and move 'em around in different directions and let's see if we can see 'em," John said, obviously enjoying himself.

"Flip on the lights and move 'em around. We're going to drive around the entire sight and see if we can see you guys."

"Why don't we just send up a flare or two," RJ said. "Maybe we can write a note, put it in a bottle and throw it through the Generals window."

"Oooorrrrr," Jason replied, obviously loosening up to RJ's humor, "Maybe we can use some M&M's to make a trail from the Generals headquarters that lead him right to us."

The two boys laughed as they hooked the batteries to the lights and dragged them to the small clearing where they would build the structure and awaited a signal. Suddenly, RJ realized that they were supposed to turn the lights on first and that they were to wait for a signal.. ......

"Oops" Jason said as he chirped his father. "See anything yet Dad?"

"Not yet," Craig replied. "We seem to be good down here by the satellite dishes."

"Good," Jason said while he and RJ held back their laughter. "Should we try it with the lights on now?"

Craig and John just shook their heads and sighed and finally Craig said, "knuckleheads......turn 'em on and leave 'em on and move them around until we tell you to turn them off."

As John and Craig drove around the entire base in the convertible jeep they couldn't see anything in the direction of the site but when they reached the top of the grade where the road dips back to the school they could see the lights clearly shining through the tops of the trees…

"Shut 'em off Jay, shut 'em off," Craig said in a panicked voice and in a flash the lights went dark.

"How we gonna keep people up here from knowing what's going on out there?" John said with a saddened expression.

"I think that we're gonna need to work by day and somehow try to muffle the sound or figure out a way to make more noise to override it," Craig said as he pulled back into the parking lot where Katie and Akiko were sitting on the entry steps talking.

"How'd it go guys?" Katie said as she walked towards the jeep.

"Great, if we could move the school on the other side of the ridge," John said as he hopped out and fumbled through his pockets for his own set of keys.

"So what does that mean?" Akiko said as she worked her way into the back of Craig's jeep for a ride down the hill.

"It means we have to figure some stuff out before we begin," Craig said as he chirped Jason and told him that he would see him at home.

Chapter Twenty-Three

As the Summer flew into full swing the town was taking shape. Most of the framing was complete and most of the structures had completed roofs. The facing of the court house and the clock tower were completed and were truly brilliant to see. The sides of the buildings were opened framing but the roofs were nearly ready for their pale concrete tiles. General Thompson was on a crusade against anything religious and had actually dismissed about 25% of the military personnel and nobody dared to ask where they had been sent. During the study group gatherings it had been discussed that in most cases up to 60% of military personnel were Christians and that meant that of the 100 or so soldiers that remained, there was a good chance that many worshiped in hiding as did they.

Ricky, while still investigating the death and resurrection of Christ while holding out hope in finding the smoking gun that had eluded skeptics for over two thousand years had devised a plan to allow for the framing of the church. He had gone to General Thompson and told him that it would be good moral builder for the construction workers to have a baseball diamond in the vacant field on the outskirts of the old stables. The stables and the surrounding area was abandoned when the Christian camp had closed its doors after the collapse. The General liked any idea that involved tearing down part of the camp that symbolized a hate filled ideology and he figured that it was better to have these hard hat fools slugging it out up at a field than in front of him every day. Ricky had explained that it would require a little demolition and some grading and landscape work but that he could have it fully functional by the middle of September and that would allow time for a short Fall league before the weather turned to rain and snow. After the go ahead from the General, John simply placed Juan in charge of the project and he used his hand held to be alerted when he would need to turn on a generator or run a backhoe to muzzle the sound of hammers and saws at the church site. This plan was working brilliantly and before long the makeshift group of builders had the makings of an actual structure formed with a composite roof and a large round void in the center of the facing where a miraculous stained glass window was to be inserted.

Mid way through the sweltering month of July the group met in the well air conditioned school when Jeff decided to change the pace a little. He had been teaching from the Bible directly and he had zero intention of stopping, but he felt it prudent to talk about the Church that they were building and the significance of it. When he had the full attention of the others he said...

"The other day when I was up at our church trying to help as best I could I got to thinking, which, as you all know can be a problem for me. Anyway, I was looking up at the sun streaming through the tall firs and I thought. "Why are we building this Church?" and then suddenly it hit me. We're not building a church we're building a body. Juan, you said that you and your brothers needed a purpose for your hands. Craig, you guys needed to find the meaning of being blessed when all seemed lost. John, you and RJ needed each other and through extraordinary circumstances you were reunited. We all have amazing stories that led us here and we all have one thing in common, we all need the Lord. Not one person here has ever said, to the best of my knowledge anyway, "Why are we building this church" We heard a dream from a man and we all believe, whole heartedly I might add, that it came from God." Jeff paused and walked around his chair and gazed out at the darkened field through the slight seams in the blinds and then continued..."God doesn't care about the church, He cares about his people and I believe that something amazing is going to happen at that site. It may sound crazy.... but I think that it involves many more people than just us. That Church is just wood and nails but Jesus is much more than that."

Ricky listened intently to what Jeff was saying and before he knew it words were flowing from his mouth....

"He is indeed more than just wood and nails." Everyone turned and stared directly at Ricky and he began to shake uncontrollably and when he flopped his forehead into his hands that had formed a resting place above his knees he began to quietly mumble, "Caroline, I can't. I can't explain it. I feel like I'm fighting something that is so much bigger than me and that the fight is already over. I just need to give up but I've always been trained not to."

"Trust me Rick," Craig said as he and the others formed a tight circle around him. "This is the only fight that you have no way of winning."

"Let it go Son," John said in his husky voice.

"Pray with me" Jeff said, "Pray with me."

Ricky fell to his knees and accepted his eternal gift of salvation while the others hummed Amazing Grace and wiped tears from their eyes. Caroline knelt down next to Ricky and whispered in his ear...

"I always knew you would come home Rick, I love you."

Chapter Twenty-Four

As the Summer wore on the wildlife became more and more active. Squirrels and raccoons busied themselves storing winter supplies and were daily visitors to the jobsite while soaring hawks would scout their young from afar. The sun was hot and the days were long, especially for Jason, RJ and 17 year old Paulie Ortiz who found themselves on the roof of the court house securing concrete tiles over the spread out, all too black tar paper. The three worked well together and had a renewed sense of worth in knowing their days that remained, belonged to the Lord. As sweat drops landed on the rooftop and evaporated a moment later they took notice of a newcomer that they had heard was soon to be arriving. Her name was Julia Weston. She wore a tie-dye shirt that hung well down past the waist of her faded 501's and her Birkenstocks completed the stereotype. Other than her fashion disaster she was actually quite stunning and her slim athletic frame and her long blonde hair woven into a tight pony tail was casting a very appealing shadow of which the boys quickly took notice. Julia was the newly appointed art Czar of the entire project, and she was not wasting time in starting her beautification as she stood there, pencil in hand, while sketching out a mural for the side of the down town movie theater a couple of blocks away...

"I wonder if she is as weird as they say she is?" Jason said.

"I heard she's a witch, voo doo and all that kind of stuff," Paulie said as he wiped the sweat from his low brow.

"I only know one way to find out," RJ said as he flung his legs around the extension ladder and started down. "If she turns me into a frog make sure you guys find me a nice home... *ribitt.*"

RJ walked down the street and around the corner to where Julia was laying out her drop clothes and wasted no time in making conversation...

"How's it going today Ma'am, sure picked a perfect day for painting."

"Don't you have work to do?" Julia said as she instantly turned away from RJ and did her best to ignore him.

"Yes Ma'am but ever since Abraham Lincoln crossed the Delaware even us Black folks get a break now and then."

"George Washington," She quickly responded.

"Excuse me," RJ said as if he were truly confused.

"It was George Washington who crossed the Delaware during a different war and in a different century."

"I know that Ma'am," RJ said with a sly, yet warm smile, "George fought during the revolutionary war in the 1700's and Lincoln was President during the Civil war in the 1860's. I know all about US history. My Old Man drilled that stuff into me for years, I was just making sure you were listening to me."

"Is there a point to any of this.....")She said as she looked back at her sketching.

"Ronald Jerome Robbs, Ma'am" RJ interrupted as he held out his hand," but everybody calls me RJ."

"Colonel Robb's son I presume", she replied with a loose gripped and fleeting handshake, "And why is the Colonel's son laying roof tiles, couldn't they find a less strenuous position for you?"

"You saw me up there, did Ya" He said slightly jabbing at the girl.

"You kind of stand out......no offense," she said with a quick look of embarrassment.

"None taken, I like standing out and to be honest I like working on those buildings. They are positively going to be something special."

"If you're into Greek Mythology I guess. Personally I would have built them in a way that reflects the earth and all its beauty," Julia said as she began to paint a few lines over her sketching.

"What is this wall going to have? Trees and rivers and butterflies?" RJ said as he tried to make sense of her scribbling.

"Actually it is going to be a labyrinth depicting the many ways to reach one goal. Whatever road you choose they will all lead you to the center... Thus is life."

"I don't know about that, but I'm sure it'll be pretty. I saw that painting in the display window of the book store with your name on it, and that was simply incredible."

"Thanks," Julia said with a half mocking smile. "It was child's play."

"Childs play," RJ said with a raised eyebrow. "I'll bet it took you years to learn your craft."

"I'm only twenty two and I didn't come out of the womb doing artful things....., but my Mom used to do commissioned paintings for churches and private homes and I use to help out on occasion."

"Speaking of churches," RJ said with an abrupt change in subjects, "I heard that we are going to build a church of sorts here in town. At first we weren't but now we are," leading his witness as RJ was known to do.

"It's a universal learning center not a dreadful church," Julia said with contempt.

"Well... maybe I'll see you there, and we can talk about universal learning and the many ways."

"We'll see," Julia said as she once again turned away from RJ and returned to her work.

"Gotta run Ma'am it was indeed a pleasure."

Julia shot a mocking half smile but only slightly turned to acknowledge his departure.

When RJ returned to the roof top he looked at his sweaty friends and said with a wide smile and a wink, "I think she loves me."

"What?" Jason said clearly amused. "You didn't tell her your whole life story did you?"

"Of course not, she's clearly a lunatic, I just catered to her ego and let the rest fall into place naturally. Now I'll need to get married, move out of my Dad's apartment, buy cologne, shower three times a days....On second thought, she's more your type Jay, she's way too skinny for me, everybody knows that we blackies like our women a little bit plump."

"You are amazing RJ. What's it like?" Jason asked.

"How do you mean?"

"What's it like in your crazy world?"

"Right now I feel like cupid, because I saw how you were looking at that girl, half drooling with your eyes a poppin'. I also know that you would never walk up to her and introduce yourself. So the next time you and I happen to walk by her, I will have an opportunity to play match maker."

That evening as the Mitchells were relaxing and resting their tired and battered bones before they needed to work their way towards the school for a study, they were startled when a news flash appeared on the 42 inch flat screen that quickly caught their attention. Apparently there had been several bombings around the country that particular afternoon. This, in and of itself, was not unusual but the amount had more than tripled the total of any other day since the end of the "Not in my Backyard" revolution. Even more alarming was who had apparently taken claim for the bombings. A new group, who conveniently called themselves "The US Traditional Christian Front" had left pamphlets around each bombing site explaining that they were doing God's work in cleansing the world from its sinful ways. There were over three dozen separate bombings in, and around every major city in the country and the most innocent amongst the remaining citizens were targeted. Daycare centers, hospitals, a couple of the new learning centers and even a few food rationing lines were hit and mostly obliterated. The red faced reporter turned into an analyst right in front of the camera and said that it was finally time to accept Christianity for what it truly is "Just another in the long line of destructive lunatic faiths." Shortly following the images of the devastation the Government controlled channel switched to the Whitehouse for a briefing from the President...

My fellow Americans, It truly is a sad day on the streets of our country. As many of you know, myself and my staff have been working around the clock to bring back a sense of normalcy to our cities and towns. We have been alarmed by a rise in civil disobedience amongst many religious groups in recent months and it was because of this that we decided to institute a universal state religion where all faiths would be free to worship as one. Obviously, many Christians never got that memo or they simply chose to ignore it. Furthermore, they have obviously decided to join in a form of their own jihad against their own brothers and sisters in their own home land. They have attacked the most vulnerable amongst us and have placed the name of their God at the top of their bloody deeds. I myself was once a Christian, but I am here tonight to denounce that faith. I was wrong to believe that there is only one way to heaven and it is now clear to me that this way of thinking is why the world is where it is today. Tolerance is the key to solving our differences and you can rest assured that I will use all resources available to keep these radicals from any further harm that they might inflict. Lastly, I realize that there are many good hearted Christians out there who simply want to worship in peace. This country does not want to keep you from your worship but we need to know who you are so we can differentiate you from the radicals. I am instituting a 72 hour time period for the Christian people of this land to register at any military facility in the country. Once again this is solely for your own protection. Anyone caught worshiping the Christian God without registration will be dealt with swiftly and severely. While it will remain illegal to gather and worship any form of deity outside our State system, the Christian faith is now deemed the most problematic and will be therefore taken the most seriously.

Thank You and good night.

"Those aren't Christians," Craig muttered. "They're secular puppets doing the dirty work needed to turn people away from God."

Katie was in tears as she started gathering their Bibles and fumbled through the hall closet for a sweater. Jason just sat there staring at the screen and then slowly looked over at his Dad and said........

"They might kill us if they find us up there building that church."

"Might!" Craig said sarcastically.........."We're going to build it anyway Son."

When the Mitchells arrived at the school they were surprised to learn that only the Wrigleys had seen the news report and the others were in no mood to wait. Maria rolled a carted television into the arena and then ran the cable from an office across the hall. Amazingly, the report was running and re-running the news report followed by the President's address in a continuous loop on both channels...

"I think we get the point Mr. President," Jeff said under his breath. "Obviously this is an attempt to gain help from the country in oppressing and eventually eliminating the Christian thought process from our history."

"Did they actually kill all those children just to make a point?" Akiko said still in shock from what she had seen and what was currently replaying before her eyes.

"I'm not sure Akiko," Jeff Said, "But I wonder how long they will continue to show the same footage. If it keeps running much longer it can be tagged as pure propaganda, that much we do know."

"What does it mean for us? Maybe we should pull the plug on the church for awhile and lay low," Dr. Daly, a nervous, but brilliant physician said while looking a tad bit frightened.

"I think that we should pray about that Frank," John said. "But I think you all know that we aren't about to quit now and I don't think that God is going to be sending anyone of us that message."

Frank, the fifty year old widower, looked at the others and in shame he said "You're right. We are all going to die anyway and our promise won't be fulfilled until then. I just got a little fearful that's all."

"Fearful," RJ said "I'm about to wet my pants.... but even that won't keep me from building that church. It's like Jeff says, we can be expecting a lot of visitors, and besides....,"

RJ paused to gather his thoughts while the group leaned in, ready to hear anything RJ had to say. They had learned that the boy was full of wit, charisma, and a strange form of wisdom that was developed way beyond his years. "We all know that whatever He has in store for us is gonna happen when we finish that church. I don't know about you guys, but I love surprises."

Jeff brought everybody back to reality by expressing his concerns about the new revelations...

"Okay guys, we are now officially enemies of the State. I know that there are others, probably right here on the base, but I kind of doubt that they are trying to sneak into the woods to build a church. We are going to need to be much more careful and bolster up our limited security. Does anyone have any immediate concerns?"

"I'd still like to see a new young Asian girl join our group so my chances of being the girl screaming in pain could go from 100% to 50" Akiko said with a sly grin.

"That reminds me Akiko," John said "Any chance that husband of yours can shed some light on whether those attacks today were staged. Maybe you can cater to his ego a little and see if he can pin point some flaws in the editing or something. Just a thought."

"I know that he hangs out with some not so nice people and he says that he hangs out with the General too, but I've never seen them together," She replied.

"I have," Ricky said. "I've seen him and a few other tech guys in and out of the Generals office reworking the computers and phone systems. I'm not sure if the General even knows his name but he's obviously noticed him fumbling with the wires. He's always polite to me but he kind of gives me the creeps."

"That's because he is a creep," Akiko said as she showed her pain for a brief moment.

"Akiko," Jeff said, as she hung her head in a momentary shame, "Start slow and don't push, but see if he can permit you any information at all. We could use some inside information because eventually the General is going to be coming for us."

"I'll try, but I talk more to you guys in five minutes then I do to him in a month."

Chapter Twenty-Five

Gencral Thompson was an avid golfer and he made frequent helicopter trips to several abandoned golf courses north of Lake Tahoe. He had made arrangements with a few local residents to keep the courses in good shape in exchange for supplies that he would deliver from the base. None of the local workers had any idea where he was coming from, they just knew that they would receive a call on the night before he would arrive and that they were to meet him in the middle of the first fairway to receive their box of goodies and then disappear and leave the General and whoever he decided to bring that day alone to enjoy the course. General Thompson always brought an extra helicopter along with highly armed security personnel for protection and his personal helicopter flew circles around the course while he was playing to watch the area for any possible intruders. General Thompson had asked John to join him shortly after he had arrived but since John didn't play the game he was never invited again. Sadahara on the other hand did play, in fact he played well. He had heard through the grapevine of the Generals excursions and he used his keen art of persuasion to get an invite.

One day, while the General was making his rounds through the tech lab Sadahara waited until he was in ear shot and then started bragging about a hole in one that he actually never made. He then continued telling anyone near him how much he missed the game that he used to play almost every day before the radicals made the leisure game a near impossibility. The General glanced over at the skinny Asian and then walked right by him without a comment. Sadahara had long accepted that the General probably had a couple of playing partners already and wasn't ready to add another, especially one who was younger and obviously more talented. About an hour later as Sadahara was eating his lunch at the Mexican cantina the General came in with Lieutenant Colonel Ramos and sat down at his always reserved booth. The two men were talking golf and seemed to be heating a little in their discussion..........

"Taganawa," The General shouted across the room.

"Yes General," Sadahara said while trying desperately to swallow his oversized bite of his chicken fajitas.

"You're a player aren't you son."

"Golf sir? Yeah I used to play anyway."

"Maybe you can settle a score for us. If I move some loose impediments behind my ball and the ball moves even though I never touch the ball is that a penalty or not."

"That would be a one stroke penalty Sir," Sadahara responded with confidence.

"Ha!" The General said abruptly. "I told you Ramos, your 89 is now officially a 90."

"Fine General," Ramos said finally giving in to his superior, "But it still bested your 92 and since I was not there on the day you supposedly fired the 80 at Coyote Moon it is still the lowest score on the course."

"I played Coyote Moon once," Sadahara said as he tried to make his way back into the conversation and this time with a truthful statement.

"Really," The General said with a little suspicion. "What do you remember about it son?"

"I remember that it has some huge boulders lining some of the fairways and a par three that tees from a cliff," Sadahara said while gleaming with pride for finally being noticed.

"You want to hit it again Son?" The General asked. "We've got plenty of new clubs at our disposal, unless your left handed."

"I would love to play Sir, anytime."

"Good," The General said. "Tomorrow morning after my morning briefing. We'll leave the heliport at 7 hundred hours and we'll find you some shoes and gear when we arrive."

Sadahara was elated that he was going to be in the presence of the man in charge. He had climbed his way to the top before and now he would have a chance to do so once again. All night long he rehearsed possible ways to gain an upper hand with the General. He knew that he hated everything about the Traditional Foundation and the project that he deemed a waste of money. He also knew that the General liked the idea of a State run religion that would hopefully bring an end to radical fringe element that appeared to be running wild. Sadahara truthfully agreed with both of those stances as he too found religion more problematic then useful. He would simply cater to the General's ego and make his way into his inner circle of elitism while leaving the other tech geeks in the dust.

When Akiko arrived home that same night she found Sadahara to be in a better than usual mood as he actually asked her how her day went. He then began to brag about his adventure the following day and how he was chosen over so many others to have the privilege of playing golf with the General. When he finally stopped rambling Akiko asked him what he thought about the attacks that happened the previous day…

"Just a bunch of Jesus freaks," Sadahara said in disgust.

"Do you think it was real?" Akiko asked.

"Of course it was real Akiko, didn't you see the footage?"

"Yeah, I saw it, but I didn't see any bodies?"

"So you think the buildings were empty?" Sadahara said with a hint of sarcasm.

"I don't know Sadie. It just seemed kind of staged to me that's all. Besides why would Christians kill people for no reason?"

"They've been killing people for two thousand years Akiko. I know that you have pretended to be a Christian since you attended a couple of services with my Mom but maybe now you can see how fruitless all this nonsense is."

"Your Mom didn't think it was fruitless Sadie," Akiko said as she looked deep into his eyes for a once known compassion.

"Yes, and now she is a widow who is losing her mind. Where is her God now?'

Akiko knew better then to push any further so she put a big smile together and showed undue excitement for Sadahara's big day...

"Anyway," She said. "That is so cool that you get to play golf with the General. Is he a nice guy?"

"He's a no nonsense kind of guy just like me, and it won't be long before I have an upper hand here at the base."

"I'm sure you'll have a great time Sadie," Akiko said as she headed towards the shower while rolling her eyes upward as she turned away from her husband.

Ricky knew some people who were imbedded in the Nation's Capitol and he also had an uncanny way of extracting information when he felt it necessary. At midnight pacific standard time Ricky called Captain Taylor Holden at the pentagon to feel the situation. Captain Holden was a true secularist. He was young, intelligent and pretty much disagreed with everything Ricky believed in. He was however, a talker and a subordinate who respected and trusted the Lieutenant Colonel...

"This is Lieutenant Colonel Richard Smalls can you patch me through to Captain Taylor Holden if he is still working the graveyard?"

"Please hold," Came the voice of a young female operator.

After what seemed like an eternity of classical holding music a voice piped through.....

"Holden here."

"Captain Taylor Holden as we live and breathe," Ricky said.

"I hope you don't mind Sir, but since it's three in the morning and you have been reduced to a camp counselor I'd like to request calling you Rick during our little chat."

"I would expect nothing else Taylor, besides you know better than anyone else that being a camp counselor has always been my dream."

"Anything to get you out of DC, right Rick?"

"That's it my friend, but believe it or not I do have a purpose for my call" Ricky said in a redirecting tone.

"And what would that be?"

"Just a little perplexed about those attacks Taylor. Doesn't seem to fit the MO of Christianity."

"Christianity, Islam, Judaism, what's the difference? They have been at each other's throats for centuries.... Bunch of crazy lunatics trying to prove they're right while ruining the planet for the sane people. Hey, you're not feeling sympathetic towards these nut jobs are Ya?"

"No," Ricky said without a pause. "You know me Taylor, I like the traditional values of our country, but I'm not a Sunday school teacher by any stretch of the imagination. It just seemed a little curious. Why now? Why target innocent civilians?"

"Beats me," The Captain responded, "All I know is that they did, and that we are moving hard to make sure it doesn't happen again."

"Taylor," Ricky said in a leading fashion. "Did you guys see any of the carnage?"

"No. The FBI along with some secret service personal cleaned it and notified the families. The President isn't going to release the names of the victims because he doesn't want people ushering in retaliation from other regions of the country."

"What about the surviving family members. Won't they be looking to get even?" Ricky said in his covert operative voice.

"That's the ingenious mind of our President at work Rick. He is relocating them to a pristine area where they can mourn away from the public eye. Nobody even knows who they are or where they are."

"Perfect" Rick said knowing that he had been given the answer he desired. "I guess we just have to hope we can put a lid on these crazies before it happens again."

"You can count on it Sir. I gotta run, anything else?"

"Nope. Just wanted to make sure you still loved me," Ricky said as he closed his eyes and silently thanked God for giving him the news that would bring a sense of peace to his brothers and sisters.

"Good night Rick," The Captain said as Ricky heard the phone click dead.

The following day Sadahara met the General and Lieutenant Colonel Ramos at the helipad and they soared high into white puffy clouds and South towards Coyote Moon golf club that was nestled in the tall pines just North of Truckee, California. Sadahara was amazed at the scenery that he had missed upon his arrival when the ground was covered with a hazy fog. He motioned to the General when he saw several men gathered around the railroad tracks in a makeshift station near the Truckee River...

"That's where all our supplies come in Son. You didn't think they magically appeared did you?"

"I guess not Sir," Sadahara said a little embarrassed.

Sadahara hadn't seen any of the containers arrive at the bottom of the hill where the jobsite was because he hadn't really ventured much beyond the base and the makeshift shops and dining areas. When the helicopter landed on the first fairway they were greeted by a few men in an old Ford Bronco who were as excited as children on Christmas morning. After the usual exchange of keys and supplies the three players walked up a slight incline towards the first tee as a dozen or so military personnel secured the area and opened the pro shop to retrieve the few sets of golf clubs left inside a locked closet and cleverly hidden by the locals under a pile of old tarps. A few moments later the same locals pulled up along the first tee with two golf carts that they obviously charged at an undisclosed area…

"If they drag those carts out here before my boys secure the ground they would be minus two golf carts," the General said with a disgusted nod.

When the security personnel arrived with the clubs and a bag full of shoes the general told Sadahara to find a pair that fit in a hurry because the chopper over head only had only enough fuel to get them through the first nine and would need to refuel before they started on the back side of the course. When the men were ready to play the General looked at the young skinny Asian and said..

"Youth before beauty Son, let it rip."

Sadahara lined up his tee shot, took a deep breath and abruptly sliced his shot deep into the wooded pines on the right side of the fairway. Deeply embarrassed he mumbled to himself, "Not now you idiot," and performed a sheepish smile and said….

"Been awhile."

"It'll be awhile until you find that one kid," Ramos said as he promptly followed suit and flopped one in the same area.

After the General hit his drive two hundred and twenty five yards down the center of the fairway he headed towards the cart and verbally hazed his playing partners…

"I guess that will be the last time I tee off last today."

Sadahara shuffled through some low rough and pine needles until he found his ball depressed into a half sunken mole hill with about fourteen trees in front of him and the green. Ramos had already found his ball and taken an un-playable lie and penalty and was waiting for Sadahara to do the same before heading back to the fairway. The General who was a stickler for rules was right on top of the situation and quickly assessed the lie…

"Better pick it up son. No way to get home from here."

Sadahara knew that it was probably the smart move but he wanted to impress his counterparts and he knew that somewhere inside him he had the shot. He would need to cut a bladed five iron under the first two trees and fade his shot around the remaining firs while attempting to run his ball around a large bunker in front of the green….

"No I think I'll play it from here," Sadahara said as he focused in on the nearly impossible shot.

"This is going to be a long day General," Ramos said as he backed up a few feet to allow time to avoid the impending ricochet.

Sadahara knew about moments like this. He had a chance to impress his superiors on the very first hole. He also knew that if it went bad that he might lose his confidence and find himself in every undesired location on the course and never be invited back. Sadahara pulled his five iron from the bag and lined up his shot. He closed his eyes for a moment, took a deep breath and then hit the ball in the middle with the bottom of his club and watched the flight with sheer delight. Sadahara's ball narrowly missed the low branches in front of him, curled around the several tall pines between him and his target and landed two feet on the far side of the green front bunker and trickled on to the green about six feet from the pin.

"Unbelievable," The General said as he shook his head in disbelief. "Great shot Son. What did you say your first name was again?"

"Sadahara, Sir."

"Sadahara...? Any shortened versions of that Son?"

"My wife and friends call me Sadie."

The General raised his eyebrows a bit and said..."Well I guess that's at least a bit easier to remember."

After that shot Sadahara played brilliantly and as expected the General and the Lieutenant Colonel warmed to him immediately. After they finished the first nine they sat around a picnic table where the security personnel had placed cold sandwiches and a few beers for the players to enjoy and the General wasted little time in bringing his usual ranting to the table....

"It sickens me that we need to have bodyguards to play a round of golf. That damn Traditional Foundation and all their idealistic ventures are holding back progress. We can secure this country in a matter of months and they want to start over from the beginning. Building new towns when we have perfectly good ones in every corner, I don't know what is going on in the minds of those morons. They seem to think that if we make self contained towns that free enterprise will flourish out of the ashes, but do they ever think about who keeps them safe and secure. They actually have plans to produce every industry needed at each of these new towns regardless of the location, green houses, cattle ranches, dairy farms, you name it. Waste of time and resources if you ask me".......Boys," the General continued after a pause to swallow the last bite of his sandwich, "I'm a traditionalist myself, but I also realize that we are headed into a global economy with a one world currency and it just so happens to be the only way we can survive. We can either be the leaders or the followers in this new system, but if these idiots have their way, our country will be annihilated while we're busying ourselves making new clock towers."

"What is the plan for the rest of the country General?" Sadahara asked with genuine curiosity.

"The Foundation is trying to prove that we can move the clock backwards and make self reliant towns and then slowly renovate the rest of the country in the same format. They control just enough of the power in vital industries to hold our country ransom and unless we want to take it from them by force and add more fuel to the already blazing fire we need to amuse them for awhile."

"So this is just a temporary situation Sir?" Sadahara said in surprise to the answer of his previous question.

"General," Ramos said trying to halt the General's banter because he felt that he had already said too much.

The General raised his hand and flipped his fingers at Ramos in a way of disregarding his warnings…

"Taganawa, listen to me Son. Do you really believe that we can slowly turn back the clocks on the way things used to be or do you think that it is more probable that we join the rest of the world in survival?"

"I hadn't really given it much thought General," Sadahara said while chomping on his tuna fish sandwich.

"Are you a religious man Taganawa?" The General asked.

"Not really Sir, always thought it was just a crutch for the weak," Sadahara said with confidence having heard about the General's stance in the matter.

"I agree Son, and we are now going to build a place for all these crazies to worship and they're complaining about a few guidelines...makes me sick. Religion caused all the world's problems and until we outlaw all this superstitious nonsense we will continue to suffer the consequences. You heard about the personnel I was forced to let go, didn't you Son?"

"It was hard not to notice the empty seats in the lab," Sadahara said.

"Well... most of those guys were resigned voluntarily. I just told them that if they wanted to freely worship Jesus they needed to do it at home and they left without incident. Now they will most likely be in charge of rounding up freaks just like themselves or be court marshaled."

"What about the Traditional Foundation Sir? What do they think about the new Universal church system?" Sadahara asked, realizing that trouble might soon be brewing.

"Oh... they want Christian churches on every corner, feel it's an important part of our heritage or something. Thankfully, that is where the President drew the line and with the recent bombings he was proven right for a change. We might have some more zealots hanging around the base but I plan on rootin' 'em out as fast as I can."

"Anything I can do to help," Sadahara said looking for a way in.

"Since you asked," The General said with a devilish grin.

Chapter Twenty-Six

Craig found a memo on his desk when he had arrived at work earlier in the morning that requested that he inform all workers that if they were Christians they needed to register as such in 72 hours or face harsh consequences. The memo also stated that they already knew which persons had stated their belief during the initial interrogation upon arrival and that hopefully all personnel will be honest in registering. The memo ended with a statement that all non-Christian personal at the base must sign a letter denouncing Christianity. Craig pondered his approach to informing the several hundred workers for most of the morning when John made his first appearance of the day...

"Let's take a walk Craig," John said as he waited for Craig at the door of the trailer.

Craig and John walked down the street and across the newly paved round-a-bout and continued beyond earshot of the working men...

"Get the memo Craig?"

"Yeah I got it, but luckily we signed agnostic when we arrived," Craig said in response.

"Well, unfortunately for the rest of us we might soon have a problem. Akiko is okay because her husband told her to say that she wasn't affiliated with any religion and I don't think the Ortiz boys even went through the process, they were just vouched for by the head concrete guy who was happy to have them before we even arrived."

"Well... if you have to register, what is that going to mean? Are they going to lift you guys out of here?"

"I don't think so Craig," John said as he gazed at the newly forming downtown.

"Why's that?"

"Because of the dream and because I have faith that at least RJ and I will be there until the end."

"So you are going to register then?" Craig said with concern.

"Yep, and so are the Wrigleys and Caroline and Rick too."

"I guess we should too then....besides we're not about to sign a statement denouncing God," Craig said while turning his head towards the ground and kicking a discarded cigarette butt.

"Everybody is going to be at the church tonight Craig. I just spent the last few hours clearing everyone's schedule and I need you to tell the Ortiz boys not to do anything until we all have a chance to discuss the matter. When are you going to make the announcement to the workers?"

"Maybe.....maybe I'll make an announcement that there will be an announcement tomorrow to buy us a little time. We can tell the General that if we wait until the crew shift at daybreak we can tell everybody at once," Craig said as he lifted his eyebrows slightly to show his delight in his good idea.

"Perfect," John said, "I'll see you tonight, I need to head up to the school and talk to Maria and make sure that she has enough people on staff tonight to allow her and the others time to be at the church by seven."

Later that same evening as Katie and Akiko were making their final rounds they ran into Ricky who had an awkward look on his face…

"What's up Rick?" Katie said as she knew his facial expressions well and didn't like what she saw.

"Plenty, but we'll talk about it tonight," Ricky said as he shushed the women with his fingers to his lips.

"Are we venturing the usual way tonight Rick?" Katie asked.

"Yeah. Just hop in the back of Juan's van around a quarter to seven and take even more precautions than usual. I'll see you guys there."

By seven fifteen all the usual suspects had arrived at the church building site. Jason and RJ along with the Ortiz brothers were prepared to work late into the evening after the gathering to finish the interior walls that were to be natural cedar and to install the last few French windows that they had borrowed from several old buildings around the abandoned Christian camp. When Jeff stepped onto the raised portion of the partially framed floor he held the memo in his hand and solemnly read it. Afterwards, everybody present began to speak at once. Most had not heard about the registration and confusion instantly set in. John rose to his feet and quieted everyone in his deep voice and stern demeanor...

"Alright, alright, alright lets settle down a bit you guys. We're here to discuss this matter and we'll stay here as long as we need until we figure out what to do."

John turned back to Jeff and motioned him to continue with a polite wave and facial gesture.

"Okay," Jeff continued "Obviously we are all given two choices; For some of us we made that choice upon arrival and trying to back away from that now would only make us more suspicious. For some others there is a choice, but I would be doing each and every one of you a disservice if I advised you to deny you have a personal relationship with Christ. I believe that this is a test from the Lord and we need to rise and meet it head on."

"But what is going to happen to us if we declare ourselves as Christians?" Doctor Daly said with a look of terror on his face.

"I have no idea," Jeff said as he reached into his pocket for a note that he had made prior to coming and after his conversation with John earlier in the Day. "But I do know this. Peter himself would have never believed that he could deny Jesus and he did it three times. If I would have asked you guys two days ago at the school if you would ever deny Jesus I hardly think a hand would have been raised. We need to register and pray that the Lord has something up his sleeve. At least that is what we plan to do."

Jeff placed his arm around his wife and kissed her gently on the cheek and opened the floor to discussion...

"They'll probably fly us out of here and drop us on the streets of East

LA," Jason said while looking at the ceiling of the cabin styled church and pondering the possibility of leaving before its completion.

"Is East LA where Malibu is?" RJ asked.

"Not hardly," Craig said as he stood up and walked to the front of the group. "Look you guys," Craig continued. "I was as taken back by this memo as the rest of you. I figured that the 72 hour deadline would be excused for people working on the base or the project, but I gotta tell you something that John shared with me earlier. He told me that he believes with all his heart that he'll be here to the end and he'll have his Son with him. We've all heard the dreams and they've been right so far, we just need to show trust and faith and hop in the backseat for a few days."

"Amen to that Brother," Ricky said as he himself made his way to the front of the group. "I do have some other news that might interest you guys," Ricky continued. "I did a little investigating last night and I can say with almost complete certainty that the bombings were staged. Apparently our dear leader has been a secularist all along and is making it his goal to rid our Nation of religion. Since Christianity is the predominant faith he is starting with us."

"How do you know that Rick?" Maria asked.

"Trust me, I know. Years of experience in the Marines and now the Army have made it quite easy to read between the lines, and those bombings were staged, and if they weren't I'm losing my mind."

"So what does that mean for us?" Akiko asked.

"It means that we might as well face the music now Akiko, because there isn't anywhere to hide anymore. They are coming for us...period!!" Ricky replied.

Everyone fell silent after Rick's final statement and they reflected on their own thoughts and fears. A moment later Caroline stood up and quickly said...

"Do you guys hear music?"

Everybody started to talk at once and John stood up and silenced them with a glaring look. As they sat there in complete silence they heard a faint sound of a guitar and the voice of people singing. The group quietly crept out the back door of the building and stopped again to listen. They could hear it more clearly now as it seemed to be coming from across the small stream and deeper in the woods...

"I better check that out," Craig said taking charge of the situation. "Jason, grab a two by four and come with me. The rest of you guys go inside and try to be quiet."

"He ain't going without me," RJ said. "Besides I'm easier to hide in the dark."

"Fine," Craig said having learned that it was always best to let RJ have his way. "But you better be able to move that giant frame of yours if we need to run."

"I'm black, running is what I do best."

As the three men worked their way through some heavy brush and up and down several ravines they soon realized that the music was coming from much further away than they thought. It was only by the echoing valleys that they were able to hear it at all. As they got closer and could actually hear the voices the singing had turned to laughter and although it was much louder they still couldn't make out any of the conversation. As they were about to move in a little closer they heard the music start again and they knelt down to listen. Ever so faintly they could hear the lyrics rustling through the leafs of the heavy woods. *"Our God is an awesome God, He reigns from heaven above"*...

"I know that song," RJ said. "We used to sing it at my church in Oakland. I'm going down there."

"Hold on a second Hotrod," Craig said as he grabbed the young man's arm. "We have no idea who those people are and they sure don't know us. Maybe it would be a good idea to wait until we can hear them talking."

"I agree," Jason said. "They might shoot you RJ and I know that its dark out here but you are still a rather large target."

"Man, is it ever pick on RJ and his size day," RJ said not persuaded. "Listen, I'll go down there alone and if they shoot me you guys can creep back to the church and pretend I got lost or something. I'll see you in five minutes with some new Brothers."

RJ gave the two Mitchells a mock wave and started heading towards the music as Craig and Jason followed behind at about a hundred feet. When RJ reached the top of a small hill he could see three men and two ladies sitting around a small campfire resting between songs and making small talk. RJ noticed that two of the men were wearing military uniforms and he figured that unless they were purchased at a local army surplus store before the collapse they were most likely from the base. RJ had never learned how to be tactful and so without warning he emerged from the trees and simply said, "How's it going out here," and was quickly on the other end of two rifles pointing directly at his head. The older of the two soldiers looked closely at RJ and said…

"You're Robbs boy?"

"Yeah, and I hope to be tomorrow too," RJ said

"What are you doing out here?" the bewildered man with the gun said.

"We were at church and we heard the music, and thought we'd check it out," RJ said as they slowly pulled the guns back to a less threatening point.

"There's no church around here Son and in case you haven't heard there won't be one for quite some time."

"Unless a group of believers like yourselves decided to build one," RJ said as he backed away a bit from his previous stance.

"What are you making one out of, fallen pines?" the elder soldier said.

"Out of scraps from the jobsite mostly," Craig said as he and Jason walked into view from behind their hiding place.

Alarmed, the men were once again at the ready with guns pointing at heads….

"How many guys are with you?" The younger wide eyed soldier said.

"This is all of us," Craig said. "Plus twenty or so more back at the church. Listen guys, and ladies we are believers just like you and we are building a place to worship. If you'd lik…

"No thanks," the elder soldier said abruptly. "We went AWOL tonight. I'm Jack Barrows and this is my wife Rebecca, my Son Travis and my daughter Emily," the soldier said as he began pointing to the other members. "And this is Rainey, a family friend. We are planning on heading North towards Oregon. We heard that there are still a lot of functioning communities there. We not about to lie about our faith and I'm not about to put my family's fate in the hands of the State and its local Gestapo. You guys read the memo?"

"We read it," Craig said realizing that they too might be on the run.

"Were going to take our chances. Kind of hoping to finish a few things here first. Do you guys have enough supplies to make it that far?"

"We have five stuffed back packs," Rebecca said. "And with good weather we can make it. Lots of rivers to fish and animals to shoot."

"Why don't you guys spend a night with us at the church before you head out," Jason said. trying to interject himself into the conversation. "It's only about a mile this way."

"No thanks Son," The elder man said. "In the morning the General will know were missing and we plan on being long gone by then. We just stopped here to rest a spell, we'll be moving all night."

"Got a final destination?" RJ said. "Cause we might be right behind you in a couple of days."

"We have friends outside of Klamath Falls, but I'd hope you guys could forget that after we part ways."

"Well," Craig said as he reached out his hand to shake the Soldiers. "God bless you guys, and good luck."

"Thanks Son," Jack said. "But I think you guys are going to need a whole lot more luck then us, and maybe a little help from above."

"We're counting on it, we're definitely counting on it."

Craig and the boys returned to the church and informed the others that the music they heard was from other believers that had decided to head north and take their chances rather than register with the General. Craig couldn't help but feel as if he were living out a childhood fantasy of being in the old west. Talking to people who had no other means of transportation other than their feet, and who planned on venturing a couple hundred miles to avoid capture. The General was the evil ranch owner who would surely form a posse to track 'em down and Craig and his minions were left to fight it out in town. When it was decided that they would simply turn in their registrations shortly after Craig's early dawn announcement the group held hands and Jeff led them in a simple prayer…

"Father, tomorrow we will truly be in your hands. We know that your purpose for us is true and we will trust in the outcome and that it will serve your will. We ask for strength, for guidance and for peace as the day's events unfold. In Jesus' name, amen."

Chapter Twenty-Seven

At precisely six am the next morning Craig stepped on top of a picnic table near the work trailers and addressed the workers. He simply read the memo and handed the microphone to the General. General Gerald Thompson looked out at the men for a moment and then began to speak...

"I recently was in contact with the Whitehouse regarding this matter. The President and his advisors are in agreement that most Christians living in the country are good people who are trying to get by just like the rest of us. However in light of the recent violence that has erupted nationwide we feel it is best for the safety of these good natured Christians to be protected by the Traditional Foundation at undisclosed areas around the country. No harm will come to any individual who registers as a Christian. We already know who made this claim upon arrival and we have done exhaustive background checks on each and every one of you. I am now going to turn the microphone over to Jeremy Kramer who is here on behalf of the Traditional Foundation with further information...Jeremy"

"Thanks General," The steely eyed and suspicious looking young man said. "I want you to know right now that I myself am a Christian and I want to offer my personal guarantee that any peaceful Christian living on the base will be transported to a safe area where they will be free to live amongst other like minded individuals. The conditions are good and there is plenty of room. It was our intention to make these new villages a place where all religions could create their own place of worship, but that dream must be put on hold until we bring about a sense of normalcy to the religious situation and all the violence. We have several buses at the ready to transport all registering individuals to Susanville, California and from there you will have several options as to where you want to call home. This is not an option as any individual Christian that does not voluntarily leave today can, and probably will be tried with treason. Trust me people, this is for your own good. Any questions?"

"What happened to the seventy two hours?" Came a cry from somewhere in the middle of the pack.

"The General felt that it would be best for the moral if we dealt with the situation today rather than dragging it along. If you are not a Christian then you can return to work as usual tomorrow but everybody must either register or sign a denouncement address today. Both options are on the same form. The stack is right here, fill it out, drop it in the box and return to your living quarters. Those who will be moved for their own protection will be notified to bring their belongings to the base headquarters. Anything else?...

"What about someone like me who marked Christian on my initial form when I arrived, but isn't a practicing Christian?" yelled someone else in the crowd.

"Just be honest, we'll take every form under consideration. The General has the final word. Thank you and God Bless you all."

John and Craig were joined by Ricky, Jason and RJ as they watched the General hop into his jeep and speed up the hill towards the mighty satellite dishes....

"I guess we're all leaving today huh?" Jason said as he gave the others a solemn look.

"I'm gonna find out right now Son," John said as he grabbed a form from the top of the stack and abruptly registered as a Christian and hopped into his own jeep.

"What are you going to do John?" Craig asked as he stopped John with a slam of the hand to the hood.

"I'm gonna show this form to the General and make him remove me himself. Personally, I don't think he's got the guts. The rest of you guys hang tight until I get back."

John looked over at the pile of papers being held down with a rock and saw the men one by one taking theirs and using the tables to file their fate...

"I'm really getting ticked off Craig," John said as he revved his engine. "And I'll tell you another thing. I don't believe that guy Kramer is from the Traditional Foundation and he's hardly a Christian."

John inadvertently flung gravel on his friends as he turned the vehicle to its capacity and floored it at the same time as he flew up the hill in a cloud of dust...

"Pop's is really pissed off," RJ said. "When he gets like that it doesn't matter if it's the Pope, the Queen of England, or God himself, he's gonna let his rage fly."

"Maybe we should try to stop him," Ricky said showing pure apprehension.

"You can't stop him when he has that look in his eyes," RJ said. "I'm his Son, remember? I've seen it before and it aint good...Nah, we better all be here when he gets back."

Colonel John Robbs was thinking about his new friends and the countless others that were going to led into possible horror as he resolutely walked into the main headquarters of the base. He didn't stop to say hello to the Generals secretary and he certainly didn't knock. John simply pushed the door open hard and it slammed into the adjacent wall with a loud crash…

"Here's my registration General. When do I leave."

The General was well trained in tense situations and used reverse tactics to gain an upper hand of the moment…

"Any particular reason you slammed my door into the wall Robbs?" The General said quietly.

"Read the paper General," John said as he handed it to the higher ranking man.

The General looked over the paper for a moment and stared back at John and said…

"It doesn't appear as if you have changed any since you arrived Robbs, so let me ask you this again, why did you slam my door into the wall?"

"I want to know when I'm leaving and I want to know exactly where my Son and I will be going," John said with his anger rising.

"I don't understand Robbs, you were at the meeting, you read the memo."

"Yes General, I have been reading since I was six and I believe that I asked you a question."

"Are you feeling okay Robbs? Seriously, am I missing something?" The General said in complete confusion.

"I am a Christian General and according to the memo, and that knucklehead Kramer, I'm on my way out of here today."

"Robbs, are you playing some kind of joke with me because I have a lot to do today and I don't need this kind of aggravation."

By this time John was just as confused as the General. He was about to start over from the beginning but he thought better of it and approached the General's desk and looked at his registration that was clearly marked Christian. John pointed to the word on the form and said to the General.....

"What does that say General?"

"Agnostic!!" The General said with his voice rising with an unsettling annoyance. "The same thing you and your Boy claimed to be when you arrived here."

John had an instant feeling of anxiety flush over him and the room began to spin. He almost fell over but he grabbed the desk with one hand and the General stood up quickly and steadied him before he fell...

"But I'm a Christian," John said softly as he slowly began to recover.

"There's nothing wrong with being an agnostic John," The General said as he helped John to a seat at the front of his desk.

Just as quickly as John had begun to feel unsteady he snapped out of it and stood strong and calm before the General...

"I'm sorry Sir. I switched blood pressure medication recently and I'm still adjusting. Doc Wrigley told me that I would have moments of confusion and dizziness for a few days but I never thought it would be like this...Wow!.... Sorry again Sir."

The General gave John a long and suspicious look and said, "Did you have a reason for coming here to see me Robbs?"

"Actually Sir I was thinking that you may need some help going over the paperwork," John said, not knowing how he was able to dig his way out of the hole he had dug and feeling God's hand directly on his shoulder..

"No need Robbs," The General said. "Kramer and his guys are going to bring me the people on the bubble at the end of the day. I'll trust their judgment on the rest."

"Okay sir, and sorry again, just got a little loopy there for a minute."

John walked over to the his jeep in absolute amazement of God. He looked up at the blue morning sky and muttered…Thank you Jesus, it's good to know somebody knows what they're doing. When John made his way back to the gravel parking lot in front of the trailers he found all four men leaning on "Old Blue" with a look of deep depression on their faces…

"Well," Craig said. "Do we need to get some shovels and gasoline for the body?"

"Tell me you didn't strangle the old boy Pops," RJ said as John approached the men and quietly said…

"It's gonna be hard to explain this one guys, but I don't think any of us will be leaving today or anytime soon for that matter."

John told the others what happened and they sat there listening like kids hearing about the tooth fairy for the first time. They were truly speechless, that is until RJ broke the silence and said…

"Well boys, sounds like we need to fill out the form and take the day off as instructed. We can call each other during the day, and on occasion not answer just to freak each other out even more then we already are."

"I have no idea if the Lord only wants me and RJ here," John said. I will be praying to see all of you guys in the morning. I need to find Jeff and tell him about an exploratory new pill he's been prescribing me and fill him in on some other details. "That reminds me," he continued, "You guys need to watch every word you say from now on. Zero tolerance, remember?"

John, still enthralled in an awestruck moment hopped back into his jeep and drove away while the others looked on amazed at what they had heard. Ricky walked over to Craig, lightly kicked the gravel and softly said...

"I'm gonna find out who this guy Kramer is. I'll come by tonight at about eleven, gonna be awake?"

"I'll be up and if we're still here we'll see you then."

All four men filled out their registrations and they went back to their living quarters as instructed. The school and base personal were also instructed to fill out forms but they were instructed to remain on duty until their shifts ended. When Katie joined her husband and son around six o'clock the entire compound was buzzing. Craig watched through his back window as people were led out to waiting vans and hurried down to the base main headquarters. Craig couldn't see beyond the corner and he was only guessing that these individuals were not coming back. Craig did recognize a framing contractor who he had gotten to know somewhat and he watched as he and his wife were being led out to the parking lot and they seemed a little upset as they were obviously arguing their point to the armed personnel. Craig was irritated by the fact that he couldn't make out what they were saying and he found himself fidgeting with his pocket knife when Jason sat next to him on the edge of the bed...

"Rayno and his wife are leaving huh?" Jason said.

"Looks that way. I haven't seen anybody come back yet and I've seen about forty people leave. Most of them seem a little set off by that too."

"I'll tell you one thing Dad," Jason said. "If Rayno is a Christian then I'm the Pope."

"Whadda Ya mean by that?"

"Well," Jason said as be laid back on the bed with his hands behind his head. "I've seen that guy drinking way more than his share, think he's been stealing bottles or something. Plus he's always taking the Lord's name in vain while belittling everyone around him. Basically Dad, he's kind of a jerk. His wife is no charmer either, she's tried to hit on RJ and I a couple of times at the pool hall. She's a bit sleazy for me so I declined."

"Let me ask you this," Craig said. "Do you think that God is supernaturally working this registration thing in our favor?"

"Maybe," Jason said as he sat back up. "At least to a degree. I don't think that the General will find himself on one of those buses, but maybe God will use the hardest of hearts to fill the seats of the believers to buy us time."

"You come up with all that on your own Jay?" Craig asked while giving him the once over.

"Nope. Just came from RJ's and they have a better view then us and as you may well have guessed, RJ knows just about half the people here and he said that he hasn't seen a nice person leave yet. Plus they seem to be going building by building, and if they are, we seem to be in the clear."

"It's just unbelievable," Craig said as he placed his hand on Jason's shoulder.

"Nothing is beyond belief anymore Dad, nothing."

Ricky made his call to the Pentagon a little earlier this time and rehearsed what he was going to say. He knew that he would be deceiving in his inquiry but he had prayed about that and figured that if he felt any guilt he wouldn't make the call, but if he felt justified prior then it would be a sign from God to continue. Ricky called Taylor Holden at 1am Eastern standard time and found the young Captain as talkative as always.

"What's up Taylor? Ricky said in an upbeat voice.

"Camp counselor Rick, how are the arts and crafts going?"

"Actually, it's been starting to cool down up here so we've moved on to making cookies. Gotta put on a winter layer before it snows."

"Good for you," Taylor said. "Are you guys a little light staffed up there yet."

"That is exactly why I called Mister Holden," Ricky said as he began his mild deception. "That guy Kramer from the Tradition Foundation, is he planning on sending over some new recruits?"

"Wouldn't count on much Buddy. The Traditional Foundation is on its way out. They took responsibility for some of those bombings. I can tell you this only because you are calling me from your personal number and we've already shut down the lines of anybody we deem dangerous. You're going to be short handed from here on out."

"Are we going to finish the projects?" Ricky asked.

"Most of 'em, but they aren't going to be used for a rebuilding of America, they're going to be used as a place of progress for an advancement of a global community, you know, a place to wine and dine the world's diplomats."

Ricky paused for a moment after being shocked by the readiness of information he was receiving and not being sure where to take the conversation from there...

"It's really for the best" Holden continued. "We need to get with the program or be swept under the rug. America has a lot to offer but we are only going to have a place at the table for so long. After that we're done"

"So the private sector is finished then, is that it?" Ricky said, unable to hide his discontent.

"Pretty much. We gave them a rope and they hung themselves with it. The UN is running things now and we are talking treaties with the Islamic Europeans. It's really now or never with these guys Rick, we just can't sustain things anymore and with religious zealots like the TF standing in the way it'll never get done."

"What about this guy Kramer? Is he going off to never never land with the rest of these nut jobs?"

"I have no idea who he is, but he was probably sent there to expedite the process. If he claimed to be a zealot it was probably to set some minds at ease."

"So where are they taking all of these Christians anyway?" Ricky asked with concern.

"Zero idea," Holden quickly replied. "But I'm sure that they'll be fine. Just out of the way."

"Good," Ricky replied. "Well I guess we just make do with who we have then."

"I guess. At least there will be fewer cookie eaters. Look man, I gotta run and remember that we are always being listened to."

"Thanks Taylor. I'll see you when you guys realize you can't get by without me."

"So that would be never then?" Holden said followed by his goodbye as he hung up the phone.

Ricky's fears had become a reality as he knew for certain that the world was no longer in the hands of the once mighty United States. He knew that they were truly alone on a mountain top and it was only a matter of time before they would be fugitives in their native land. Rick walked over to the Mitchell's home and told them the news and they prayed for the persons who had left that day, not knowing their destination and certainly not their fate.

Chapter Twenty-Eight

A s the days became shorter and the work continued onward, it didn't take long for Craig to realize that he needed to reorganize the schedule. Fortunately most of the structures had roofing and the exteriors were close to completion, but he knew that the interior work would be a struggle to complete during the hard winter that lay ahead. John had a morning briefing with the General and he divulged the same information that Ricky had learned the night before, but said that he wasn't convinced that they had rid themselves of all the religious zealots and that he was going to be in high alert to root out the rest. As John was leaving the meeting he practically slammed into Sadahara as he was entering the Generals office at the same time. John had seen the Kid several times but was never properly introduced. As he left the building he couldn't help but wonder what the General had in store for the young Asian and what it meant for the rest of them.

Sadahara sat quietly across from the General as he began his usual rant. He informed Sadahara that it was a provision of the TF to make all communication from private areas of the compound off limits to any recording or listening devices. He also informed Sadahara that the military had never felt the need to bug the construction site or the school with the secure nature of the base. Currently however, with the rise in zealotry violence and with the traditional vermin out of the way things were about to change…

"I want to be able to hear every conversation that takes place within these fences. Will that be a problem for you?" The General asked.

"Not really," Sadahara replied. "Just gonna be a little suspicious.... unless....."

"Unless what?" The General said annoyed with the leading proposition.

"Unless we act as if we are upgrading the system and we need to enter all sites including the living quarters."

"Fine" The General said. "Do whatever is needed, just get it done."

"Do you want phone conversations or any conversations General," Sadahara said realizing the implications of bugging personal living spaces. "I mean...well.....it's just that if we bug them we'll hear everything."

"I'm not a pervert," The General practically yelled. "But we need it all and I need you to keep it between you and me. Can I count on you Taganawa?"

"Yes General, I'll get it done."

Sadahara was given clearance to all sorts of new privileges including a pointless card that enabled him to drink freely. That same night he downed seven shots of sake and his bragging nature quickly reemerged. He informed Akiko that they would need to be quiet during their lovemaking because somebody might be listening. He then bragged that only he knew how to shut off the listening devices and that maybe he would make an exception for Akiko on that rare occasion that he felt so inclined as to touch her. It took Akiko all of about fifteen minutes to inform the others of the new listening devices after Sadahara had finally passed out with a pride filled smile on his face. Craig, John and the others knew that they had little time to speak freely and decided it best to avoid openly speaking about the church or anything else unless they were clear of any structures starting immediately.

Chapter Twenty-Nine

As Summer became Fall and Fall turned into a bitterly cold, snow filled Winter, the remaining workers shuffled through the heavily beaten trails to warm structures where they worked day and night installing drywall, electrical fixtures and plumbing. Storefronts were decorated and restaurants were supplied with state of the art kitchens. The courthouse and clock tower was near completion as Craig's crew that was mostly left intact knew that there were other areas that would need extra help. The remaining personnel watched nightly as the State propaganda machines showed images of so called atrocities committed by religious zealots across the globe. Some were Islamic, but most were Christians. They bombed schools and hospitals; they burned buildings and murdered thousands in the dark of night. A proposed one world government was championed between any break in the programming where they showed people living in a peaceful way far removed from the shackles of the devastating religions that once enslaved them.

The sheer beauty of the village that they were constructing and the bi-weekly meetings at the mostly completed church were the only things that kept the group of believers going. Their numbers had grown to over fifty and they needed to arrive at different times and by different routes. Some had devised a way to enter the school in the back of the gymnasium and then one by one they would slip out the back and into the trees about a hundred feet away. From there they would follow the snow packed trail for three quarters of a mile to find the warm fireplace blazing inside the sanctuary and another outside in a large pit when the weather allowed. Others would gradually leave the building sites at the end of town and sneak into the back of an abandoned shoe store and then one by one they would walk out into the darkness, across the interstate and into the trees. They too would follow a snow packed trail for over a mile to the church. At the church they would sing songs of praise, read the word and discuss any relevant matters, of which there were many.

The General had many pawns and their numbers seemed to be growing as well. It became clear to everyone present that the General was suspicious of everyone who wasn't directly under his thumb. Sadahara had become his most loyal companion after Lieutenant Colonel Ramos had been surprisingly removed during the registration reduction. Apparently he had put up quite a fight and the General himself had a few lingering scars from the scuffle that took place that day in his office. Sadahara had quickly taken Ramos office and was basically estranged from his wife, coming home only on rare occasions to change his clothes and check on her in a demeaning manner. Mostly he slept, showered, and ate at his new home away from home that provided all those needs. The General and his new sidekick could be seen walking down the ice free sidewalks of the newly painted exteriors of the village pointing and laughing at what they would soon possess. They had constant security when they made their rounds and they talked down to everybody who engaged them. John had seen his briefings reduced to once a week and most of those scheduled meetings were canceled at the last minute as the General saw no need in meeting with a guy who would be rendered useless when the project was complete. Ricky, on the other hand, was never asked to meet with the General. He was considered even more useless than John in the eyes of the General other than it was he who was to reeducate the children about the new world order and their eventual role in it. Ricky, Maria, and Caroline were sickened by the new secular propaganda that they were required to teach the children. The material was riddled with hate speech mostly aimed at Christians and the kids were buying into it hook line and sinker.

As the Winter rolled on and the town was nearing a sense of completion the group of believers were becoming more and more alarmed at the situation at the school. They knew that they were being listened to and yet they hated the fact that they were turning good kids away from the truth. They needed to act before they would become responsible for adding more subordinates to the General's minions, all the while subtracting from God's Kingdom. In late March, as the calendar declared Spring, the church was filled with chatter and the talk began to heat up...

"Look," Jeff said as he tried to get control over the group. "We can't bring these kids up here one at a time and tell them that we've been lying to them. They're kids for crying out loud, they'll be singing like a bird the minute they get back."

"If we keep going on like we are they will be hard to reach," Maria said while fumbling with her jackets zipper. "Plus I can't speak for everyone, but I die a little inside every time I read that stuff to those kids. I don't think I can do it much longer. Today alone, I told a group of fourth graders that George Washington was an atheist and that Abraham Lincoln was gay"

"We don't have any choice Maria," Doctor Daly said. "Unless we want to hop on a bus to God only knows where."

"We put ourselves out there before and we're all still here," RJ said. "Why don't we just tell these kids the truth and let the Lord settle the score."

"He's right," Jason said as he stood up to punctuate the point. "We must know by now that God has our backs. I think that we should just say what we need to say and pray for protection."

The room exploded in a combined conversation that formed a humming gibberish until John stood up and yelled in his distinctly heavy bass tone...

"Settle down. This isn't going to solve the problem. For the time being we are still a democracy. I say that we spend the last forty minutes of this gathering praying in small groups. After that we can privately vote. Either we forget about who may or may not be listening in the classrooms and tell these kids the truth about God and their country or we protect our situation and go on as before. Jeff and I will read the votes and we'll reveal the findings on Thursday."

John seemed to command respect from just about everyone short of the General and the group nodded in agreement and about an hour later John, Jeff and Courtney were alone in the church counting the votes under candlelight...

"It appears if we are about to test our faith again," Jeff said as he threw his stack of votes into the fireplace.

"Same here," John said as he did the same.

"I do have one vote for the status quo," Courtney said. "And I think we all know who it is probably from."

"I know, I know, I need to talk with Dr. Daly about his faith," Jeff said. "You would think that by now he would have learned to trust God a little more. I realize that's a scary proposition, but it's time we get used to it. Things are starting to boil down to the end."

"The end of our time on the mountain?" John said. "Or the end of times all together."

"Listen John," Jeff said. "Courtney and I have been praying almost every night to better understand the meaning of your Pastor's dream and yours as well. I know that I've mentioned it before but I think that something amazing is going to take place within these walls and I think that time is coming soon."

"The bright light," John said. "Is that going to be the second coming?"

"I'm not sure John, but whatever it is we need to be ready."

Chapter Thirty

The next morning as Craig and Jason were sipping their coffee and watching the reruns of the previous nights televised lies, a loud and quick knock came at the door. Jason slowly walked over and opened it to find Ricky as white as a ghost. Ricky held a sign up that simply read *"We need to talk now"* and motioned Craig and Jason towards the door. The three men walked out to the snow covered parking lot together watching each other's breath turn to vapor and just as quickly disappear. Ricky rubbed his hands together to fight off the bitter morning cold and said that he sure could use some new shoes as he hopped into his jeep and sped down the icy hill towards town. Craig and Jason waited a few freezing minutes in "Old Blue" for RJ and then quickly followed...

"The calendar says that its Spring and I'm as cold today as I was on Christmas," RJ said as he warmed his fingers against the heat vent in the backseat.

"Jay," Craig said. "I'll head over to the shoe store and see what has Ricky all spooked but I need you guys to act normal. If that's at all possible" Craig shot RJ a glance when he made his final point.

"I'm always acting normal. My normal might not be the same as your normal, but I'm always being me," RJ replied. "What's up with Ricky?"

"I'm gonna find out," Craig said. "You guys help the electricians get those freezers in place at the new "Chateau ala Whatever" place down the street. I'll be back soon."

Jason and RJ hopped out of "Old Blue" and Craig drove down to the edge of town and started taking pictures from different angles until he was sure that nobody was watching him. He then walked around the backside of the shoe store and lightly rapped the sequenced knock and the door ripped open....

"Craig, Thank God," Ricky said as if it may have been somebody else. "They're planning on sending the kids packing."

"What? When?"

"As soon as they have their big celebration on the thirteenth of July. They plan on bringing in about five hundred people who will be permanent residents. The kids, and most of us will be leaving on the buses that bring 'em here."

"How do you know that, Ricky?"

"Last night, Caroline and I were walking around the base when we heard a heated exchange happening in the General's office. We crept up a little closer to the partially opened window and did some ease dropping. It didn't take us long to realize that it was the General yelling at somebody over the phone. He said that he didn't want to wait to get kids out of his hair. He said he wanted to exchange these idiot workers for sophisticated people as soon as possible. After a moment or two he said with disgust "Fine!! Immediately after the Christening celebration on the thirteenth, but if they're still here on the fourteenth I'll shoot 'em myself," and he slammed down the phone."

Ricky had just finished his sentence when the sound barrier was interrupted with a sonic boom that made the old wooden shoe shelves bend and wobble...

"What the hell was that?" Craig said as he reached to steady the shelves.

"Oh yeah," Ricky said as he rolled his eyes upward. "I forgot to tell you that they will be testing the new missile defense system all week. The General is planning a big military display in July for all the new residents."

"Good grief Ricky," Craig said in amazement. "That probably just scared my remaining workers half to death."

"I was supposed to tell you last night and you were supposed to tell them about forty-five minutes ago," Ricky said as he checked his watch. "My bad."

"Are they going to shoot those things down up here in the woods?"

"Not now," Ricky replied. "They're firing friendlies from over in Nevada, tracking 'em from here and shooting 'em down in the Eastern Oregon desert. On the thirteenth of July they plan on doing all three from right here."

"That'll be some cool fireworks," Craig said while avoiding the matter at hand. "Look Ricky, I need to tell the guys to be expecting more of those missiles flying by and as for the kids man, I don't know, we'll need to talk about it tomorrow. We'll know about the vote and maybe we'll figure something out."

"Craig," Ricky said while grabbing hold of the door disabling Craig from leaving. "If they try to take those kids away in some bus headed to God only knows where, they'll have to kill me first."

"Me too Buddy, me too."

Craig crept around the back of the old shoe store and took a few extra pictures just in case somebody might be watching him and then drove "Old Blue" back to the new French restaurant to check on the boys. When he made his way to the door he glanced over his shoulder and saw Jason talking to Wade Philson, a plumbing contractor from San Francisco who Craig had placed in charge of the other plumbing contractors because of his unique ability of connecting old systems to new. Wade worked mostly from midday to late in the evening so he could be present to coordinate different projects with the other plumbers.

Wade was waving his arms and showing distress as steam flew from his mouth in the brisk morning air. Craig walked around a few rusted trucks and interrupted the conversation........

"Problem, Wade?"

"Craig, good. I need to talk to you it's about my mother," Wade said appearing a little relieved that there was somebody who might be able to solve his dilemma.

Craig motioned to Jason that he should probably head inside and help the others with the massive freezers and that he would handle the situation.

"What's going on Wade?" Craig said while believing in his mind that it was a trivial matter and that it would pale in comparison to what was troubling him.

"I can't get a hold of her. That's what's wrong. I can't call anyone outside of the base and neither can anybody else for that matter."

"Since when?"

"Since about an hour ago. I went home and I tried to call my mom and the phone simply wouldn't ring. I thought that it was just a glitch in the system so I called down to the base and they said that phone calls were no longer allowed. My mom is old and she has a lot of health problems. Craig, if I can't call her or her friends at the church then I'm outta here."

"Who told you that?" Craig asked.

"The General's secretary herself. Said there will be a memo later today."

"I'll find out what's going on, Wade, and I'll come by your place around noon. Good enough?"

"I guess Craig, but I'm serious when I say that I'll be on my way if I can't talk to my mom."

Craig walked back to "Old Blue" and let out a huge sigh. He knew that the "powers that be" would eventually clamp down on their liberties and that while studying the word of God and listening to Jeff and others who had a far better understanding than him, he had come to realize that the clock was indeed ticking. Craig fired up the engine and bowed his head for a moment to pray for the strength that he would surely be needing.

Back at the construction trailer turmoil had already set in. Ryan was enraged that all of his orders were now to be made by the General and his staff and that he was no longer allowed to have direct contact with his suppliers. John was sitting at his desk with his head down, obviously irate as well that he could no longer witness to his loved ones back in South Carolina. Putting the finishing touches on the newly built town had for the first time in months taken a back seat and when Craig opened the door about twelve people instantly leapt towards him with questions and revelations...

"Wow, wow, wow, I heard you guys. And I don't know anything about it. Has anybody seen the new memo?" Craig said as he made his way to his desk.

"It's here," John said as he pointed to Craig's computer screen. "We all got e-mails"

Craig opened his inbox and read the memo that required him to read it to all the workers. Craig was taken aback by the insensitive nature of the words that he was reading and the audacity of the General himself...

"The United States government, along with its allies towards a united world, has deemed it necessary to eliminate all communications outside of a ten mile radius. Calls to emergency facilities and certain government entities will be allowed to those living in rural areas. The new restrictions are being levied to eliminate those wishing to destroy our unity by engaging in and promoting religious zealotry. It has been deemed that those who wish to cause harm and engage in unlawful activities are present in every group or community including our own. When the time comes when we have weeded out the few remaining obstacles of a freer and better society all our liberties will be restored."

Craig read the word a few times and then simply shrugged his shoulders and said...

"Well guys, get ready for a mass exodus."

"I don't think so Craig," Ryan said as he leaned against Craig's desk. "The General already informed John that anybody who wants to leave can start walking and he already has the roads blocked off. He says that the vehicles here belong to the Military and he is going to be taking a nightly inventory."

"Great," Craig said in disgust. "Were stranded here unless we want to try to scale a mountain or two find our way back to the ruckus party on the streets of debauchery."

"Pretty much," Ryan said. "There's something else Craig, and based upon your apparent love of the General I'm not so sure you're going to like it."

"What?" Craig said while slumping back in his seat.

"The big July celebration. The General wants to have a party for the new arrivals at his new house that he wants done in about a month."

Ryan laid the plans on Craig's desk and informed him that the General simply asked for plans that were in the Santa Barbara data base of homes that were built by Craig Mitchell Construction and it appears as if the General picked a home that might appear rather familiar.

"These are the plans for my house," Craig said as he sat up straight and stared at the plans with wide gazing eyes. "Where does he want me to build this thing?"

"On the ridge on the opposite side of town. He's got guys out there now plowing a road through the snow."

Craig sat there motionless as he gazed at the plans when John walked up to him and placed a hand on his shoulder and sarcastically said...

"Having a bad morning Son?. Let's take a walk."

Chapter Thirty-One

On June 1st 2017 a foundation was poured for the General's new home. Over seventy five men went to work a week later framing while others were being pressured to finish the interiors and store front signs in the new town. The workers had been shut off from the outside world and although some, including Wade, had taken their chances and had left the base, Craig and his crew defiantly scrambled to finish what they had started. God had once again answered their prayers and had protected them from persecution and the children were boldly being taught the true history of their country and about Jesus and his amazing love in the old gymnastics arena and were taken in groups to the church as well.

None of the Hat Creek believers had a clue as to the rapid decay happening in the towns and cities across the land. People were being arrested and executed at an alarming rate as the power of the State had grown into a global monster. Christians were at the brunt of most of this hatred as their churches were bull dozed or burned to the ground. State run universal churches were being constructed as fast as the others were destroyed and a new Christian underground had emerged that was in constant danger and losing members on a daily basis. The Group of isolated believers were left to only presume this was happening and it only added to their detestation of the work that they were performing for those who could never deserve it.

On a particular Thursday evening Jeff had taken notice of the hopeless attitudes on the faces of the now over seventy-five regular attendees.

He too was filled with many emotions, and although it was up to him to place God above their troubles he decided that it was time to address the situation. While Akiko and Maria read Old Testament stories to the handful of children outside by the open fire, Jeff rose to his feet and began...

"Brothers and Sisters I know that you are hurting. I'm hurting too. We can only imagine what is happening to other believers around the globe and I know that many of you have contemplated fleeing to help those in need. I can't make any decisions for you, but I want to help put your hearts at ease the best I can when I tell you that building this church has been a noble effort to bring others home. When we started out a year or so ago there were only a few, now we are many. I believe that our numbers will grow around the world and we will be as numerous as the grains of sand on a long beach. I don't know how, I simply believe it. I also believe that we are here for a reason and that God has a plan for each and every one of us"

Jason glanced up at the round void in the wall and felt the cool evening air brush against the un-covered portion of his neck and in an attempt to add a moment of humor he said...

"Do you think he has a plan for that stained glass window Jeff?"

"Well, like we said before Jay, the General didn't like the idea of any stained glass work at the village because it reminded him of a traditional church, so to answer your question, no."

"Why does it have to be a stained glass window?" Juan said while looking around for an agreeing nod.

"I can't answer that Juan," Jeff said. "But I believe that it will be and someday soon."

The group had finished reading from the word and was lounging around the fire when out of nowhere they heard somebody quietly say "Craig, Craig Mitchell" The group froze momentarily and looked into the heavy wooded direction to the North.

"I'm Craig, who's there?" Craig said with authority as he stood up.

Out of the woods came Jack Barrows with his family intact, including Rainy and about twenty others. The group of believers were immediately alarmed but were quickly put at ease when Craig said that he would vouch for the new arrivals. Jack walked over to Craig and shook his hand and then looked at the others and said...

"We have a lot to tell you guys and it's gonna take some time. Maybe we should go inside."

The group of nearly a hundred made their way into the small crowded church and Jack walked to the front and began to speak to listening ears...

"I expect that you all heard about our journey North. Well, by the time we arrived in Klamath things had dramatically changed. The place was on fire. People were scared and hiding out in abandoned warehouses and storefronts. The military was rounding up anyone they remotely expected of believing in Christ. Our friends and Family were nowhere to be found and their homes were either burned to the ground or were confiscated by soldiers. We hid out in the mountains outside of town and eventually met others who were trying to find their family members. We were resigned to stay and fight when we stumbled upon Amy here" Jack pointed towards a young teenage girl who was sitting in the back with her head down rocking repetitively while Emily Barrows rubbed her back. "She is autistic to the best of our understanding and she hasn't spoken a word since we heard her moaning in a nearby ravine while we were cooking up a deer. After about thirty minutes trying to calm her down she reached into her pocket and handed me this," Jack held up a piece of paper with a few lines of information and a couple of numbers. "We tried to make sense of this for about a week or two but other than the heading that reads 'My name is Amy' and a list of ingredients to build a stained glass window, we were clueless."

The seventy-five previous members let out a collective "Whoa," and that momentarily stopped Jack from proceeding but he eventually re-collected his wandering thought process once more and continued...

"Anyway, after looking at these numbers and trying to make sense of them we eventually realized that they were longitude and latitudes and amazingly they pointed us right back here," Jack took a deep breath and said. "And the final line in the note is written in Arabic and when we finally happened upon James here he deciphered it for us. James was the President of North West Bible college until they.....well, until burned his school to the ground. Pastor James, do you want to take it from here?"

James was an elderly white man with a partially bald head and a over grown beard. He was filthy and withdrawn as were all the other new arrivals. When he made his way to the front of the church and looked out at the people he hung his head for an instant and quietly said...

"You must excuse me, but I lost many a friend not long ago. You see... I was away for a week at my cabin when the fictitious attacks began to happen and when I returned I couldn't find a living soul that I once called a brother or a sister. I not only taught theology at the school I was also the senior pastor. My wife had passed several years ago and my only daughter had been taken home when she was only six. I saw so many dead bodies near the school that it almost took away my spirit to go on............Until......until I saw this note in the hands of a young student who was aspiring to spend her days doing missionary work abroad. She had been murdered execution style on the grass in front of the school along with many others. Inside their pockets I found the same note and although I cannot make any sense of the ingredients for the window I can tell you what the words in Arabic read.…

James pulled his reading glasses out of his pocket and blew hard on each lens and quickly wiped away the condensation…

"For those who are willed, meet me at a place of peace, for those who are not willed but are at peace, I will see you in eternity. The time is near, and the independence we once had we will celebrate no more in this age, or on this land."

The room went into confusion before Jeff stepped forward and halted the decibel level with a loud whistle…

"Listen up people," Jeff said when the roar had subsided. "We have two groups of people here with half the story and I think that it is time for somebody to bring it all together. Please give me a minute to fill in some blanks."

Jeff spent the next thirty minutes explaining the entire situation to the newcomers. He retold the dreams and spoke about the supernatural protection that God was providing. He talked about the window and the apparent ability that Amy might have to construct it if they could find the supplies needed. He spoke about the idea that had been rolling around in his head for months that there would be many more newcomers in the days ahead. He spoke about the needs that these people would have and that they would be in hiding here at the church. He then spoke about the shortcomings that he felt hindered him in Biblical prophecy and his personal prayers that someone would come along to better explain the happenings in the world. Then he softly looked at James and said that he felt his prayer had been answered today. When Jeff had finished talking he looked at his watch and noticed that they were pushing their luck being out of sight for so long and he asked Juan if he could stay long enough to show the newcomers where they could find water in a nearby stream and if he could sneak back late at night with some food and laundry supplies. Juan shook his head in agreement and the group dispersed after a few introductions and loving hugs.

Craig had scribbled down the supplies that were listed on the note when he came to a startling, yet awe inspiring revelation. He was copying something that was directly from God himself and at that moment he was permitting Craig to play a part in his will. He had learned from Jeff about the early Hebrews and how they carefully copied the scripture over and over again to insure the Word of God and it gave him a moment amazing wonder as he wrote the words a little more carefully. On the way down the trail Jason looked over his shoulder at Amy and said.........

"Do you really think that girl can build that thing Dad?"

"I don't know," Craig said. "But I know that somebody is. We just need to find all this stuff in a hurry."

Later, in the early morning hours, Dr. Daly returned to the church to examine the young autistic girl. He noticed that her impulse reactions were delayed and that she hummed a negative response to every technique the doctor used in the examination. When Doctor Daly used photo images to further his exam she turned away from each photo and began to moan. He asked Jack if he had any information regarding her behavior that might be useful and Jack simply replied that she would eat when they gave her food and she would follow them wherever they went. He told the Doctor that his wife and daughter would help her with hygiene matters and that they kept a careful eye on her but other than that they didn't have much to offer.

Doctor Daly then pulled a picture from his pocket that he had torn from an old home and garden magazine with a stained glass window prominently displayed in front and showed it to the young girl. Her eyes popped open wide and she began to writhe around in excitement.

She then grabbed the photo from the Doctors' hand and started to hum loudly as she starred deeply at the photo....

"I think this young gal might know a thing or two about stained glass windows," Doctor Daly said as he stood up and looked at the others who were still awake at that hour and the others' who were awakened by the loud moans of the girl.

"This stuff is really starting to freak me out Doc," Jack said as he and Rebecca tried in vain to calm Amy down.

Doctor Daly wanted to give the girl a tranquilizer but he knew that autism was not his area of expertise and that it would be best to consult with Dr. Wrigley before doing so. He told Jack that he would be back later that night with Jeff and they would examine everyone on site and have antibiotics at the ready in case there were any infections that needed treatment.

When Juan arrived back at the church with supplies in the mid morning he found that the entire group was fast asleep. Jack and a few others gave Juan a friendly smile as he crept in and quietly left some detergent, towels and blankets on a table near the back. A moment later Paulie came in with a bag of canned goods, some fruit and a couple of gallons of water that he plopped down hard after his tiresome journey. The boys gave a gentle and sheepish wave to the sleeping group and quietly left the church just a mere moment after they had arrived.

Late in the evening Doctors Daly and Wrigley returned to the church and began examining the newcomers. Several were noticeably ill with a virus that had caused there trek to be much longer than it should have been, but nobody appeared to be in a dire situation. Doctor Wrigley started each and every one of them on a seven day regimen of amoxicillin and instructed them to load up on multiple vitamins every day. Jack knew about boiling water before use and basically how to survive in any situation. It had been his survival skills that he had learned from his father and later during his Army Ranger days that had led the group to prevail against the harsh elements during their journey north and then back once more. Jack had also taken charge of the group and everyone looked to him when a problem arose....

With ample supplies provided, Jack shook the good doctors' hands and said that they would be fine hiding out here until they returned on Tuesday. Jeff said that they would love to figure out a way to get Amy down to the base hospital for a cat scan to determine her degree of autism, but Jack quickly disagreed with Jeff.....

"I believe that you have her best interest at heart Doc, but I think that the poor girl was sent here for a reason and I believe that the good Lord will provide her what she needs to fulfill that purpose. Besides, we don't have long for this dying world and she will be renewed soon enough. No sense in scaring the living daylights out of her."

Jeff looked down at the wooden floor and realized that his doctor days were indeed coming to an end and that he would no longer be needing to search for ways to heal others of their maladies. He was in fact, a bit embarrassed that he had forgotten that the world was ending and if they were wrong there would be plenty of time to help the young girl at another time. Jeff looked up and said quietly.....

"Sorry Jack, of course you're right."

Chapter Thirty-Two

Over the next couple of weeks Craig and his crew built the Generals house in record time. Akiko was hard at work trying to convince Sadahara that it would be a nice housewarming gift to present a stained glass window to The General for his front door. She knew that if he made the initial order from his laptop at home she could alter it and increase the order. Sadahara was deeply embedded with the General at this point and he had more clearance than anybody else at the base. The General trusted him and actually gave him the only other large office at the base headquarters. The two had become attached at the hip and Craig couldn't help but notice that when the General stopped by to check on the progress of the almost finished home that Sadahara was always in tow. The General asked for Sadahara's advice at every question that Craig presented before him and Sadahara was arrogant and demeaning to the workers in his response.

The General liked the idea that he was going to live in the exact designed home that Craig had built for himself and his family and he reminded Craig of that fact every day. The childish demeanor of the General and his skinny Asian subordinate had been gnawing at Craig's side during the entire project and it was reaching a boiling point. Craig new better than to let this obvious attempt to belittle him by making him construct his own personal design intended for his family for somebody else get to him, but he was still a human being and still entirely attached to his prior nature. Sadahara would take jabs at Craig and his design and tell the General that the home he had in the Napa valley was indeed a better design. As the granite counter tops were being installed and the painters were doing their final touch-ups the General and Sadahara made their daily visit to the site….

"How's it going today Mitchell?" The General said as he walked in through the un-finished garage. "What's left to be done?"

"Morning General," Craig said as he set his coffee cup down on the corner of his worksite desk. "Not too much, just need to get the landscape guys out here to do their stuff. We should be outta here by early next week."

"Good," the General said as he rubbed his hand over the new counter top. "So I can have my furniture delivered on Monday?"

"Bring it today General, the carpet is in and all we have left is a few fixtures and some minor touch-ups."

The General looked around the house and then back at Craig and sarcastically said…

"Does this place hold up par to your house Mitchell? You're not holding out on me are you son?"

"It's designed the same and built the same General, what more do you want? the Pacific Ocean?"

"How about a little respect?" Sadahara said as he glared at Craig in a failed attempt to intimidate.

"Listen Junior," Craig said as he stepped a bit closer to the skinny Asian. "I'm not in the military and neither are you. I build quality structures every time and I have had about enough of your childish remarks that you have been squawking at me and my guys during this project. So I'm going to say this once and it would do you good to listen, Shut the hell up!! Got it?"

"Watch your attitude Mitchell," the General shouted. "This man works directly for me and I won't have you threatening him under any circumstances."

"With all due respect General," Craig said as his voice began to rise bringing others into the kitchen. "I have over seventy-five men here who want to take this idiot outside and smack him around. We'll finish the project and I guarantee the quality of the finished product, but we don't need his input."

"You'll get it when I give it," Sadahara said feeling his power that the General seemed to be backing.

Craig walked straight over to Sadahara and moved to within an inch of his face and said…

"Walk out of the house right now."

Sadahara knew that he was out matched in strength and began to slightly tremble with fear but his pride pushed him onward in his verbal assault…

"I'm not going anywhere Mr. laborer, maybe it's time that you left."

Craig did his best to calm his agitated nerves. He thought about the ultimate judgment belonging to the Lord, but he couldn't muster up the strength to stand down. Instead he started counting with a stern warning of what would happen if he reached five.

"One, two, three…."

Sadahara looked over at the General who was speechless at the new found bravado that was being displayed by the builder…

"Four…,..'

Before Craig could reach the magic number Paulie walked by Craig's shoulder and simply grabbed Sadahara by the waist, flipped him over his shoulder and quickly carried him through the garage and plopped him in the front seat of the Generals jeep while Sadahara screamed and clanked his fists against the Hispanics back.

Paulie stared at Sadahara for a moment after depositing him securely in the vehicle and said in heavily accented voice....

"You hit like a little girl," then he chuckled, winked at Sadahara to further the insult and walked away.

By this time the entire group had made their way through the garage and while many were laughing, the General was steaming mad and his face was a bright red.

"You're done Mitchell," The General said as he made his way to the front of his jeep where Sadahara sat with tears welling up in his eyes. "You and your entire crew, you're all done." The General fired up his rig and let the tires spin hard as he blew dust and dirt at the onlookers as he angrily fled the scene.

Within a minute of the incident Craig was on the phone to Ricky at the school. He told Ricky what had happened and asked what to expect. Ricky was never one to sugar coat anything and he told Craig to stay put and that he would be there in five minutes or less. As Ricky hurried to his jeep he saw Katie tending to a scraped knee through the glass of the nursing station and he realized that they would most likely be coming for her as well. Ricky open the door in a flurry and told Akiko that Katie was coming with him and that he would explain later. Ricky and a flabbergasted Katie made quick work of the hallway and were soon heading down the hill as Rick did his best to inform Katie of what had happened.

Five minutes after Ricky and Katie had arrived at the General's new house on the other side of the small valley a military cargo van pulled to the front of the structure and two well armed military personnel hopped out. The older soldier who appeared to be about thirty-five walked up to the crowd of about twelve and said..........

"We have orders to escort Craig Mitchell and his family along with the four Ortiz brothers off the base permanently."

Ricky walked straight up to the soldier whom which he out ranked and said...

"What if I said that I wasn't going to let you do that?"

"Then we'd be forced to shoot you Sir," The lower ranking soldier said.

"Shoot me!!" Ricky said in unbelievable disbelief. "You have direct orders from the General to shoot people?"

"If anybody gets in our way, that is affirmative Sir."

"Where do you plan on taking us?" Jason said as he looked deeply into the soldiers eyes.

"Somewhere safe, that's all I can tell you."

As a standoff was about to ensue another cargo van pulled up alongside the first and two more soldiers made their way to the back and ordered the other three Ortiz brothers to move to the back of the other van.

"If you guys are going to remove my best friend from this base then you

215

can consider this my resignation. I go where they go," Ricky said in a resolute voice.

The elder soldier motioned to the other three that he would be back momentarily and he walked about fifty feet away and used his radio to contact the General. The General had little use for Lieutenant Colonel Weeks and was simply glad to be rid of him sooner rather than later. Before he signed out he reapplied his command one last time..........

"You know what needs to be done soldier, correct?"

"Affirmative sir," was the quick reply.

The soldier flipped the switch off on his radio and rejoined the group that was engaged in a threatening staring match.

"It's all set," The soldier with the radio said. "If you want to leave with them, hop in."

Ricky and the three Mitchells were extremely apprehensive about boarding a vehicle bound for God only know where, but along with Paulie they joined the other Ortiz brothers and were quickly shuffled off the base and seemed to be heading south to the best of their recollection. Ricky placed his finger over his lips to insure that they didn't say anything that would further their already dangerous plight and the group sat quietly and silently prayed during their bumpy ride to the interstate.

Back at the main construction trailer, John was about to delve into his pastrami on rye when his phone rang. He sat the sandwich down, sighed and said to himself...."As usual, perfect timing."

"Robbs here."

"Robbs, General Taylor here. Listen you need to find a new project manager to put the final touches on the village. I sent that no good Mitchell and his family packing today and I don't want this to slow down the process any. I've got a lot of people comi...."

"Whoa, whoa, wait a minute General. Did you say that you sent Mitchell and his family packing? Are they already gone?"

"All three of 'em and that kindergartner teacher Weeks too."

"What?" John said trying to digest what he was hearing. "Why? what happened?"

"Mitchell was threatening one of my men and I ordered him to stand down and he disobeyed my order. Then one of his Mexican guerillas attacked my man so I sent him packing too along with his three brothers. Those four were never properly vetted anyway.

"So there all gone just like that?" John said as his confusion was turning to rage.

"Yes, and I need you to assure me that it won't cause any problems with our scheduling."

"I'll see to it General," John said as he hung up the phone and then instantly flipped his desk over in a violent rage filled response. Broken coffee cups, pens and paper were quickly strewn all over the floor and Ryan and a few others stood there momentarily frozen by the anger displayed by the seemingly gentle giant...

"What's wrong John?" Ryan said in complete shock at what he had just seen.

John was about to tell Ryan what had him so upset when he suddenly thought better of it. He merely nodded a "not right now," and walked out the door to find RJ to muster up a plan that they would need to implement immediately.

Chapter Thirty-Three

As the military cargo van drove east on Highway 44 they came upon a check point where the road had been destroyed and a temporary bridge was installed to clear a small creek. After the soldiers made there brief comments to the check point personnel they continued south east for about another two miles and then quickly pulled into the woods about a quarter mile deep....

"Everybody out," The elder soldier said as he waved his gun at the occupants.

The group slowly unloaded and quickly realized that either they were going to shoot them or they would be waiting for a flight. Based upon where they were with no visible clearing the first thought was on everyone's mind. Craig held tight to his wife and son as Katie silently wept. Ricky made threatening glances at the two soldiers but he realized that he was no match for the assault rifles pointing directly at his head. The soldiers ordered the group to head deeper into the woods and as they began marching behind the group the younger soldier made a quick and suspicious owl tone and pointed to his radio. The elder soldier rolled his eyes upward in embarrassment and the two trotted back to the van and simultaneously threw their radios on the front seat and made their order again.....As they reached a small brook about a half mile in the soldiers lowered their guns and the older one said.....

"We're not going to shoot you people, you can relax."

Ricky walked straight up to the soldier, looked him straight in the eyes and said....

"Were you ordered to?"

The soldier sighed and said in a mono-toned voice....

"We were."

Emotion ran wild in the group as they were caught between two separate feelings; one of relief and another of disbelief. Katie was merely kneeling on the ground trembling in fear and while at the same time thanking the Lord for sparing her and her loved ones. Craig was filled to the brim with adrenaline and he wanted answers........

"What's going on guys? Are you just going to leave us here?"

"Listen" The elder soldier said. "Contrary to what the General believes, or what he wants to believe, the military is made up of mostly God fearing young men. Most of the turmoil happening around the country isn't being caused by Christian zealots, it's being cause by Christian soldiers fighting back against the global control. I'm a Christian, so is Jensen here and there are many others on base. We thought that we would have been removed by now but our God doesn't seem to think the time is right. Anyway, we hav...

"We're Christians too," Jason said. "Each and every one of us. In fact we even built a church in the woods outside the base."

"You're kiddin' me," The elder soldier said. "If that's true then I guess we'll know where to find you because I was just about to give you guys a compass, a rifle and some blankets for your journey. I gotta tell you guys, things are getting pretty fierce at the base. The General has that Asian kid tapping everything that is humanly possible, but luckily we have a guy who is one step in front of him. We just found out the other day that our radios are tapped on the exterior now. Even if the darn thing is off they can hear everything that happens within a fifty foot radius."

"So what direction do we take from here?" Craig said. "It's not gonna be easy to find the base without certain settings."

"Craigo," Ricky said, "You're talking like a builder. Trust me guys, give me the compass and we'll find it."

"Names Kevin Wilkes," The elder soldier said as he reach out his hand to shake Rick's. "And I can do better than that. If you guys are really quiet I can show the exact direction on the GPS in the van, but you need to remember if you guys get caught we're dead. But first I need to put on a show for the hidden microphones." With that, the soldier blasted his assault rifle for a solid thirty seconds and it made all the detainees shiver at what might have been.

After the soldiers and the group parted ways Ricky led a brisk march that would have the group back at the church by early morning the next day, and the group briskly trampled through heavy woods to a clearing where they were better able to find their bearings.

Back in the General's office Sadahara and the General sat in a moment of complete silence and shock. They had heard every word of the conversation that had taken place between the two soldiers and the group of exiled workers. The soldiers hadn't realized that Sadahara had placed small listening devices into the stitching of their uniforms while they were hanging in lockers to be cleaned and the newfound revelation had the General spitting mad.........

Hyperventilating and swearing like a drunk sailor the General screamed out a proclamation.."We're going to track them down like the cowardly dogs they are and put bullets between their eyes."

"Do you want me to send some men to find this church, General?" Sadahara asked.

"Yes, and I want it burned to the ground," The General yelled as he slammed his fists of rage hard against his desk.

"Consider it done sir," Sadahara said as he stood abruptly and started to leave.

When Sadahara reached the threshold of the General's office door he turned back towards the red faced man who was still breathing hard in anger and said…

"Or…………we can hide our cards until we lure out the rest of them."

"What are you talking about Taganawa?" The General said while showing his annoyance with a second thought that wasn't his own….…

"We heard Wilkes say that there were many others and God only knows how many people there are in Weeks and Mitchell's group. If we play all our cards now they will fall deeper into silence and it might be harder to seek 'em out. Why not take the people out with the church….…two birds with one stone?"

"I knew there was a reason that I trusted you Son," The General said with a smile. "But I want those two soldiers to take their last breath at the checkpoint. I know all too well that you can't get information out of zealots. We'll just tell their wives and friends that they tragically went off a cliff or something."

"I've been monitoring the checkpoint from time to time General, and I think that it's safe to say that those guys are not zealots. If you tell them that our two conspirators are planning to terrorize the base I'm sure that you can get them to shoot to kill."

"Fine, I'll do it now. That'll be all.

Chapter Thirty-Four

John had found RJ cleaning construction debris off the store front windows in the shiny new village and he pulled on top of the curb and shouted to his son to simply get in and buckle up, and in a flash the two were heading south in the direction that RJ who had no idea what was happening at the time saw the cargo van heading only minutes before. John knew that they would not be trying to make a trek over Lassen peak because the road wouldn't be passable until late August and that left only one option and that was to head east on highway 44 towards Susanville. John also knew that there was a checkpoint about two miles in because when he had first arrived on base the General had driven John around the area to show off his security measures with great pride.

As John drove like a wild man he told RJ about the incident and the two then went silent, each pondering the events that might soon unfold. John was stoic in his demeanor but his mind was reeling with "what ifs" What if they were already dead? What if he and RJ are heading into an ambush? How will he be able to explain his whereabouts? As they turned left onto highway 44 John realized that he had left in such a rush that he had left his radio back at the trailer and he was bitterly upset with himself when he thought to radio ahead to the van's driver and use his superiority to temporarily halt them. John also left his jacket on the chair's arm in his office and although he had no idea, it probably saved his life.

Less than a minute later they could see the checkpoint come into a view. It was a small cabin looking structure with a round lookout deck that surrounded a tiny second story room. Before they had even begun to foster a plan as to how they would make their way through the checkpoint they saw the cargo van coming from the other direction and John violently swerved the jeep between two mighty pines and rolled to a stop up a small embankment. John quickly shut off the engine while the jeep that sat resting at a 30 degree angle let out a fume of steam.

"Good Grief Pops," RJ said as he flopped back in his seat after practically being expelled from the vehicle. After he composed himself he found that he was trailing behind his old man through the pines to get in a little closer to the checkpoint without being noticed.....

"That's gotta be the van," John said. "Is that the van RJ?"

"Looks like it Pops, but there is about twenty of those things comin' and goin' all day. I can't say for sure."

John and RJ looked on from about fifty feet away while cleverly hiding behind several trees. As they watched they saw two soldiers emerge from the cargo van and approach the checkpoint personnel who were waving them towards a pit that they had dug at the side of the structure. The men had dug the pit in the early spring to hopefully capture wild animals to relieve their boredom. When the two un-suspecting soldier peered into the pit one of the checkpoint personnel crept up behind them and simply shot them in the back of the head with his military issued 9mm Beretta handgun and they quickly fell face first into the pit.

RJ jumped in shock and let out an abrupt though deep scream and his father put an arm around his neck and pulled him into a dirt-filled face plant, narrowly avoiding the trunk that they were hiding behind. John's eyes were popping as he motioned RJ to silence and by sheer luck the gunshot echo seemed to hide the boys momentary scream. John's mind raced and he hadn't even taken a breath when he decided what he needed to do. He told RJ to stay put as he stood up and gained his bearings. He then looked down at RJ once more and extended his arm with a flat hand in a repeat of his earlier command and then pumped it once to punctuate the point. John then made his way back towards the jeep and then walked back to the road and then started running towards the structure while shouting...........

"What's going on here, I heard gun shots?"

Three soldiers emerged instantly in front of the structure with guns pointing directly at John, but when they realized who he was they just as quickly stood down. John didn't recognize any of them but they had been in town way too many times to not know who he was. It is a soldiers duty to know the higher-ups and John being second in command combined with his rather large build made him rather easy to notice and certainly remember....

"Terrorists Sir," one of the soldiers said. "They were plotting to bomb the base and we had direct orders from the General to take 'em out."

"Where are they?" John said, although he already knew.

"Over here," the same soldier said as he motioned John towards the pit.

John looked down at the two bodies that were missing large portions of their heads and then he looked at the mixture of blood and brains scattered on the side of the building and he trembled with shock, horror and anger. After he took several deep breaths he looked at the much younger soldier with a glaring fire in his eyes and said........

"These are human beings Son....Get me a ladder"

John made his way to the bottom of the pit and reached for the neck tags of the older soldier. When he pulled the tags to the front of the blood soaked collar he saw two military tags and a cross. As he examined the cross; the soldiers who were keeping a watchful eye on the proceedings proclaimed, "He was a zealot, look at the cross." John, who's back was to the others grasped the cross and tags firmly in his hand and closed his eyes and prayed for the strength to remain calm. His every instinct was to rise and take out his anger on the three soldiers standing above him who seemed so far removed from common decency that they could hardly be described as human. He knew that he was in the end times and Jeff had said on more than one occasion that there would be an increase in the purely evil deeds that man might occupy, but that wasn't easing his tension. After about a minute of remaining still and offering his prayer he opened his eyes and again started to examine what he held in his hand. The tags were typical military issue and after reading the name and serial numbers he looked closely at the cross. It was a bright silver with a small diamond at the top and two others at either end of the horizontal. When John flipped it over he read the words that answered his prayer. It simply read....

"I live for Jesus, I die for Jesus. If you are reading this I am with Jesus"

Somehow the words gave John the comfort and the strength he needed. When he rose and made his way up the ladder he actually and genuinely felt more sorrow for the three men staring directly at him then the two in the pit. John took a couple of deep breaths and looked at the men who appeared to be without life in their eyes and said in a deep voice.........

"I was out for a drive today because I was feeling a little stir crazy. I have my son with me, but when we heard the shots we locked it up and flew off the road. My Son is hiding in the woods.........

"RJ come on out," John yelled and the four men could hear RJ trampling his way closer.

"Anyway," John continued. "I might need a little help getting my jeep back on the road."

Chapter Thirty-Five

Katie was glad that she had worn tennis shoes to work that day as she would have been miserable if she had worn anything with a heel and she marveled at the small details that God somehow took care of. The group had made their way through several clusters of trees, up and down a few moderate hills and across a couple of chilly streams. It was late in the evening when they stopped to rest near an abandoned cabin deep in the wooded area about three miles south of the base....

"Anybody in the mood to check out the interior?" Jason said as he pointed to the run down wooden shack...

"Go ahead honey," Katie said. "I have a feeling that there might be one too many spiders in there for me."

"I'll go with you," Juan said, and the other Ortiz brothers followed suit as Craig and Ricky sat down next to Katie to rest their weary feet.

Jason and the Ortiz brothers walked with caution onto the small five by five front porch that led to a door that was slightly ajar....

"Anybody home?" Jason said in a mocking tone as he pushed the door open as it let out a long overdue creaking noise. The night was closing in and coupled with the heavy woods, the interior of the cabin was barely visible to the five men. When they realized that the place was mostly gutted other than a table and a cot they decided to leave as quickly as they had walked in. Jason being the first in was the last in line to exit when he noticed something shining in the corner of the otherwise darkened corner of the room.....

"Wait a second guys. What is that?" Jason said as he pointed to the small shiny object in the corner.

Paulie was the only Ortiz brother that actually heard Jason and he looked carefully at the shiny object and started to make his way over to it with Jason close behind. Paulie squinted his eyes and slowly reached for the object when he noticed that some type of cloth was covering it. When he pulled the covering away he could see that it was a bright green LED light attached to rectangular box that had wires running down to a larger box below. Before the boys could react to the menacing looking device it exploded with a mighty crash that blew a gaping hole in the side of the shack and slammed Paulie instantly into Jason and sent both of them flying across the room into a pile of stacked fire wood. The three other Ortiz brothers who were knocked off the small porch by the blast were instantly joined by Craig and Rick as they made their way into the smoke filled cabin. The men covered their mouths and made their way across the floor only to find Paulie and Jason lying in a puddle of blood on the opposite side of the room. The men quickly pulled the two from the structure to an area where a slight clearing would add some light to the situation. As they laid Jason and Paulie down on the frost covered ground and their eyes adjusted to the light they were sickened at the sight of Paulies disfigured body. His arm was completely missing from the elbow down and his mid section had been torn completely open. Paulie was dead and his brothers dropped to their knees and wept uncontrollably. Jason had been protected from the blast for most part by Paulies body but he laid there unconscious with burns across his face and he had several lacerations from his tumble.

Craig knelt next to his son as Ricky who was trained for situations such as these checked Jason's vital signs and then examined him for broken bones. Katie was hysterical as she looked on wishing she could do something to help, but she had no idea what to do…..

"He's just unconscious Katie," Ricky said. "He's gonna be okay," Ricky said, while not completely convinced of his own words.

About an hour later the group had made a fire and were engaged in deep prayer. The Ortiz brothers had not yet left their state of shock and after a few more hours passed Craig and Rick went to work digging a grave by hand while Katie attended to her son who was awake but could only mutter words of confusion. Shortly after the blast Rick had used what little water they had remaining to clean Jason's wounds and they used torn off pieces of their blankets to wrap them. With a soft glow of a distant fire on his face Craig said to Ricky…

"What the hell was that Rick? Who would set explosives in a cabin out in the middle of nowhere?"

"I have an idea," Rick said. "But it's a little farfetched."

Craig turned his hands upward to suggest that Rick share his thoughts…..

"Well," Rick continued. "We can't be too far from the base, so as I see it, either these explosives were set as a booby trap for anyone who might be making their way towards the base or it set primarily for us."

"What do you mean for us?" Craig said with a confused look on his face.

"That blast was not an amateur set. An amateur would have had it explode at entry. Nah, they wanted everybody inside before it blew, a pro set that up, a military pro. I don't think that the General is too concerned about a few nomads trying to make their way onto the base. I think he knew we would be making our way through here and he might be watching us right now."

"Are you serious? Why wouldn't he just fly in here and shoot us down?" Craig said as his eyes scoped the surrounding area.

"I don't know Craig, maybe they set the trigger and are planning on checking it tomorrow or maybe later tonight, either way we need to get out of sight soon."

The two men began digging at a hurried pace and soon the final prayers were said for their fallen brother and with the strength of four men they carried Jason deep into the woods to rest for the night.

Chapter Thirty-Six

Later that same night John and RJ along with the Wrigleys made their way to the church, only to find Caroline crying and being consoled by Jack near a stump outside the front steps. Rick and Caroline had planned on announcing their engagement during the next gathering, and hoped to be married that same night. Caroline had heard about Rick and the others from Maria, who was forced to make the announcement at the school. Akiko had left the grounds immediately, hoping to gain some details from her husband, whom she still loved, but hardly trusted. Since her departure at around two in the afternoon, nobody knew her whereabouts.

Near a small clearing Amy was hard at work. Craig had ordered a small amount of crushed glass and lead to be used on the Generals front door. He told Sadahara that it would be a nice gesture when Sadahara had brought the idea to him. Fortunately for Craig, Sadahara had no idea about the amounts needed and when the materials arrived, Jason and RJ had simply helped themselves to the larger portions. Maria had done the groundwork of how to assemble a window of that size and when Jason had finished the framework the autistic girl came to life and was building the window during every waking minute and it was beginning to take shape. The others were forced to gather up wind from the smoke that poured out of the large iron pots that were melting the colorful glass, but nobody seemed to mind.

When Caroline saw Courtney she rose to meet her embrace and the older Sister hugged her tight and told her the reasons to not give up hope. The news seemed to calm Caroline, but her anger over the death of brothers that she never knew brought a new anguish to her still reeling mind. As John and Jeff watched Amy pouring smoldering glass into lead molds with oversized welding gloves, that covered her arms about six inches above her elbows, worry started to set in...

"Did you talk with the General at all after you returned today, John?" Jeff asked.

"Nope," John replied, "But he sure wanted to talk to me. Guess he heard that I was at the checkpoint and wanted to interrogate me."

"How'd you get out of that one?" Jeff said looking a little perplexed.

"Told him I had a headache, and that I'd see him in the morning. He started blathering and I hung up. He called a couple more times and then sent one of his minions to my door, but I yelled that I wasn't feeling good... Eventually they left."

"Do you think there is any way they followed us here?" Jeff said in a frightened tone.

"Yep, I do. I really think that anything is possible at this point, but what are we supposed to do. I'm here, you're here and I guess we'll keep coming here until they gun us down."

"Let me ask you this John. Do you think the others are making their way back here to the church?"

"I think so Jeff, but if they're not here by morning I'm gonna start looking for them."

"After you meet with the General?" Jeff asked.

"Before" John said. "I'm gonna try to get a couple of hours of shut-eye here and at about 4:00am, if they're not here, I'm heading south through those woods."

"Is that going to give you enough time John?" Jeff asked while looking at his watch.

"I told RJ to call the Generals office at about 7:00am and tell him that I have the flu and that when I feel better I'd call....That'll need to do for now."

When the Wrigleys along with Caroline and RJ had left the church John and Jack shared some war stories and then they each found a spot in the chilly church to hopefully sleep while others wandered about.

At 4:00am John's watch started to chirp and Jack sat down on a pew next to where John was rubbing his eyes with a cup of coffee in his hand...

"I'm going with you John," Jack said as he handed John the coffee. "I've been through these woods a couple of times now and I have a decent bearing."

"I won't argue with that, besides I could use the company."

"Well, we better get going then," Jack said. "There's a lot of creepy, crawling things that are still sleeping, best to get a head start on them."

"Great," John said as he sat up and tried to gain his bearings.

The two men left about twenty minutes after four and quickly made their way over a few small streams and a couple of hills that left John gasping for air. About three miles into their journey they saw a group of people sleeping near a half lit fire and they quickly realized that it was the people they were looking for..."Didn't think it would be this easy," Jack said as he watched John run down a slight decline while he trailed close behind. Their sudden arrival caused Rick to spring to his feet in a battle ready stance as the others slowly flapped their heads in every direction trying to brush off the morning slumber....

"John," Ricky said in a loud un-expecting voice. "How did you find us? How did you know to even look for us?'

"That's a sad story son, but I'm glad you are alright."

"Not all of us," Katie said as she rubbed her son's head.

"What happened to him?" Jack said as they stepped forward to have a closer look.

Jason was now conscience but he said that he could barely hear and that his head was reeling with pain. Craig had him stand and try to see if he could support his own weight. Jason seemed fine, other than his hearing and his headache and the group revealed the previous days stories to one another. Jack and John were sickened when they heard about Paulie, and John hesitated to tell them about the two brave Christian soldiers who had given their life so that he might be able to find them. When the group made their way back to the church at about 8:00am they were happy to see Jeff awaiting their arrival who quickly went to work attending to Jason. James who had taken on the role of the church Pastor was consoling the Ortiz brothers within minutes of their arrival and the four men were in deep prayer. Rick, Craig, John and Jack added some wood to the outdoor fire pit and began the most serious conversation that any of them had ever engaged in....

"This is getting way out of control John," Craig said. "Those two soldiers told us that the battles taking place outside the base are being waged mostly in defense by Christian soldiers fighting back against the State. Americans are killing Americans."

"It's a civil war," Jack added.

"A holy civil war," Rick said as he slammed a final log on to the fire. "Only this time, there are no boundaries."

"And no honor," John said as he slightly turned to address the others in a more steadfast and stoic manner. "It looks like RJ and I are going to be the outside ears for now, so you guys are going to have to hang tight. I don't know what all the General knows, but if he knows about this place he must be waiting to do something bad. For the life of me I can't see why he would wait."

"He's using the church as a lure," Akiko whispered as she suddenly appeared at the edge of the fire and motioned the men to follow her inside.

"Akiko," John said once they were safely inside. "Where have you been? We've been worried sick about you since last night."

"I've been with my husband, trying to talk some sense into him. He doesn't know that I am a part of this group, but he knows about the church and they're planning on a raid."

"When?" Craig said as he looked around at the others.

"I have no idea, but I plan on finding out. Last night when I went home I found Sadahara drunk. I guess his run in with you guys had him feeling a little shaken. Anyway, he started bragging about getting the last laugh so I started catering to his ego. It wasn't long before he started telling me about what he had been up to. You guys wouldn't believe what he knows."

Akiko went on to explain that the General has recently found out about the church and he knows about most of the people who make their way here for worship.

"He has had people watching the pathways since early yesterday afternoon so anybody who has been back and forth since then, he knows about."

"That pretty much means all of us," John said.

"And now me," Akiko added.

"Why did you come here this morning Akiko?" Ricky said with a withdrawn voice. "You could have stayed in safety."

"I don't care anymore, and besides I had to inform you guys. The way I see it, I have about two hours this morning to get whatever information I can from Sadahara before he finds out that I'm part of his problem and that is what I intend to do."

"Let me see if I have this straight" Craig said. "He knows where we are, he knows what we're doing and he's just going to wait until the right time to slaughter us."

"He doesn't know that we know," Jack said. "So we need to play that angle."

"For a couple of hours he won't know that we know," John said. "As soon as Sadahara finds out about Akiko then the gig is up."

"What now?" Craig said in frustration.

"We get everybody here now, and I mean this morning, and we wait," John said. "If he knows what, where and when, then we might as well not hide it anymore. I'll have Jeff get whatever supplies he can get and RJ and I will do the same. We'll round up the others and make a stand for however long it takes, but first I need to have a talk with the General."

"Isn't that a dangerous proposition," Jack said, "The man is a hard nut to crack, what do you hope to find out?"

"I played the power game for a long time too, son," John said with raised eyebrow, "I have a few reverse psychology tricks up my sleeve. Plus I'll be packing heat," John said as he winked and moved towards the lower, endearingly labeled "Shoe trail." "I am not about to be detained with Jesus on his way," were John's parting words as he and RJ disappeared through the mighty pines.

Chapter Thirty-Seven

ulia Weston had seen the van fly by her as she was on a trail south of the base. She also took notice of a particular occupant that she had been secretly watching for well over six months. She had seen Jason that first day when she met RJ and was drowning in her own shyness ever since. Julia was an avid hiker and it was last fall when she found this particular trail and was all too quick to avoid the boundary signs and the not quite as advertised electrical fence. Julia had seen the highway from the trails elevated points, but always hid herself well when she heard any vehicle bearing down from a distance. As she knelt down in the overgrown narrow trail she saw the van barrel by and she was sure that she saw Jason with a solemn look on his face peering out the back window.

Julia did not need to channel Sherlock Holmes to realize what was happening. Personnel did not go for rides in vans unless they were not coming back and that particular van seemed full to its limit. Julia was about to turn back towards the base, imagining their destination would be a far greater distance than she could walk, when the van abruptly pulled off the road into a small clearing. She was well over three hundred yards away, peering through a fully blossomed maple and was instantly horrified when she saw two uniformed men with assault rifles quickly lead Jason and about six others towards the woods. She sat there breathless as the soldiers suddenly returned to the van to toss their radios on the seat, apparently not taking any chances of someone hearing there brutality. The men returned at the rear of the group and whisked the terrified people out of site at gunpoint.

Julia had not been that scared in her entire life. She had been an only child, turned orphan early in her teens when her parents were lost in a small aircraft accident over Mojave desert while venturing towards Death Valley for artistic inspiration. Julia became a ward of the State for her remaining four years of childhood living in one foster home after another. She became withdrawn and introverted in her new existence but she found an outlet in her art and never ventured far from it. Now lying still amongst the pine needles that formed a thin blanket on top of the hardly visible trail, she felt as if she was a foreigner in the beauty that had always inspired her. Moments turned into minutes when suddenly she was brought back to a horrific reality with a flurry of gunfire that lasted for much longer than she would care to imagine.

Julia let out a slight scream that she quickly muzzled and than simply started to run. She ran so fast that before long she had lost track of the barely noticeable trail and was suddenly lost deep in the woods. She knew that there was a road to the South and another to the East, but the midday sun was not helping her situation as she simply picked a direction and moved forward. Within minutes she heard another van in the distance. She crept low and listened for its direction and then slowly moved that way until she came to a high ridge overlooking a wooden lookout station. The station was placed directly in the middle of a highway with a small single lane bridge crossing a creek over a blown out part of the road. As she knelt there quietly wondering who to trust she saw the van approach and she watched silently as several men came out to greet the occupants. Julia felt a cold trembling shiver over take her body as she saw the same two men who she had, mere moments before seen, march others to their death and she thought to shout out a warning when she realized that these people were probably on the same team. Seconds later she saw the two murderers walk with a curious look to the side of the building and out of Julia's vantage point. She did however, see one of the station guards pull out a hand gun from behind his waist and fire two shots in that same direction of the unsuspecting men and then she heard the horrific thumping of what must have been two bodies landing lifeless into a hole.

Julia was now terrified, silently weeping and completely frozen as she saw Colonel Robbs arrive at the scene. She knew that she had seen too much and she knew that it went much deeper than a few wayward soldiers. She needed to find a safe haven and the base was not going to be it. She laid there for over an hour listening to conversations that she could not make out clearly and then in a state of shock she started heading Northeast, by the best of her sun gauging ability.

Chapter Thirty-Eight

Every church member knew that this was going to be the last day and the last chance to be at the base and gather whatever information they could and to stock up on supplies. John and RJ would go directly to the General and pretend as if he didn't know about the church and see what secrets and urgency he might show in his bravado attitude. Meanwhile, as others scrambled for supplies, Akiko would awaken her husband and pry, pry, pry before heading for shelter from the coming storm.

The General was fuming mad. After several attempts to speak to Sadahara by phone he had sent two men to pound on his door and they found him barely audible and holding his head when he finally did open it up. Sadahara told the men that he must have eaten some bad chicken and that he had spent the night throwing up. He said that he would need about an hour to clean-up and that he would be at the General disposal the rest of the day. The men radioed the General who rolled his eyes in disbelief at the same moment his buzzer rang on his desk..."General Robbs and his Son to see you sir. Should I send them in?"

"Yes, and bring us some coffee too, would you Christine?" the General squawked in his husky situational deep voice. John motioned his son to wait outside with a low wave of his hand, and opened the door.

"Robbs, where have you been?, I have been trying to reach you since yesterday. I heard you saw a little justice at our lower check point. Hope that didn't turn your colors too much Colonel."

"Seemed a little severe General, and with all due respec..."

"Severe," the General shouted while flailing his arms and knocking two full coffee cups off a carefully carried tray that went smashing to the floor. "What do you mean severe? Those men were planning on bombing our facility here Robbs," the General said while his nervous secretary busied herself wiping droplets of hot coffee from her bosses forearm. "You should know better than anyone that we can't tolerate that sort of treason in times like this."

"What times are these General?" John asked while remaining completely stoic and appearing oblivious to the crash of coffee and cups that narrowly missed his leg. "Are we now living in a time where all decisions about the mortal destiny of others are determined by one man? Are we currently suspending all due process and simply executing personnel that we deem a threat?. Who's making all the rules General,? You!!"

"I don't make the rules, Robbs," the General yelled, clearly agitated, "I follow them."

"So you were ordered to take justice into your own hands yesterday? Just exactly how many days before that were you given authority to administer your brand of justice?" John said while staring directly into his superior's eyes.

"I know about you Robbs," the General screamed as he pounded his desk. "I know about you and all your treasonous friends too. I know about the Church that I plan on blasting back through the woods. Whether or not there are zealots inside is going to up to you. I'll give you and your friends until dusk tomorrow to surrender. After that.... the blood will be on your hands Robbs."

"General," John said in a quiet voice. "I forgive you and I will join others to pray for you, but you do not have cannons big enough to destroy the church that I belong to. In fact, only God will let you try, if it is in his will."

"Nonsense," the General shouted again even louder than before. "You have until dusk tomorrow Robbs, dusk tomorrow you hear me?" he continued as John quietly left the office.

RJ had been wondering if his Pops was going to need his Glock to make a break for the church and he was happy to see that it wasn't the case. RJ hated guns and he knew that with the eyesight of his Old Man in their weakened condition, he might end up a friendly fire victim. John told RJ to hop in the jeep as they were going to make one more round through the town before they abandoned the jeep for the last time at the old shoe store.

Chapter Thirty-Nine

Akiko arrived home before Sadie had checked his inbox that would most assuredly contain news about his wife's participation. He was showering and she offered a pleasant hello and said that she was home for a quick bite and that she would see him when he got out. Sadie grunted something under his hung over breath and started his final rinse of his shampooed head. Akiko quickly scrambled together some bread and lunch meat to cover her story and made one for her husband too. When he appeared half dressed drying his hair with a bleach white terry cloth towel she started her stealth interrogation.

"So where is that church you were telling me about last night Sadie?" Akiko said while smiling wide.

"It doesn't matter it will be gone soon enough along with all the loonies," he replied.

"What will you guys do with all of them?"

"Deport them to Cuba, I guess," he said with a sly grin, approving of his own humor.

"Will they hurt these people Sadie? I would hate to hear that they were in danger because a few of my friends at the school might be part of the group."

"There are people from all over the compound heading up there in the dead of night. You should see all the footage from yesterday alone," Sadie said with disgust. "I can't imagine who has been taped since then.".

"What happens now?" Akiko asked, finding it harder and harder to hide her ill feelings towards the man she somehow still loved, though loathed in many ways.

"The General and I are going to wait until we get them cornered and then we are going to blast them to hell....nah, we'll give them a chance to surrender first...I guess...but then, Bam! right in the kisser," he proclaimed while pumping his skinny arms in a humorous show of machismo.

"Why would they need to surrender? What did they do besides worship God?" She replied lowering her head and raising suspicion.

"They stole, they cheated and snuck around, and worst of all they have been planning to attack our base, the crazy zealots," Sadie said as his voice raised to a new level.

"No they're not," she replied quietly. "Either you are a liar or you are being lied to," she said while rising to her feet. "The reports from all over the country are lies too. We have an inside man who has been unwittingly giving us all the details we need."

What do you mean "We have?" he said as he pulled his freshly washed USC T-shirt over his dampened head." And how are you suddenly speaking such good English?"

"I am one of those hated zealots and I helped build that church Sadie. I have been reading the Bible every day and night whenever I have time and maybe that has helped with my English. To tell you the truth I hadn't even noticed. It's amazing how you have noticed all of a sudden after ignoring everything about me for so long. I could have been on fire during the last year or so and you would have thought the neighbors were having a BBQ."

Akiko sighed and paused. She somehow felt the deep sorrow for her husband who appeared so weak and petty before her eyes. She did not want to argue with him, she wanted to help save him. She closed her eyes and quietly prayed for God to loosen his heart and let him see the truth. A long moment passed and then she said with genuine love and in a completely different tone.

"I want you to come with me Sadie, there is still time for you, we can help you." Again she paused and looked down at the floor and then continued, "I still love you Sadie, doesn't that mean anything to you? Please come with me, please! we can help you!"

"Help me! help me!" he said as moved within inches of his beloved betrayer. "They're the ones who are going to need help. They are the ones that are going either surrender or be blown into ashes."

Sadie began to breathe hard as he walked around the room turning on occasion and giving his wife death stares. "As for you Akiko, you are not going anywhere. You will be by my side until this whole thing is over and then I'll decide your fate myself."

"I already made that decision Sadie, and it was the right one, can't you see that?" She paused and waited for a response that never came, and so she slowly turned and headed towards the door.

Sadie sprung after her, grabbed her at the elbows and pressed her arms hard into her waist. As she struggled against him he overpowered her and spun her around until she was facing the kitchen table. In a moment of passionate rage he abruptly gave her one violent shove that sent her flying over the table and with a loud crash into the glass doors of the modern china cabinet, followed by a limp flop to the floor. Sadie's eyes were bulging as he saw what he had done. He never knew that he had that kind of anger inside him. He froze, standing silent, trembling with adrenaline pumping through his veins making his breath hard to catch. Sadie felt a million emotions flood his brain; sorrow, sadness, loss, self anger and loathing followed by a preserving sense of justification that somehow his wife had brought this all on herself. His stillness was interrupted as he saw the entire upper portion of the cabinet begin to tip down towards his lifeless wife. In a flash, Sadahara performed a jumping slide over the table and leaned his shoulder into the upper portion of the cabinet all the while being careful to not trample his wife below. Sadie's Shoulder was torn open by the jagged glass protruding from one of the broken doors and blood trickled down his arm as he steadied the heavy decorative piece. Still in shock, he backed away from the scene of his violent act and stared at his wife from across the room as she lay there motionless.

Moments later Akiko came back to life. She had been rendered unconscious by the blow to her head on the side of the table following her crash into the glass doors. She stood up and stared at her husband who was dripping blood on the rather new carpet and he simply stared back at her. After a grimacing first breath she knew that she had more pressing injuries than the knock she took to the head. She pulled up her shirt and saw a deep gash that had ripped through her rib cage and was quickly soaking her shirt and jeans.

"Wrap that towel of yours around that arm Sadie or you'll bleed to death," she said in a stern voice. "Better go get stitches too."

Sadie had no words for his wife. He watched as she took a sheet off their bed and folded it into a long narrow wrap and then tied it tight around her waist.

"I'm leaving now Sadie," she said. "Please don't try to stop me again, it might not be so one sided this time." Akiko lifted his signed Ichiro baseball bat that his father had bought him several years before and showed it to her still frozen husband. Akiko opened the door and ran down the hall, dropping the bat at the exit and painfully began heading towards the church, completely bypassing the school that would force her to form a new trail through heavy brush and fallen pines.

Chapter Forty

John and his son walked down the newly paved road and truly marveled at the beauty of the new town. The store fronts were shiny and clean and the sun was casting a short and stocky midday shadow of the clock tower in the center of the roundabout. John looked at the plaque, then back at his son's smiling face and realized that this is what Albert must have seen. John placed a warm hand on his son's shoulder and said, "I'm tired RJ, let's go home." As the two men drove the jeep towards the shoe store John had a revelation. "No reason to hide anymore RJ," he said as he turned the jeep around sharply and with a loud screech of the tires headed for the far end of the field at the back of the school to save his poor feet some anguish.

Akiko was light headed before she had reached the edge of the wooded outline of the base. Her pain slowed her but her heightened adrenaline and pure anger drove her on through the heavy and dense woods. She knew that within minutes she would be within earshot of her brothers and sisters if she simply continued in the right direction and she was quite sure that she was. Her blood had now soaked through her makeshift bandage and was clearly visible straight down to her foot. She realized through her years of medical training that she was running out of time, and worry followed by panic made her pulse rise and her eyesight blur. As she slowly crept under a fallen pine she saw a slender figure to her side, frozen and trying to hide. Akiko locked eyes on Julia Weston, took a deep breath and passed out half way out from under the giant log.

Julia had been hiding between the base and the church overnight. She wasn't sure where to go and wasn't sure who to trust. What she had seen the day before had left her in a state of disbelief, shock, anger and deep worry. She had seen the news reports about the Christian lunatics and how they seemed to be murdering non-believers and she was certain that she didn't trust the military. When she saw John Robbs at the church the night before she stopped dead in her tracks. Surely this man had something to do with the murders she had witnessed or he wouldn't be alive himself. All she was sure of is that she was alone, scared and looking for some kind of answer that would send her in the right direction. Now as she knelt down to attend to a young lady who was obviously bleeding to death she had a choice to make; Help the girl and expose herself or let her die and take her chances alone. It was a choice she knew she needed to make now, and that prospect didn't help much in her anxious state. She stood still looking upward towards the darkening sky as many thoughts raced through her mind. She thought for a moment to pray and it was that particular thought that would need to be her sign. She looked once more at the bleeding girl and then ran towards the gathering of believers yelling for help.

Dr. Daily stitched Akiko's wounds and ran an IV that Dr. Wrigley had brought to the site not more than an hour before and he and several others stood over her and simply prayed. She had lost a lot of blood and there really was not much more they could do. Her vitals were low and she had not yet regained consciousness. The group had no idea what had happened to her, but they were sure of one thing, glass was involved. Dr. Daily had pulled out several small pieces that were actually lodged into her ribcage and while cleaning the wound he also noticed four cracked ribs.

"The poor girl was in some kind of struggle, Jack," Dr. Daily said, "Look at the bruising on her arms starting to form, plus she has a nasty knot on her head."

"Is she going to be okay?" another replied.

"That is a question for God, I'm afraid. I have done what I can."

Ironically it was the third of July and the General had unwittingly given the group a Fourth of July deadline to give up their independence. As the believers hustled children from the school in small groups, others arrived carrying whatever supplies they could muster as the day began to turn dark. What was once a brilliant sunny afternoon was suddenly darkened with heavy gray clouds that were joined by a stiff chilling breeze. Still the work continued and by the late afternoon the final framing around the stained glass window was complete and it was secured into its final resting place at the front of a now darkened wooden church

Outside by the open fire Julia was warming her hands. She was welcomed warmly and felt safe and as if she made the right decision for now but was still on high alert. Julia had always kept religious people at an arm's length, believing that they were more of a hindrance to peace rather than protectors. She had been schooled in the secular world and was deeply entrenched in the multi-cultural tolerance mindset that had always made sense. Now the very conveyors of the message were gunning people down and showing zero tolerance while doing so. Julia had seen her world turned upside down in a matter of hours and she was spinning with anxiety while mumbling quiet questions to herself not expecting answers.

"The book of Revelation," Jason said as he made his first appearance from the back of the church and into the cool evening air.

Julia looked at him in shock followed quickly with amazement but couldn't find the words to express her confusion. She was sure he was dead and his bandaged body left more to her imagination. She stood there still as a statue.

"Are you okay?" Jason said as he made his way alongside her and the reached his hands to warm by the flames.

"I saw you yesterday," She said in a low mono-toned voice. "I saw you in that van. I thought you were murdered."

"Nope, alive and getting well," he replied. "What about you? What brought you to this neck of the woods?"

Julia explained about the previous day and how afraid she had been ever since. She told him about how she had been hiding out all night not knowing what to do. She even told him about her fleeting thought to say a prayer and how she used it as a sign. After a brief pause she looked at Jason and realized that she had been rambling on for quite awhile so she took a deep breath and in an attempt to lobby the conversation his way she said...

"Anyway..I'am glad that you killed yesterday."

"The two soldiers who helped us escape were murdered after saving us," Jason said as he lowered his bandaged head. "They were Christians and they didn't much care for the orders they were given."

"So what happened to you?" She said.

"That's another story," Jason said, "But maybe I can help fill in some blanks for you first."

Julia nodded in agreement and Jason settled down in a makeshift chair and told his story. He told her about his brother and his death. He told her about John and his dreams, and why they built the church. He told her about his hope and his faith and he told her about his fears.

After several more moments of casual conversation she remembered what he had said as he first appeared from the church. "You said something about Revelation, didn't you?"

"Oh Yeah," he said with rolling eyes that showed his tendency to lose focus. "I just had a feeling that you might be wondering about some of the same things that I have been trying to get a handle on.... Finally did though. Found some answers in the book of Revelation."

"That's the end of the world stuff in the Bible, right? She said in a leading manner.

"Yep," he said while nodding in a dreaded agreement. "Amazingly" he continued, "I barely understand any of it, but it answered my most troubling question and that is all I was looking for when I read it."

"And what was that?" She said.

"I couldn't understand how people could turn so ugly and so evil in such a short period of time. People who seemed normal and upright a few years ago are now killing people and lying to cover it up. I guess that lying, stealing, murdering people...That kind of stuff has always happened, but usually people would feel some sort of guilt. Take the General for instance. He surely didn't get to be where he is in the military by killing people and self justifying it along the way. Somehow, that normal feeling of sorrow for evil actions is being eased and it is allowing people to do otherwise unheard of things. It just seemed unbelievable that humanity could turn so bad so quickly and I needed to understand how that could happen.... Anyway, when I saw you there I just figured that you were probably wondering the same thing."

"That is one of my many questions" She replied.

"Well," he said as he leaned forward to continue. "As I have come to learn through opening my heart to God, is that we are all evil by nature and flawed to our very core. I have also come to realize that it is only God's permitted grace, which is available to all of us, that keeps us from tearing each others' eyes out. The book of Revelation says that God is becoming impatient and is now simply letting people who have hardened hearts succumb to their own desires."

"I don't know if I'm ready to believe that I'm evil," she said with complete confidence.

"It is a hard jagged little pill to swallow," he said, "Unfortunately it is a requirement that you recognize that fact or you won't truly see the need for a savior to free you from your nature."

"I like my nature," she said. "I like who I am."

"I like you too," Jason said while nodding in agreement. "I just met you and I can tell that you are a sweet caring person, a good person....But, that is only me judging what I see. God judges on a different scale."

"If God judges me," she said as she abruptly sat upright to form a protective pose, "Then he will see that I'm a good person, right?"

"I'm not the right person to answer all of your questions, Julia" He replied. "There is a Biblical scholar here who you should talk with and I really think that you should do that now."

"I don't know, I guess," she said.

Jason gave a friendly wave to Pastor James who was listening to the conversation from the other side of that fire, where a few others were standing alongside of him. Pastor James walked over to Julia, placed an arm on her shoulder and said in his elderly kind voice..

"let's go inside and take a look at the book of Romans. I think we can find some answers for you there."

Chapter Forty-One

As the final minutes of July third were wearing down, the General remained in his office self-justifying his actions and the further action he might need to commit the next day. His mind was reeling from the lack of guilt that he felt. The less guilt he felt the more justified his mind became. The General knew in the far reaches of his existence that his ultimatum was extreme but he was quick to tell himself that these were extreme times. The General was an educated man and he knew that his greatness would be judged in coming generations and that he needed to be strong and do what needed to be done. He thought of President Lincoln who had choices to be made that led to the death of thousands. "Thousands of Americans," he mumbled to himself to punctuate the guilt easing fact. The General pulled out his directory and woke several officers and called for a six am meeting. He then pulled a silver encased flask from his top drawer, unscrewed the top and took a deep draw of Kentucky's best as he leaned way back and deeply sighed. As he sat there motionless he looked blankly into the engraving and the fine details of the silver as he silently read the words of a close friend and giver of the gift he held in his hand....."No man is an island, except of course you, Gerald."

John used Maria's influence to shuttle the remaining kids from the school to the church in the dead of night, and the place was now about as crowded as it could be. There were over forty adults surrounded by over a hundred kids standing around or near the fire and surely the inner walls were filled with tired souls and sleeping children. John and Craig emerged from the trail after making one final walk to be sure there were none left behind. When they took a long look at the people surrounding their once quiet and intimate site they both stood still and the obvious question came to life....

"What are we going to do with all these kids?" Craig said when he came to the realization that they had not really thought this through.

"I don't know son, I don't know," John replied. "Not even sure how we can keep them warm overnight."

Just then, as if it were staged, a roll of thunder came from a distance and it began to lightly rain.

"Or keep them dry," John added with a smirk and a nod to the heavens.

John and Craig walked to the fire where Jason and RJ were listening intently to a story of redemption from one of the new arrivals when the rain began to come down a little harder. Craig let out a deep sigh and said that he was going to see how many people they could fit inside and he asked Jason and RJ to look for tarps among the supplies that had been gathered earlier that day.

Craig walked up the steps to the door of the church and turned around to get a visual of the amount of persons who were now covering their heads and scrambling towards the small eaves along the side of the building. He knew that it was going to be a long night and he knew that there was no way they could provide shelter for all of these refugees, but he needed to do what he could. Craig opened the doors, stepped inside and was quickly sent into a state of shock. There was room, plenty of room in fact. As he looked around the sanctuary his head became light and he nearly fainted. Just as he reached for a stabilizing table or banister, Jeff grabbed his arm and lowered him down on a pew.

"Are you alright Craig?" He said looking into Craig's glassy eyes. "You look like you've seen a ghost."

"Is it me," Craig said with his eyes darting around the heavily candle lit room, "or is the church getting bigger?"

"Bigger," Jeff said as looked at the several others working diligently to cover sleeping children and tend to the sick. "I don't know wha...." Dr. Wrigley noticed two things. One was that it was a lot less crowded in the room than it was a mere half hour ago, and two, was that the pile of supplies and food in the back of the church had tripled in size.

"When was that last time anybody brought food supplies in here Craig?" he said while feeling a little loopy himself.

"Well before sunset Doc," Craig said as he began to come to terms that another supernatural event was unfolding right before his eyes. "Well before," he continued. "I'm going to ask everyone to come inside now Doc. I don't know what to expect, but I have a feeling that God doesn't want his children in the cold rain anymore."

Craig walked to the door, opened it and said in a broken, barely audible voice, "Everyone inside."

The crowd mumbled a few "what did he say's?" as they looked up from their down turned heads before he repeated himself in a much deeper and pronounced way..

"I said, everybody inside."

At once the children who were cold and hungry made a move towards the door while the adults, Jason, John and RJ included, looked at Craig as if he were crazy. The church was only built to hold fifty or so people and the last time any of them had checked it was wall to wall with well over seventy. Jason and RJ dropped the tarp they had just began to unfold and together with John, Pastor James, Julia, Jack and a few others made their way to the side of the church where Craig had led them to the two small windows on the South side of the structure. Craig looked through the window and shook his head in amazement and then slowly turned to see several sets of eyes looking directly back at him.

"We worship an amazing God people, look for yourselves"..

The group took turns in pairs looking in sheer amazement inside the well lit interior of the church, followed by several steps back to see that the exterior had not changed at all. Back and forth they went looking in amazement, shaking their heads and then backing to see the outside dimensions. Inside, the room continued to get larger as the people outside slowly came in. There were plenty of beds, blankets, food and candles for all to see. Every time one of the peepers blinked there would be something extra in the room. There were those who had been in the room all along who were now in complete realization that God was supernaturally intervening and they were weeping and on their knees in worship. Some were in groups praying, while still others, including Maria, Katie and Caroline softly sang as they attended to the sick and wounded. As the rain began to fall much harder than before the group decided that it was time to join the others and they slopped their way towards the door. All, except Julia who had stepped back from the group after having her once stable naturalistic existence shattered right before her eyes. She was rocking back and forth and seemed to be in the middle of an acute panic attack with her knees pulled tight against her chest when Jason joined her and sat close with Pastor James occupying her other side.

"It's okay Julia," Pastor James said as he rubbed her back. "Let's go back inside now."

"I can't go in there again," she said with a trembling voice. "I didn't believe until I saw it with my own eyes....I don't deserve to be saved like you guys. Julia took a deep breath to gather a moment's composure and looked directly at the Pastor's caring eyes and said, "I kind of understand what you were explaining to me pastor, I just don't think I deserve it."

"Nobody deserves it," Jason said. "I know that I don't. But if you truly feel that you don't deserve it..... and it sounds like you do......... then you are ready to accept the free gift"

"He's right young lady," Pastor James said with a warm smile. "It's time Dear, it's time."

Julia took several deep breaths and listened intently as the Pastor explained what was about to happen and that her only part was to allow God his rightful place in her heart. As others watched from the south windows she accepted Jesus on his terms. She wept, lowered her head in shame for several moments but then looked upwards and raised her hands in praise as the now heavy rain seem to wash her clean before a cheering audience of onlookers.

Chapter Forty-Two

In the wee hours of the morning on the Fourth of July the original group of the church's founding had gathered around a table in the vastly expanded church. They knew that they were meant to be there at that particular moment in time, but they still were uneasy as to what lay in store. They knew about Pastor Albert's now legendary dream and how it ended in a peaceful rest, but they also knew about a terror that preceded it. Was it going to happen tomorrow or would this drag out for months? They were unsettled with unanswered questions, but they also had a level of peace that none of them had ever sensed before. It was an amazing time and the dialogue of the meeting went in many directions but each thought ended with hope and joy and a praise to God for allowing them to be used in his amazing will. After about an hour of thoughtful prayer, John, who had become the group's leader had some final thought before they were to find a quick nights rest on one of the many beds....

"Tomorrow when the General arrives with his minions, only I will go outside to greet him. He will have some intimidating guns and a few hand held rocket propelled grenades that the US confiscated from the Afghanistan war. He wants a battle, I could see it in his eyes. Somehow he has justified it, I guess he sees it as ethnic cleansing for the good of the State.....Anyway, he will fire upon us if we don't surrender to his commands...We are not going to surrender people. God didn't bring us here for that. He didn't provide for us, protect us, and lead us to this moment so we could hop on a bus to a re-education camp or probably something far, far worst.....No!.... he wants us here to make a stand. I'm not sure why, or what it will prove, but we stay put and stand firm...And to make sure we all understand, I greet the General alone.."

Amazingly nobody added a single comment. It was as if they knew that John was speaking words from God. The remaining Ortiz brothers quietly walked away first followed by everyone else except RJ who remained silent and then kissed his Dad's forehead and then peered over his shoulder for a bed and crept away. John was now alone with his thoughts as he rehearsed the next day's events in his mind. He had always relied on his own bravery and intelligence but now they were useless. He was only a pawn in a greater scheme set forth by his Lord. John knelt down before the table's edge and began to pray for the strength he would surely be needing just as lightning began a steady flash through the darkened clouds outside.

Several miles away a small group of twenty or so believers, living in makeshift cabins, were awakened by the sound of a distant thunder. They stood glaring at a single dark cloud that hovered over a small area while the surrounding areas were clear and brightening with the early morning sun. They were not surprised when their leader asked them to grab what they needed and start moving. It was as if they had been waiting for a sign for months and the darkened cloud that might loom danger at any other time, brought them a curious and heart-filled hope that they couldn't explain. As a group, they simply knew they needed to go. Like the Wise Men and the Shepherds two thousand years before, they would be making a journey of faith to a welcoming homecoming feast that awaited them. They were not to be alone in their journey, as many others would be following early dawn's magical sign and making their way to a bustling new wooden church as well.

Sadahara sat quietly in his apartment staring at tightly framed family pictures while he slowly sipped his glass of gin. His freshly stitched shoulder throbbed and his drunkenness was not nearly enough to absorb the pain. "How had he fallen so far" he thought as he peered at much happier times on the photos adorning the walls and the dresser top. He looked at his father's photo and felt a shame that bit down to his very core. Tears began to fall as he realized that he had lost everything that ever mattered to him. His dad was gone and his mom was barely understandable. He had lost his wealth, his home and now his Wife. "How could he had hurt her in that way," he thought as he replayed the moment of violence over and over again in his mind. He thought sadly about the way he had distanced himself from her since the collapse, how much love she continued to give, and how he had time and again, abused it. Now he was an abuser of the worst kind, a man without a soul, a man without a place, a man who deserves to die. Sadahara let loose of the glass and it fell crashing to the floor as he dropped hard to his knees. As the early morning light, peering through heavy rain, began to form a shadow on his wall, he lowered his head began to cry. Soon his cries turned to low sobs and he eventually passed out on his cold hard wood floor, knowing what he needed to do.

Chapter Forty-Three

The General was startled by a knock on his office door at exactly six am. He had nodded off not more than an hour before and his head went into an instant state of ache. When he was joined by his officers, and coffee had been poured all around, he slowly and methodically explained what was going to happen as the sun set on their little facility in the woods. He carefully detailed the two options that he would give the zealots and the consequences of each. One would mean instant departure and the other would mean instant death and the destruction of the church. As the other six men listened, two were in shock, though they carefully hid their apprehension. They could only hope that these men could not find it in their hearts to do them harm, but they were also afraid of the fate that might fall them or their families if they refused an order. The other four men seemed callous and simply nodded in stoic agreement. The General told the men to gather about forty more men armed with assault rifles and about 5 RPGs. They were to meet at the school field at 7:30 in the evening and be ready to march through some heavy woods to the site.

As the early morning turned to mid-morning the church was rustling with people who were curiously unconcerned about the pending deadline. Conversations were roaring and anticipations grew wild, although nobody had even a fleeting anxiety about what was to happen. Maria and Katie attended to a now conscience Akiko while John and Craig lay sleeping nearby. RJ and Jason were making small talk with Julia as the three lay on cots side by side. Ricky and Caroline were talking with the Jeff and Courtney at a table while children ran around in the great open spaces that God had provided. There was an amazing peace that ran through the church that seemed to touch every soul. People laughed and sang and not a harsh word was spoken. People prepared food and tended to the sick and wounded who seemed to be healing at a rapid pace. It was as if they were getting a glimpse into what life would be like if love were the rule of the day.

Somehow it did not appear strange as others appeared through the woods. They simply knocked on the door and came inside. People quickly helped them to dry and clean, and they gave them blankets and fed them with an always increasing food supply. As the day wore on more and more people made their way inside and new friendships flourished in record time. Nobody seemed to notice the rapidly growing church. It was as if they had finally let go of the world and placed Jesus in control. They had a new peace with the supernatural because they now had no doubt who was in control, and they knew He loved them.

John awoke with a smile as he saw two young boys trying to tie his shoe laces together while snickering to each other and then quickly running away. John felt a new peace as well and almost forgot completely about the showdown scheduled for dusk. John grabbed a cup of coffee and found his way to Jack who was watching the rain through the side window.

"Morning Jack," John said with a warm hand placed over the shoulder of the suddenly startled man.

"It's amazing isn't John," Jack said as he glared back out the window. "I've been sitting here all morning marveling at our God. He really thought of everything, didn't he? I mean....How did you sleep John?... good right?.... look around John, this church is full of playing kids and yet we can sit here and have a conversation without being bothered in the least and we don't need to raise our voices...He's controlling the sound levels for each and every one of us. I can't even hear the generator unless I go outside under the tarp to add gas to it, which by the way it never needs....It's crazy...and so unbelievable amazing."

John looked around and realized that Jack was right. It was just another in a long list of miracles that God was using to help his children. John shook his head and gently replied to his new friend, "Nothing should be a surprise to us anymore Jack, nothing."

"Are you worried about tonight John?" Jack asked.

"I'm not," John said while raising his eyebrows. "I guess I should be, but actually I'm just excited. I don't know if this is going to be our rapture or just a start to a new adventure, but either way I have no worry at all.... and it's strange."

"I'm not worried either John, might not even watch," Jack said with a warm smile as they parted ways and John went looking for Pastor James. John had a question that should be causing him trouble and although it wasn't, it did perk his curiosity.

When John found the Pastor they convened to a small table near the front of the church, under the great stained glass window and started going over his prior Pastor's dream. John was perplexed as to why, in the dream, there was a look of terror on the faces of the believers when the dream came to an end. John looked around at all the people gathered within the walls and said...

"Does it look like these people are going to be scared by the General and his planned showdown tonight, Pastor?"

"No it doesn't John," He quickly replied, "But that doesn't mean that the God has completely taken away all of our fears, at least not on this side of forever."

"I don't understand," the big man said, "What does that mean?"

"God can give us a new found peace for a time John, but he only promises eternal peace after our time on earth is done." The Pastor thought for a moment and then continued, "If God did not provide us with this temporary peace and comfort we might be at each other's throats. There would probably be others trying to dethrone you as our leader and others me as our Pastor. We would be arguing over food and bedding, it would be chaos if, we alone were in charge......No..... he did what he needed to do and I think that he might have one last reminder to us all of our falling world to throw our way tonight....a peek of the hell we will be leaving behind."

"So you think that we are leaving this planet tonight Pastor?" John said as he peered deep into the graying man's eyes.

"I have little doubt John, but then again, I'm not God."

"Then what about the description of the rapture then, it is supposed to be a surprise, a thief in the night and all of that," John said as he thought hard about what he had been learning during his short time as a believer.

"I've been troubled by that too my Son," James said as he nodded in agreement. "The way I see it, is that this is a soul harvest of sorts. I think for most it will be like the two men in the field and suddenly one will be gone, but for others, like so many here, God needed to use extreme measures to bring them home. Also John, we must remember, God will not lose a single one of his children."

"But what about you and the other lifelong Christians, what are you guys doing here?" John asked while he seemed to be getting more and more confused. "What about the Wrigleys for crying out loud?" he added to punctuate his point.

"We are just servants John" the Pastor replied, "We are to be used where the Lord leads us and He obviously wanted me to be here with you right now. We cannot forget that we worship a sovereign God and that he is in complete control, John. I don't have all the answers, but I hardly think that God is going to contradict himself. It just appears that way from our limited view."

John lowered his head and nodded in agreement, and almost instantly his curiosity left him and joy filled his heart as he saw his good friends Craig and Ricky heading his way with an extra plate of microwave sausage and buttered bagels. The men joined in fellowship as the day blew by without incident.

Chapter Forty-Four

As the early afternoon began the dark clouds turned white and puffy, but they remained low and still. The General's men were busy gathering their forces and loading their weapons as the day became ten degrees warmer in a matter of minutes. The soaked ground started to dry and the musky covered pines spewed out a pleasant fragrance, that no one paused to notice. The soldiers barely spoke a word as they readied themselves with helmets and body armor. Some were deeply worried and some were confident and bullish, but all were on high alert and it could be seen, though not differentiated in their faces. It was six thirty when they began to load the several jeeps that would transport them up a small hill to a now abandoned school to meet the General. The living quarters of the remaining work force had been placed in lockdown for the entire day as the chosen soldiers worked on a silent base wondering if they would need to do the unthinkable, fire on American civilians.

John asked everyone to stay inside as he stepped out onto a small front porch, sat down on a whittled chair, and waited for his moment of destiny. He still felt no fear but his anticipation was rising fast. Inside the mood had turned to curious but with so much to attend to only a handful seemed to care. As the day grew slightly darker and the last few refugees had waved hello to John and stepped inside a slight rumble gently shook the ground. Just as John was sure to think that it was the soldiers coming in full force he felt it again, only this time it rattled much more violently...

John stepped back inside the church and quickly came to the realization that the quake had shaken everyone back into a state of fear. It was as if God was saying, "Not so fast people, we still have the matter at hand." Children were beginning to cry and they were comforted by others who had terrified looks on their faces. It was more than the quake that had everyone spooked, it was the coming moments of confrontation that had been cleverly hidden from their fears that was now being realized once again. Fears of the coming onslaught that was only minutes away and moving fast.

As the soldiers made their way to the small clearing on the front side of the church, the General stepped to the front and with a bullhorn bellowed out a command...

"Robbs, front and center soldier..... now soldier!!!"

John looked at his family of believers, shrugged his shoulders and said, "I guess it's time people."

And while everyone held their collective breaths he reached for the door, opened it and saw a small army of men pointing guns and RPGs directly at him. As John closed the door behind him and started down the steps he felt another slight rumble and he grabbed tightly to the handrail. The quick rumble was then followed by a violent jolt that knocked everyone off their feet and caused several bullets to inadvertently fly by John's head and into the wooden structure behind him. John scrambled behind a nearby stump and began checking himself for bullet holes as the General rolled on to his stomach and screamed for everyone to cease fire. Seconds later the ground shook again and was followed by an even larger Jolt that sent men flopping to the ground once more and holding on for dear life. Inside the church the actual structure was holding up okay, but people were smashing against walls and into each other. Akiko had been thrown from her bed and her half healed wound was reopened and she was screaming in pain as blood poured from her side. Maria and Katie were scrambling to her aide, but through the shaking they could do little to help. Ricky had snapped his arm as he tried to steady both Caroline and himself when the final jolt had hurdled them to the ground. RJ and Jason looked on from their knees and were trying to get close enough to help, but were rendered useless as the building continued to shake violently. Terror was in the eyes of the believers and they were at a point where they simply couldn't take anymore when suddenly, just as quick as it had began, the shaking stopped.

John slowly rose to his feet and watched as the soldiers did the same. A few of the men tried to help the General to regain his lofty position on the front line but he angrily shook them away and gave them an evil glare. It took several minutes for the group to regain its composure. Some were bent at the waist, holding their knees, and hyperventilating while others held their arms out wide trying to overcome their feelings of vertigo. Inside the church, Katie was now holding Akiko's hand while Maria was pressing hard on her wound with a blood soaked towel. RJ and Jason had made their way to Ricky who quickly waved them away to help the children who were screaming and lying in small puddles of blood throughout the sanctuary. When Craig had regained his composure he slowly moved towards the door while picking a two inch splinter out of his forearm from his sudden crash into the backrest of a pew. He stopped at the door and looked back at his friends and said...

"I need to go out there...I mean....I feel led to go out there, I can't explain it... I just need to go."

"I need to go too," came the faint voice of Dr. Daly. "I need to go with you Craig," he continued, "We need to go now, before the God given courage escapes me."

Craig shook his head as he opened the door the very moment that the General started his final warning followed by a slow countdown from ten. Craig and the Dr. walked down the partially caved in steps, avoided the protruding nails, and joined John on either side.

John saw the men at his side and gave them a warm smile. The two men smiled back and showed a new bravery and a calmness that seemed to further infuriate the General...

"This is it Robbs," the General screamed in a now hoarse voice. "A little earthquake is not going to buy you any more time, I will blow that tiny church of yours to kingdom come."

The term the General used "Kingdom Come" caused the men to snicker and when that snickering turned to laughter, the General became incensed to a boiling point. He ordered his men at the ready and resumed his interrupted countdown at four. At three he was interrupted once again with a sudden and shocking sound of rifles falling to the ground. The General was swearing and spitting at several soldiers who had abandoned their ready stance and were walking with their hands held high in praise toward the wooded structure. The uniformed men walked in a trance and seemed to not even notice the three men who were amazed and frozen as they watched what was sure to be their new brothers walking towards their impending death. As John, Craig and the Dr. looked directly at the General he shouted his final command of violence....

"Fire, I said Fire!!"

Chapter Forty-Five

The whistling sound of three rocket propelled grenades fired simultaneously together with several assault rifles popping made a rather hellish sound as John, Craig and Dr. Daly turned slightly and closed their eyes in fear. The pure silence that followed the initial onslaught of gunfire was curious to the still standing men as they opened their eyes and turned back towards the frontline of soldiers that were sure to have ended their lives. Inches from John's head were two slugs and alongside were dozens more heading towards the torso and heads of the bewildered men. The three believers quickly jumped back and dropped low in a stunned amazement. Only a few feet from the men who had launched them were three RPGs with a fiery smoke tail that stood still in suspended animation. Everything was frozen except the three men who were standing still in a shocked amazement. Moments later they found themselves creeping around the vessels of annihilation, like a curious cat carefully examining a new piece of furniture, and observing them from all angles. Not a sound could be heard as they walked back and forth and around the bullets. The men crept towards the frontline and could see the anger on the Generals face. He was placed still in a ridiculously looking, angry, scrunched up face with a splatter of spit flinging outward, yet as frozen as he. The men looked in every direction and they could see birds, squirrels and clouds remaining perfectly still as if God was giving all creation a moment to catch its breath.

Craig walked up to a fired rocket and gave it a light knock with his knuckle while peering at the man who had fired it. His eyes were closed tight from the initial blast and he too was frozen like all others and all things...

"Are we dead?" Craig said as he looked over at the Doctor who was staring at a squirrel that was in a full running jump at the moment and was frozen in mid air.

"I don't think so," the Doctor replied while checking his pulse. "I have a pulse, a really good one too," he continued with a nervous smile.

The men spent several more minutes walking around the site in a stunned, yet curious state. It was as if they were astronauts on a distant and foreign planet where everything is the opposite of what they had always known. They would share smiles at each other and then explore more like children at Christmas time. But it wasn't Christmas and somebody needed to remind them of that.

"It's extraordinary boys," John said as he literally dipped his head to avoid the rocket Craig was standing next to and joined his friend with a hand on his shoulder. "But I think we are supposed to go home now."

Craig and Dr. Daly agreed and as the three men turned back towards the church a beam of light from high above blazed through an opening in the heavy clouds and made its way directly through the stained glass window and it turned the structure into a brilliant lamp. The tiny church was glowing so bright that it illuminated the area as far as one could see, and yet the time remained perfectly still. The men simply walked to the door, opened it to a flash of light that zipped like a laser beam into outer space the very second they were inside and then vanished as the canyons came back to life and brought time back into flow.

Epilogue

kiko stood in the presence of the Lord, as did they all, individually, and without exception. He cradled her and wiped away her remaining tears. He spoke softly to her and told her about love, a love she could never know or understand until now. Akiko felt all her fears and worries melt at her feet as she embraced Jesus with all her might and he gently rubbed her hair. Jesus pulled back for a moment and held out a hand and said....

"You continued to love him when he did not deserve it, just as I have continued to love you......Observe, my Child." Jesus said as he waved his hand gently towards the density surrounding her.

Akiko looked on as the clouds parted and a surreal vantage point came into view. It was as if her entire peripheral vision was a monitor and she was simply watching a three dimensional vision from her mind. In a matter of moments she saw Sadahara rummaging through the bathroom drawers of their home looking for razor blades to end his life, when, by God's pure grace, he found her note. It was a note she had intended to leave on his desk prior to the dreadful happenings of their final encounter. The note he held in his hands simply read...

> *"Sadie, I will always love you, but there is someone I love more. The good news is that He loves you too. I am going now to be with Him and if you love me I can only tell you this...If you find Him, then you will find me too."*

Akiko looked on as she saw the remaining four years, four months, and twelve days of Sadahara's life unfold in a matter of seconds. She saw him pray to receive God in a darkened, abandoned hotel room. She saw him imprisoned and beaten on several occasions. She saw him lead others away from the fallen world and into God's light and she looked on with delight as he sang praises and read from the Word of God. Finally, she saw him die a martyr's death in which he bravely endured, and she saw him buried with countless others in an unmarked field near Reno under a frozen pile of rubble.

Still staring at the brutal end to her husband's life she was startled when a touch lightly brushed her shoulder...

She quickly spun to see Sadie looking back at her with Jesus at his side...

"I found Him" he said to her softly as she looked deep into his eyes in amazement...

"And now I have found you too."

The End

About the Author

Robert Segotta is a retired Contractor who enjoys studying theology and philosophy. He began writing several years ago while living in Southern Oregon with his wife Christine and their son Kyle. The three now live in Salem, Oregon where they study, learn, and teach at Calvary Chapel Salem. When he is not writing he enjoys the fellowship of his friends, playing golf and watching his beloved Angels.